C000125241

JOHNNY TUDOR is an actor, entertai embraced all forms of the industry in hi encompassing musical theatre, drama, tel appearing in productions for BBC, Thames,

He has appeared in *Gavin & Stacey* and *Stella*, directed three pantos and a musical for the Welsh channel S4C, and co-wrote *Say It With Flowers*, a drama on the life of Dorothy Squires, which opened at the Sherman Theatre in Cardiff before going on to do a successful tour. Johnny's last venture was a biography on the life of Dorothy Squires entitled *My Heart is Bleeding*, which was published by The History Press in April 2017 and has just gone into re-print. *Peg's Boys*, a semi-autobiographical novel, is his latest project.

Find out more at www.johnnytudor.com

PEG'S BOYS

JOHNNY TUDOR

SilverWood

Published in 2020 by SilverWood Books

SilverWood Books Ltd
14 Small Street, Bristol, BS1 1DE, United Kingdom
www.silverwoodbooks.co.uk

Copyright © Johnny Tudor 2020

The right of Johnny Tudor to be identified as the author of this work has been asserted
in accordance with the Copyright, Designs and Patents Act 1988 Sections 77 and 78.

All rights reserved. No part of this publication may be reproduced,
stored in a retrieval system, or transmitted in any form or by any means,
electronic, mechanical, photocopying, recording or otherwise,
without prior permission of the copyright holder.

This is a work of fiction. Names, characters, places and incidents either are products of
the author's imagination or are used fictitiously. Any resemblance to actual events or
locales or persons, living or dead, is entirely coincidental.

ISBN 978-1-80042-022-9 (paperback)

British Library Cataloguing in Publication Data
A CIP catalogue record for this book is available from the British Library

Page design and typesetting by SilverWood Books

*In memory of Philip and Barry,
the best friends I ever had*

Prologue

I am an old man now and recent happenings seem to slip through my ever-decreasing memory, but the memory of that day and the guilt I felt then is as strong today as the day it happened.

London, January 1963

A cold wind whipped the rain down the grey city street. Passing cars were kicking up spray, soaking the old lady squatting next to the bus stop – chilling her to the bone. Her plea for 'Any loose change' was falling on deaf ears; it was as if she were invisible to the waiting commuters huddled under their umbrellas.

A red Routemaster splashed to a halt. I was about to step onto the open rear platform when I noticed the old lady staring at me.

'Hello, Jono,' she said. Her deep-set eyes held my gaze, willing me to remember.

How does she know my name? I thought. Embarrassed, I turned and mounted the bus. As it pulled away from Dolphin Square I ran the image through my mind. It slowly dawned on me who she was but it was too late. I watched helplessly through the sealed windows, running with tears, at her lonely diminishing figure. I wanted to get off the bus and go back…or maybe I didn't; in truth I'd chickened out and I've felt guilty about it ever since. I couldn't face what Peg had become. I just wanted to remember her as the vibrant young woman she was, and how she and her boys had touched my life back then.

Part One

Chapter One

Cwm Teg, South Wales, 1951

Jono

It was the first coal tip I'd ever seen close up. It wasn't a tip in the conventional sense but a mixture of coal dust, slag and debris from a nearby abandoned iron foundry. The top of it had been flattened off and grassed over and a gang of local kids were having a great time using it as a rugby pitch. A piece of the tip had broken away from the cliff-like side and fallen into the river below, its land-slip of slag adding to the already polluted water. My eye was drawn to a colourful glassy piece of rock glinting in the water. It looked like a precious stone to my eight-year-old eyes. Its green and blue swirls shone like a rainbow as the sun caught it. I put my bike down, clambered down the slope and picked it up. I was studying its razor-sharp edges when I was confronted by a boy of about my own age.

''Ave it out, *was*,' he said.

I turned to face the skinny kid. He was holding a soapbox cart by a piece of rope. One leg of his too-long underpants was peeping from below his dirty, patched union flannel shorts, his elbows were poking through the sleeves of his argyle knitted jumper, and his black lace-up hobnailed boots, which most of the valleys kids wore in the fifties, were scuffed and dirty.

''Ave it out, was?' He repeated, fixing me with his gypsy-looking eyes.

I didn't understand the boy's lingo but his clenched fists told me he wanted a fight. I was about to find out that '*Have it out, was?*' was South Wales valleys vernacular for 'Do you want a fight, friend?' A paradox if ever I'd heard one.

He raised his fists and took a step nearer, invading my space. I just stared at him, not knowing quite how to respond.

'Are you going to fight me, *was*, or not?' he goaded.

'What do you want to fight me for?' I said. 'I don't even know you.'

'Tell me your name, then.'

'Jono,' I said. 'What's yours?'

'Pip, everybody calls me Pip… Give us a go on that, then,' he said, nodding towards my bike.

I hesitated. I'd just been given the shiny new two-wheeler for my birthday and I wasn't about to give this scruffy kid, as he'd said, 'a go on it'.

'Come on, Jono. You can have a go on my gambo if you like,' he wheedled, pointing to his cobbled-together contraption.

His gambo, as he'd called it, was just a wooden box nailed onto some rough planks precariously perched on top of a set of old pram wheels. I'd never seen anything like it. It had an old piece of rope tied to the front axle to guide it by and, as far as I could see, no visible way of stopping it.

'Is it a deal, Jono?' he asked, flashing me a cheeky grin.

The vehicle, if you could call it that, didn't look safe to me but I was intrigued. So, against my better judgement, I said okay. He tied the rope of his gambo to the back of my bike, mounted it and peddled off down the road at breakneck speed, dragging me behind him. I hung on for dear life, terrified but exhilarated at the same time.

'What do I do if I need to stop this thing?' I yelled.

'Use your foot against the wheel,' he yelled back. 'You'll soon get the hang of it.'

This was fun. At least it was until Pip hit a pothole in the road and I was flung out of the gambo, crashing headlong into a lamp post.

I took a deep breath. I was immediately hit by a searing pain. I put my hand to my mouth and felt a sharp edge; I'd broken my front tooth, exposing a live nerve. I gingerly checked it with my tongue. The gap felt enormous and there was a taste of blood in my mouth; the jagged end of my tooth had gone through my lip and I was dripping blood all over my jumper. Pip pulled out a grubby-looking handkerchief and tried to stem the bleeding but he wasn't having much luck.

'Where d'you live, was?' he said. There was that word again.

'The Collier's Arms,' I spluttered.

'Come on, then. Let's get you home.' He bundled me back onto his cart and dragged me down the street to my father's pub. I was greeted by my not-too-happy mother, horrified to find me bleeding on the doorstep.

'What the hell have you done, Jono?'

I sheepishly raised my top lip, exposing the cracked tooth.

'Oh my God! Your new teeth! Bert,' she yelled, 'come and see this.'

Teeth were important to my mother; hers were the talk of the pub. They were so straight and white that the punters would take bets that they were false. So, the fact that I'd just smashed my brand new gnashers was a major disaster to her. Pop, her father, had instilled upon her to look after her teeth as he had done. He still had the gold fillings he'd had as a young sailor in Hong Kong. He'd gone back every day for a week for a Chinese dentist to painstakingly hammer gold leaf into the cavities and they were still in place till the day he died.

Pip, foreseeing a serious bollocking for his part in the heinous crime, untangled the rope from my bike and beat a hasty retreat, dragging his gambo behind him.

'Don't forget to come to my party, Jono,' he yelled as a parting shot. 'I'll tell Peg to expect you.'

'And who was *that?*' snapped my mother, looking with disdain at the retreating urchin.

'It's Pip. I met him up the tip, Mam.'

From that day on, Pip, my new butty (or buddy, to give it the English equivalent), and I were inseparable. I didn't appreciate it then but the next eight years were to be the happiest years of my life and the first real roots I'd ever known.

Chapter Two

I was born backstage in a provincial theatre. Showbiz was in my blood but living most of my young life out of a suitcase wasn't easy. My mother and father were show people, always on the road. In a leafy suburb of what is now Greater London was 40 Linden Avenue, the first and only house my father ever bought, albeit to keep my mother happy. She'd had enough of touring and the three-bedroom suburban semi-detached in Ruislip Manor was her idea of heaven. But it didn't last; eighteen months later we were on the road again; every week a different town, every town a different boarding house, some good some bad. Digs, as we called them, were usually cold unwelcoming places but Mrs McKinney's welcoming hearth in Aberdeen was different.

Appearing as Man Friday in *Robinson Crusoe* wasn't a role my old man relished; having to daub black make-up on his face twice nightly wasn't what he'd signed up for after gaining a Licentiate of the Royal Academy of Music. Stage fights weren't his speciality either. He'd broken his leg during a performance and been sent home.

I was only young but I have this vivid memory of a man in raggedy clothes hobbling into the digs on crutches, face all blacked up and a plaster cast on his leg. Who was this black man in funny clothes? Frightened, I ran to Mrs McKinney and buried my head in her lap.

'Don't be alarmed, Jono,' he said. 'It's only me, Dad. Tell him, Nanna McKinney.'

Nanna he'd called her. I see an image of *my* nanna, baking bread in her house in Tiger Bay and Pop, my grandfather, smoking his thin roll-ups under the wall clock and singing one of his comical Irish songs. It plays in my head.

There were plums and prunes and cherries,
Citrus and raisins and cinnamon too,
There were nutmegs cloves and berries.
And the crust it was nailed on with glue.
There were caraway seeds in abundance,
Sure t'would build up a fine stomach ache.
It would kill a man twice after eating a slice
Of Miss Hooligan's Christmas cake.

This was my refuge, my nanna's house, my sense of belonging, the only stability in my nomadic life. We were like gypsies and my education was lacking, to say the least. I'd been to about ten schools in my short life; I'd learnt more about the backstage workings of a theatre and the characters who inhabited them than my nine times table. I would sit side stage watching in awe as the jugglers, magicians and song and dance men performed their well-rehearsed routines. I even learnt to tap dance by watching the line of beautiful chorus girls who took me under their wings.

When my father made the unfathomable decision to give up show-business to run a pub in South Wales, I couldn't believe it. The reason he gave for his decision was to give me some grammatical grounding. True, my accent *was* a mixture of cockney and Aberdonian but it came in handy when my mother wanted me to translate some rhyming slang or '*Fit like's the time?*' – Aberdonian for '*what time is it?*'

To me the theatre was education enough and I couldn't figure out for the life of me why Dad would want to leave such a colourful life. His protestations that it was for my education didn't fool my mother though. Truth was she'd caught him up to no good with one of the chorus girls and given him an ultimatum: it was either showbiz or her. He strongly denied the affair of course but my mother was no fool; she'd been a chorus girl herself and knew the temptations of the long-legged scantily dressed dancers. That's how she'd hooked him. And so, as the final curtain fell on *Robinson Crusoe*, Dad, with tears in his eyes, gathered his props and said farewell to the only life he'd known.

The following day Mam and Dad packed up. I said a tearful goodbye to Nanna McKinney and we caught the train to Edinburgh then boarded the overnight Pullman for Cardiff.

As the train thundered across the Forth Bridge, I tossed a penny from the window and made a wish as I had done before, then settled down in my bunk for the journey home. The carriage had three bunks – one each for my mother and father, and I had the upper bunk. I was too excited to sleep, but the soothing rhythmic sound of the train over the tracks and the sway of the carriages back and forth soon had me dreaming of pantomime villains and the haven of my grandmother's house in Tiger Bay.

I came round in the morning to the sound of a cheery 'good morning' and the rattling of cups; it was the steward arriving with a tray of tea and biscuits. My mother patiently helped me to wash in the lukewarm water that swashed from side to side in the small sink, helped me dress, and combed my hair; I was ready. The train pulled into Cardiff General Station. I stepped down onto the platform and filled my lungs with the cold morning air. Familiar smells of coffee beans being ground at the nearby Costa Rica Coffee House, the aroma of hops wafting from the local brewery, and the sound of passing trams rattling by stirred my memory… I was home.

'Home for long, Merville?'

It was Mrs Samuels who, dress tucked in her bloomers, down on her red knees, rubber-gloved and pinafored, was scrubbing the already gleaming pavement outside her house as if her life depended on it.

'Not long,' replied my mother, tight-lipped.

The front step of my nanna's house had been scrubbed squeaky clean too. Even the pavement leading from step to gutter had been washed down. I noticed that most of the adjacent houses had done the same thing; the dark polished stripes of the blue pennant stones contrasting with the grey unwashed ones looked like some gigantic piano keyboard.

Inside nanna's house was just as painstakingly polished as the front step. The brass stair rods gleamed and the oak banister, hall stand, and oil-clothed hallway all shone with lustre from my nanna's elbow grease. As we entered the kitchen we were welcomed by a coal fire glowing in the black-leaded grate and the delicious smell of baking doughnuts wafting from the scullery. I went through my usual routine of hiding behind my mother, pretending I wasn't there. But I was soon sniffed out by Taff, the Welsh terrier who tried to lick me to death.

My grandfather, or Pop as I called him, was sitting in his favourite chair next to the fire. He was reading the *South Wales Echo*, which he devoured every day from the first word to the last. He looked up, a smile playing about his lips as he witnessed my childish ritual. He opened up his well-worn baccy box, pulled out some fine strands of golden tobacco, reached for a packet of Rizla Blues, deftly filled one of the cigarette papers with the tobacco, moistened the paper with his tongue then, skilfully, rolled the thin cigarette with one hand. As he lit up, the wall clock above his head seemed to tick in protest at the clouds of smoke that seeped into its movement. I can still smell it now. Whenever I open Pop's clock to wind it up, the sweet aroma of his Golden Virginia that still lingers brings back visions of my nanna's house, as plain as if I were still there.

'Where's Jono?' asked Nanna, wiping the flour from her hands on her apron. She shot Pop a mischievous glance. 'Did you leave him in Glasgow?'

'Don't tease the boy, Emily,' he said, folding his paper and picking a strand of tobacco from the tip of his tongue.

Realising my cover was blown I made my grand entrance in true showbiz style and ran to my nanna's outstretched arms. As she held me in those arms, her familiar smell, a mixture of freshly baked doughnuts and Pears soap, wafted over me, comforting me; there was nowhere safer than in my nanna's arms. She always had time for me. I would listen spellbound as she told me fascinating stories of when she was a girl in Ireland and sang old Irish songs, and how her uncles had sailed to America to make their fortunes.

'Times were very hard, Jono,' she said. 'The Irish potato famine caused everyone to leave.'

'What's a famine?' I asked.

'The potato crop failed, Jono. People were starving. A million people died and more than a million left for America, my uncles amongst them.'

'What were they like, Nanna?'

'They had guns and daggers all over them...beautiful!' she said, smiling as she remembered her long-lost uncles.

Visions of cowboys and Indians, like the ones I'd seen in the Saturday morning pictures, fired my imagination: outlaws holding up trains, wagon trains surrounded by whooping Red Indians firing flaming arrows, tumbleweed blowing down dusty streets and gun slingers facing each other down to see who was the fastest on the draw.

She brought down a tin box she kept on the dresser and opened it. Amongst the faded dog-eared photographs of her childhood were pictures of her uncles, shovels and picks in hand, standing by a railway track in some far flung part of the Wild Frontier. With their gun belts, long hair and goatee beards they reminded me of Wild Bill Hickok. She pulled out a tin-type photo of a smiling young woman wearing beach pyjamas, blew the dust from the faded image and polished it with her sleeve.

'That was my mother when she was a girl,' she said with pride. 'Ellen Brennan on the beach at Coney Island.'

She carefully unrolled a dog-eared sepia sailing bill of the American Steam Ship Company and Pennsylvania Railroad. 'This is the ship she sailed on, Jono.'

Underlined was the good ship *City of Limerick* and, next to Wednesday July 19, 1876, scrawled in pencil, was 'Nelly Sailed'.

'Who was Nelly, Nanna?'

'My mother, Jono. We all called her Nelly. She sailed out to see her brothers when she was only eighteen, a brave thing to do in those days. She wanted to go again but my grandmother wouldn't let her.'

As Nanna read from the bill, I was transported to a different time, a different place.

'*For the princely sum of six pounds six shillings,*' she began, '*steerage passengers will be furnished with an abundant supply of provisions of the best quality cooked and served by the stewards; but they will have to provide themselves with bed, bedding and mess utensils, the whole of which can be bought for ten shillings.*'

'Is that a lot of money?'

'It was a lot in those days.'

She carefully rolled up the fragile bill and pointed to a photo of a young girl in a leotard and ballet shoes. 'That was your mother in her dancing class. She loved to dance and she led me a merry dance, I can tell you.'

My mother shot Nanna a good-humoured smile.

'I wasn't that bad, Mam.'

'Oh no...? What about the time you ran away to join that so-called actor-manager called Sylvester and his ragbag troupe?'

'Tell me, Nanna... Go on,' I pleaded.

I always loved hearing stories about when Mam was on the road. And Nanna's memory of my mother's one and only experience of touring with this group of broken-down actors was very colourful.

'I don't think it was what she expected,' she said. 'They had to travel to the North East of England on the back of a coal truck, if you please.'

Pop puffed out a billow of smoke and slowly shook his head at the memory.

'It gets worse. When she arrived it wasn't a theatre, at all; it was no more than a disused village hall. They had to do everything; help fit up the scenery, sell tickets, bottle the crowd.'

'What's that mean?'

'What…? Bottle the crowd? Well, they had to go around after the show shaking a bottle for donations, said it was for charity but I know different. He was a right crook that Sylvester. Anyhow, your mam had learnt the script off by heart but Sylvester said he didn't have any red crepe paper for Red Riding Hood's cloak. So they had to do *Babes in the Wood* instead. Nobody knew it so he stuck bits of the new script on various parts of the tatty scenery.'

'What happened?'

'What do you think? The show was a flop. No one got paid and they had to scarper-de-leti.'

'Scarper…de?'

'Scarper-de-leti is showbiz slang for they had to do a runner from the digs. Pop had to call the police to bring her back home. It was a disaster.'

It was no wonder my mother got the bug for the stage. She'd been intoxicated by the theatrical atmosphere that pervaded my nanna's house. Being just across the Taff River Bridge from the Playhouse Theatre made it easy for Nanna to supplement Pop's meagre earnings; a humble postman's wages didn't go far in those days. Nanna would put up actors from the touring revues. They'd come in tired and hungry after their twice nightly performances, sit down to a fine supper prepared by Nanna and shoot the breeze. My mother told me she would listen spellbound to their banter: what had happened on stage and off, who'd missed an entrance, who'd forgotten their lines, which one of the girls fancied the juvenile lead? Oh how she'd longed to escape Tiger Bay, to be part of that colourful life.

The docks or the Bay, as it was known by the locals, was more reminiscent of New York than South Wales. Its diverse ethnic mix was a melting pot where Somalis, Chinese, Jews, Arabs and Greeks all lived cheek by jowl. Life in the Bay had a ferocity that was second only to Marseilles.

21

I'd overheard Pop talk of knife fights and stabbings, prostitution and gambling dens but 'What d'you expect?' he'd say. 'It *was* Tiger Bay.' He told me of the times as a humble postman he'd rubbed shoulders with ship owners, millionaires and coal exporters in the Big Windsor and the Mount Stewart Hotel. That's where he'd met my nanna. He boasted that she'd served Scott of the Antarctic and his crew with their last pint of beer before they sailed, full of hope, towards their unfortunate destiny. He lamented the glory, if somewhat dangerous, days, when men were shanghaied, millionaires lived in Mount Stewart Square, when there were six post collections a day, and the first million pound cheque was signed at the Coal Exchange. He spoke with pride of the Tiger Bay that had exported over nine million tons of coal a day in its heyday. It was the envy of the world.

The glory days might have gone. The magnificent buildings that had once buzzed with commerce might now lie empty or derelict but I can still remember the atmosphere of the place. The re-developed foreshore may have been turned into an homogenised playground of cafes, bars, and shops for the hoi polloi but it doesn't have the allure of the sights, sounds and smells of my childhood: the aroma of freshly baked bread wafting from Mr Zemlar's bakery on the corner, the whiff of garlic from Sammy Wong's Chinese restaurant, the heady smell from Sadie's Curry house and men as black as coal playing dice on the pavement outside The Casablanca Club where jazz riffs from harmonicas and twelve-string guitars bled into the street.

Later, snuggling down in the feather-filled mattress in my nanna's brass-bedded box room, I listened to the sound of the steam-belching trains hooting from the nearby railway station. The memories of the many journeys I'd taken with my parents and the different towns we'd visited came flooding back to me. I didn't know it then, as I lay cocooned in my nest like a coiled dormouse, but my life was about to become very different.

Showbiz had been my life until then and my father's salvation. His talent as a musician had saved him from following his father into a life of hard graft at the coal face. Although, trying to find work as a musician in London hadn't been a walk in the park either. He'd slept on a park bench more times than he cared to remember, with only newspapers stuffed up his shirt for warmth, and tramped the streets, knocking on agents' doors until he landed a much welcome gig in a dance band.

His father, a wiry little man weighing no more than seven stone wringing wet, was affectionately known as Dai Gaff. This was on account that he'd been the gaffer haulier in charge of the working ponies that had taken the place of child labour in the pit. From the tender age of fourteen, he'd worked underground from morning till dusk, never seeing the light of day in winter. The only thing he had to show for his toil was pneumoconiosis or dust as he called it, and the blue scars where the coal dust had seeped into his tender young skin, indelibly tattooing his body. The last thing my dad wanted to do was to follow in his footsteps. But he returned to South Wales all the same, not to work underground but to run a pub, and he'd regretted it for the rest of his life. In his own words, he'd sold his soul to peddle pints and pork scratchings.

Chapter Three

The next day we left Nanna's and made the short journey to Cwm Teg. As the train puffed its way into the heartland of industrial South Wales I was amazed at the difference in the landscape. The journey was just ten miles from Cardiff but it couldn't have been more different. From the city with its busy streets, department stores, tramcars rattling on rails and street hawkers plying their trade, I was looking at green hills that had been scarred by ripping coal from their bellies and tips standing incongruously like black pyramids that had been dumped next to them. I couldn't help wondering why people would dig coal mines in such beautiful countryside.

We steamed further up the valley, passing rows of miners' terraced cottages that clung to the side of the mountains as if they'd been put there by mistake and towns with names we couldn't even read. My mother had a brave try but she made Caerau sound like the capital of Egypt. Little did I think then that I would grow to love the little valley town that was to become my new home for the next eight years.

I don't know why but I always felt Welsh. It was probably because of my paternal grandfather, Dai Gaff, or Taid as I called him, and his influence seeping into my subconscious. He being born and brought up in North Wales, Welsh was his first language. When I would visit him I would often find him sitting on a park bench with the old men of the town shooting the breeze in what he called 'The language of heaven', or sipping tea and listening to the news in Welsh on the radio.

Taid was meticulous to the point of being obsessive. I was never allowed to pour the tea. 'Don't pour it,' he'd say. 'I haven't turned it yet.' Turned he said, not stir. It was a literal translation from Welsh. Although the industrial revolution had been in part the reason for the slow demise of the language, the people of the valleys were still speaking Welsh. They were just using English words, that's all.

I watched Taid's ritual as he made his tea. He warmed the pot; he even warmed the spoon then dried it. He spooned in the best Darjeeling then poured the golden liquid into a bone china cup and added one lump of sugar. His painstaking ritual was a paradox; coal miners usually drank their bog-black beverage from tin enamel mugs. He was fastidious in everything he did. He got up every morning at six, did his deep breathing exercises in front of an open window, winter and summer. This helped with his dust, he would say. Then he shaved with his cut-throat razor, got dressed in his suit, shirt, stiff collar and tie then sat down to a breakfast of bran, followed by a lightly boiled egg – three and a half minutes, no more no less. This was accompanied by Allinson's brown bread toast slathered with copious amounts of butter and topped off with his favourite Frank Cooper's marmalade, rind and all. 'I like to see my teeth marks in it, Jono,' he'd say.

Pop was a bit like Peg, no one knew anything about his background. He never spoke of his mother who'd been in service to the local doctor. He was brought up by his grandfather. Being illegitimate, he didn't know who his father was. It was rumoured that it was the doctor who'd taken advantage of his mother, which might explain his fastidious and gentile way of preparing his breakfast; perhaps it was in his genes.

'You don't understand this, do you, Jon bach?' he would say alluding to the Newyddion Cymraeg coming from the radio. I didn't at the time but it was somehow comforting to let this musical tongue with its strange consonants and vowels wash over me. I made up my mind there and then that I would learn to speak my own language one day.

It opened up a whole new world to me. There was a parallel culture that I had been totally unaware of although it had been around me all the time. The Mabinogion, a collection of Welsh myths, was every bit as exciting as the Greek or the Roman. It puzzled me to think that the English knew little of it. After all, old Welsh *was* the original Celtic language of Britain before the conquering Roman legions turned up.

The Romans weren't the only ones to try to stamp out our Celtic culture. The Victorians tried their damnedest too but the village of Cwm Teg seemed to have survived the 'Welsh Not'. My grandfather, who'd been a victim of this oral ethnic cleansing, told me of the time he'd been flogged in front of the class for speaking the only language he knew. He told me how his teacher – a cruel, cane-swishing bastard with a red beard down to his waist – had caught him speaking Welsh and made him wear a rope around his neck with a wooden plaque attached to it. It was inscribed with the words 'Welsh Not'. He wasn't allowed to take it off until he heard another kid speaking Welsh. The last one wearing this humiliating abomination got a bloody good hiding with his whangee cane. Unfortunately for Taid, he was often the last one and 'The bastad diawl' – his words not mine – 'made me bend over the desk, to prepare for the thrashing of my life.'

Even after all these years, I still really miss my taid with his stories of Wales and regret that I was not there when he passed. I have this recurring dream about him, where I remember that I haven't seen him for a long time. I go to his house. It's all in darkness, no sign of life. The garden is unkempt and the curtains are drawn; it looks as if no one has been there for years. I still have my key so I let myself in. He's in his chair, listening as usual to the Welsh news on the radio. He's in his best suit, starched collar and tie, shoes polished. 'Where've you been, Jon bach?' he says. 'I've been waiting for you to comb my hair; I want to go looking tidy, see. Don't be frightened, Jono,' he says. 'I won't hurt you; I didn't hurt you when I was alive so I'm not going to hurt you when I'm dead.' Then I wake up and realise he's been dead for years. As I pass the hospital now it crosses my mind that I should have called in to see him that night but it was late – two o'clock in the morning late. I'll wait till the morning, I thought, but by the morning he'd gone; he'd died in the night, calling for me to comb his hair.

Chapter Four

When the train pulled into Cwm Teg Station I was amazed to see a herd of sheep roaming the streets. They'd come down from the nearby mountain and were attacking the dustbins, looking for food. A young ram with its head stuck in a bucket was running wildly through the high street, trying to dislodge the offending object, and young lambs, bleating for their mothers, were being answered by the ewes' hoarse voices; they sounded like old men coughing. I tried in vain to catch one of these newborn lambs but no luck; they were as quick as greased pigs.

It was Friday, market day, and the market square was as full as an egg. People, all hoping to snag a bargain from one of the visiting market traders, crowded around the stalls where barrow boys, fruiterers and fish mongers were bawling out their wares. There were men selling crockery, women with reams of fine fabrics draped over their arms selling the swathes of cloth by the yard, be-turbaned women in white pinafores selling Penclawdd cockles in baskets, stalls selling goldfish in plastic bags filled with water, and Petrelengo Boswell, the gypsy, selling an evil-smelling preparation, yet to be discovered by chemists, that he'd made from ground ivy. He swore it would cure everything from coughs and colds to athlete's foot. A manic street preacher was banging a drum and bellowing something out in Welsh, which I didn't understand but by the drama in his voice it was obviously religious. This was fun. I was beginning to like my new home already and the market square became one of my favourite places.

All the wide boys would come to ply their wares. Frenchie, a Jewish man from North London in a long navy overcoat with an astrakhan collar, sold china. He was a real showman; I would skip school on a Friday just to watch him perform.

'Who'll give me fifteen shillings for this tea set,' he would bawl as he expertly rattled and spun his plates. 'No, I tell you what I'll do, lady…don't give me fifteen shillings, not even twelve and six… I'll tell you what I'll do; I'll chuck in a matching tea pot as well. So, not fifteen shillings, not even twelve and six. Go on, I'll tell you what…give me ten bob and it's all yours.'

The first one to put her hand up was usually a plant that would start a stampede of ladies thinking they were getting a bargain. Little did they know that the whole lot wasn't worth more than ten bob in the first place.

The grandly named Collier's Arms Hotel was anything but. The old ale house, built before the Great War, was a dark and gloomy place. Inside, the yellowing nicotine-stained walls and ceilings ran with condensation and smoke hung in the air like a cloud, stinging my eyes.

The previous landlords had lived in a dark and dismal basement flat, which suited them and the abundant amount of black beetles that scuttled about, but not my mother. She decided there and then to move the living quarters upstairs and as far away from the black pats as possible.

The staff came with the building. Victor, the theatrical barman with a cut-glass accent, nicknamed Nigel because it sounded more upper class, fantasised about being a film star and had a suit for every occasion. 'This is my Dirk Bogarde suit,' he would say or, while struggling with heavy crates of beer, he would boast that he was like Marlon Brando in *The Young Lions*. His party trick at lock-ins was the Jack Hawkins speech from *The Cruel Sea*. He insisted that he be soaking wet for the atmosphere. Horace, the bar cellar man whose mother and father came from Antigua, would oblige by chucking buckets of water over him much to the amusement of the rest of us.

The only other black face in the village, if you discount Mansel Morgan the coalman and the unwashed miners coming home from their daily grind, was the colourfully named Aloysius Augustus Gums, affectionately known by the locals as Chalky; it would be seen as a racist slur today but no slur was intended. To us, Chalky was just another Welshman.

Mrs Huntley, mother of twenty kids, twelve still living, was in her eighties but was still the best barmaid we'd ever had. When my father caught sight of her slipping two-shilling pieces down her cleavage he turned a blind eye; he knew her till would show no shortfall. How she did it he never quite found out but he suspected she made it up by overcharging the punters.

With Mam and Dad busy in the bar, I was left mainly to do what I liked. I would sit on the stairs watching the colourful characters that came and went and listen to their banter. Albbie Defoe the town drunk, having been thrown out a number of times during the evening, returned through the back door only to be confronted by a not-too-happy Bert.

He eyed my father up. 'Are you the manager of every pub in this town?' he slurred.

Dad told him to get out and quick. Albbie turned slowly then danced out singing, 'Quick, quick-quick quick slow,' with my old man trying his best to stifle a laugh. Living above a pub was a new experience for me and I was loving it.

Chapter Five

Clutching a birthday present, I made my way to Pip's house. The large Victorian villa was not all it seemed; there was forlornness about it. The house, sandwiched between rows of terraced miners' cottages, was badly in need of repair; there were cracks in the pathway and most of the windows were curtain-less. In the overgrown front garden stood an old Volkswagen Dormobile up to its rusty sills in weeds. It had a fading paint job of gold star-bursts on the side panels and sported a painted banner announcing: '*Peggy and the Playmates!*'

I tentatively knocked the door. It burst open to reveal a woman of about my mother's age. She was wearing a glitzy dress of iridescent peacock colours of green and blue, her shock of black hair sparkled with silver glitter dust, and her glamorous eye make-up accentuated her dark

Celtic eyes. It was the first time I'd met the flamboyant Peg and her magnetism was instant. She kissed me on both cheeks as if she'd know me all my life, gave me a twirl and said:

'Come on in, Jono. Come join the party.'

I followed her, through a room that was littered with artwork. Weird collages all inspired by Rhineland castles. Some of the half-finished ones were scattered about the sparsely furnished room. Mobiles, in various stages of completion, were hanging on hooks from the ceiling. A mess of plaster of Paris, glue, pieces of glass, paint pots, brushes stuck in jam jars and bits of material all festooned a coffee table. The walls were plastered with photos of Peg in various showbiz poses: smiling outside the Vagabonds Club in Wiesbaden, arm in arm with a GI in uniform, and a poster that announced 'Appearing Tonight at the "Snake Pit" Mainz – Peggy and the Playmates.'

A sound like drumsticks beating out a rhythm on plates and glasses was coming from the next room, becoming louder as we came closer. The party was in full swing. I'd never been to a kids' party like it. There was no jelly, no blancmange, no sandwiches, no crisps, no lemonade. The table had been laid with knife, fork, spoon, cigarette, and glass of wine. Pip was sitting at the dining table, drumming with his knife and fork, and five other kids were sitting next to him, puffing profusely on their ciggies.

'Hiya, Jono,' said Pip handing me a glass of wine. 'Glad you could come. This is Frankie, my brother, and that's Dai Sideways,' he said, indicating a kid wearing national health glasses with one eye blanked out. 'Dai got a squint in his eye, see,' he said, noticing my quizzical look. 'He got into the habit of walking with his head on one side and now he's stuck with it. Oh…and that's Bounce next to him, cos he bounces when he walks. That's Barry Beef over there; his old man is a butcher and that's Winkie Waklin. We call him Winkie cos he got the biggest winkie in the school. Where's the food, Peg?'

I found it strange that Pip called his mother Peg; I would never have called my mother by her first name but with Peg it seemed okay somehow.

'Just coming,' she yelled back and arrived with what looked like poached eggs on toast and announced in a grand voice that it was eggs Benedict – it just looked like poached eggs to me.

Peg was a mystery; nobody seemed to know where she came from. Even though she lived in this little mining town, she had a posh accent and cooked French toast for breakfast; not the usual spread for 1950s South Wales. But then, Peg wasn't usual. Pip started puffing expertly on his cigarette. Frankie was blowing smoke down his nose, much to the amusement of Dai Sideways and Bounce.

Barry Beef and Winkie were getting stuck into their eggs Benedict.

'What do you think of this, Peg?' said Frankie, and took off his tee shirt, inserted the end of his cigarette into his belly-button and started to blow smoke rings out through his pursed lips then inhale them back up his nose.

'Very funny,' she said and left to get the cake.

I exploded into laughter. I had a mouthful of wine at the time, which was unfortunate; it squirted out of my nose, soaking my shirt, staining it a vivid red. Pip lit a cigarette and passed it to me.

'Go on, Jono. Take a drag.'

I shifted nervously in my seat. I'd never taken a drag before but not wanting these streetwise kids to think I was a wimp, I took the cigarette, held it between two fingers, as I'd seen the boys do, and took a lungful. I thought I was going to choke to death. The acrid smoke attacked my throat. I dropped my cigarette on the polished surface of the table and coughed and spluttered till I threw up. I was in a hell of a mess; my once spotless shirt that my mother had so lovingly laundered was now decorated with a mixture of red wine and vomit. Pip shrieked with laughter; tears were running down his cheeks.

'It looks better now, Jono. It's in Technicolor.'

'You rotten sod,' I spluttered. 'You knew that would happen.'

'You little bastards, what have you done?' It was Peg, returning with the cake. 'Jono is our guest; what will his mother think? Take your shirt off, Jono. I'll wash it for you; you can't go home like that.'

'That's more than you do for me,' said Pip. 'I have to wash my own in the bath.'

'You cheeky little bastard,' she said and gave him a slap for his insolence. She spotted the half-empty wine bottle. 'You were only supposed to have the one glass each,' she yelled and grabbed a thin stick she kept by the fireplace.

The boys knew what was coming and ran howling with laughter into the garden. Peg gave chase then, seeing the funny side, she started to laugh too and all was forgiven. I was in awe of this unconventional household. Apart from nearly choking to death on cheap wine and cigarettes, it was the best fun I'd had since my dad had left show business.

'Why don't you come and stay with us, Jono,' said Pip. 'It'll be alright won't it, Mam?'

'I don't know, Pip. Depends what his old man says. Here you are, Jono,' she said, handing me a small tray. 'A present for you; I don't do balloons and party bags.'

The three-dimensional collage replicating a Bavarian winter scene was quite a work of art. There was a mirror representing a frozen lake with figures made from pipe cleaners skating on it, twigs had been glued around the perimeter to represent trees and cotton wool had been stuck on to represent snow. Clutching my strange present, I followed Peg down the street towards my father's pub. As her dangerously high-heeled shoes tapped out a percussive rhythm on the pavement, she started to sing along to the rhythm of her own foot falls. I tried to remember where I'd heard the song before, then it dawned on me; I'd heard my father sing it.

Chapter Six

Heads turned as we entered the Collier's Arms. Peg's glitzy outfit looked totally out of place amongst the regular customers who, apart from a smattering of regulars, consisted mainly of coal miners dodging a shift.

There was a natural segregation in the pub. The old men frequented the long bar and the more colourful characters congregated in the small bar off the black and white tiled hallway. The few women, brave enough to be seen drinking without their husbands, could be heard raucously singing popular songs of the day in the smoke room. The accompaniment was an out-of-tune piano being thumped by Harry Humphries or Liberhumphrey as all the wags called him on account of his idol being Liberace.

There was a camaraderie and banter amongst the regulars that only people who toil hard for their living have. Everyone had nicknames: Blodwen, the cleaner, was affectionately known as Blod's thicker than water; the local cinema owner as the Abominable Showman; Mr Huntley, husband of Mrs Huntley, her of the twenty kids, was known as what-a-man-Huntley; and the dentist was Harry the extractor. Then there was Dan the Yank, my favourite. The nearest Dan had ever been to the Wild West was watching *Wagon Train* on TV. Dan was a rag-and-bone man who made his living totting for anything saleable on the nearby tip and flogging it to the local scrap yard. He'd got *his* nickname when his older sister ran off with a GI during the war and sent him a postcard from Texas. He'd spoken with an American accent ever since. He cut an incongruous figure in his turned-down wellington boots, bootlace tie and Stetson hat. His suntanned, handsome, if somewhat lined face, was enhanced by a black pencil line moustache, in honour of his hero, Errol Flynn, which added to his confident swagger that most good-looking men have.

Dan eyed Peg up. 'Shake hands with a millionaire,' he drawled, proffering Peg a grubby hand crammed with cheap rings. Dan was as far removed from a millionaire as was possible. He lived in a trailer on a bit of waste ground called Bates' Field with his cross-bred fox terrier, Bing, and his common-law wife, Liz, who, it was rumoured, did a bit of hooking on the side. Unfazed, Peg grasped Dan's dirty digits, responded with 'Howdy, pardner,' winked at him then seductively slid onto a bar stool.

'Scotch, please, barman,' she said.

Dad looked on as Victor filled a glass at the optic and pushed it towards her. Victor eyeballed her glitzy get-up and quipped, 'Didn't I see you with Burt Lancaster in *From Here to Eternity*?'

Ignoring his obvious pickup line, Peg shot out a manicured hand that sported blood red nail varnish, grabbed the glass and sank it in one.

'Hit me with another, Nigel,' she said, sliding the glass back. This one she drank more slowly, like a connoisseur – lingering on the taste.

'Very nice,' she mused, 'even if it isn't my usual single malt. You must be the new landlord,' she said, flashing Dad a flirtatious smile. 'I must say you're an improvement from the last incumbent.' She offered her hand. A look passed between them. Victor noticed the look. He also noticed that they held hands a little longer than was necessary.

'Where's the dance, love?' Dad asked.

'Oh there's no dance,' was her flippant reply. 'I just dressed up for the children.'

Peg often got dressed up in the most outrageous outfits for no apparent reason, except to please us kids; to Peg that was reason enough.

'Jono wants to stay with my boys for a bit,' she said flashing Dad another disarming smile. 'It'll be okay, won't it?' He didn't answer.

'Can I stay with the boys, Dad?' I pleaded. 'Please, Dad, can I?'

Before he could reply my mother appeared behind the bar with a tray of her home-made pasties. She fixed Peg with a steely look. Mam, with her hazel eyes blazing and her long black hair tumbling around her shoulders, reminiscent of Ava Gardner, Yvonne De Carlo and the like, was every bit a match for the exotic Peg. My skinny, five foot seven, bespectacled old man, trapped between these two glamorous women, looked like a startled prawn.

'And *who* is this?' Mam snapped. The crowded bar stopped mid sip. Dad pushed his glasses up his nose with his middle finger as he always did when he was nervous and my mother knew it.

'Oh…this is…er…'

'Peg,' she said, cutting in. 'My name is Peg. My boys are friends of Jono's.'

There was an awkward moment when nobody spoke. My mother was staring unblinkingly at Peg. Dad was looking sheepish; he'd been caught flirting again and he knew he was in for it. The whole room had gone quiet by now, reminiscent of a cowboy film when the stranger rides into town. Peg took the hint, sank her drink and slid off her stool. The eyes of all the men followed her as she slowly sashayed in sections towards the door. She turned, gave my mother a withering look, winked at Dad, then made what can only be described as a theatrical exit.

My mother hit the roof. 'Are you at it again? Your cock is like a Geiger counter always divining for your next conquest. I gave up showbiz to get away from women like her. If I catch you at it again you and me are history.'

'I can't help being sexually charismatic, can I?' Dad quipped.

Victor tried to stifle a giggle with not much success.

'What you laughing at, Victor?'

'Nothing, missis,' he said and beat a hasty retreat mumbling something about needing to change a barrel.

'I was only trying to lighten the mood, Merle,' Dad protested and was rewarded for his flippant remark by a flying dish cloth hitting him smack in the face. It really upset me when my parents fought, which was often, usually over my father's weakness for a pretty face and his spendthrift habits, and the thought of escaping to Peg and the boys for a few days was a very appealing prospect.

'Can I go to Peg's, Mam? Please, can I?' I wheedled.

My mother went ballistic. 'You come home here, smelling of smoke and reeking of alcohol, and expect me to let you stay with *her*? You're never to go to that woman's house again, do you hear me?'

I knew it would be impossible to persuade her otherwise while she was in this mood so I started putting pressure on my old man. He was really hassled that day and I knew it; the last thing he needed was an eight-year-old kid getting in the way and he cracked under the pressure.

'Go on, then,' he said. 'But if I catch you smoking again I'll chop your bloody hand off.'

'What the hell do you mean, "*go on then*"?' screamed my mother. 'And *you*,' she said, turning to me, 'get upstairs. I'll deal with you later.'

It all kicked off again. I could hear the shouting match from my bedroom and my mother was winning. I laid low for a while, waiting for my inevitable bollocking but it never came. She'd either forgotten me in the heat of the moment or thought better of it. Anyway, it wasn't my bloody fault that she'd caught the old man red-handed.

After about an hour I decided to chance my luck. We'd had the builders in and fortunately for me they'd left the scaffolding still in place. I climbed out of the window onto a wooden platform, grabbed a rope that had a bucket on the end and slid down to the garden. Then, making sure the coast was clear, I made for Peg's house.

Chapter Seven

I rang the bell. No answer. I pushed the door; it was unlocked.

'Pip…Frankie… Are you there?' Still no answer.

I stood in the hallway, listening for any sound – nothing. I ventured further, through Peg's art room to the dining room; the remnants of the party were still in evidence. And then I found her. She was huddled over the ashes of a dying fire, shivering. Her lovely eye make-up had run down her cheeks in rivulets and her usually beautifully styled hair was hanging loose and lank exposing a grey re-growth.

An empty whisky bottle and tumbler lay discarded by her side. Not being content with the generous doubles she'd downed in the pub earlier, she had managed to down a bottle of Scotch as well. How she'd sunk it in such a short time was anyone's guess. I didn't know what to say. I just stood there gawping. She handed me the tumbler. Her hand was shaking uncontrollably.

'Get me a glass of water will you, Jono, there's a good boy.'

I went to the kitchen, ran the tap until the water was cold, filled her glass and handed it to her. She grabbed the glass, drank it down in one gulp and flopped back into the chair.

'Are you okay, Peg?' I muttered not knowing quite what to do.

'It's undulant fever, Jono,' she explained, noticing the look of concern on my face. 'I caught it from contaminated milk.'

Only Peg could have thought up such a crazy excuse – she didn't fool me though. It was the booze; she had the bloody DTs.

When Benny came in I was surprised to see how much older than Peg he was; an older pot-bellied bloke with a bald head and comb-over was not what I'd have expected the exotic Peg to have shacked up with. After downing the bottle of single malt Peg had sent her long-suffering partner to get another one.

'Do you love me, Benny?' she schmoozed, grabbing the fresh bottle and pouring herself a large one.

'You know I do, Peg.'

'Then show it in cash,' she said with a smirk and tipped me a wicked wink.

Resigned to the fact he was only the paymaster, Benny sighed, pulled out a wad of notes, stuffed them into Peg's hand and left. There was an awkward silence.

'Don't look at me like that, Jono. How else was I expected to keep the family together? He knows I'm only with him for the money but the poor bastard's nuts about me. Anyway, he won't miss it – he's bloody loaded.' She poured another drink and started to laugh hysterically. 'His mother's furious; she's worried I'll inherit the family furniture business and I'm not even Jewish.'

'How did you meet him, Peg?'

'Met at a dance in Cardiff. I was singing with a band; Benny was the drummer. He wasn't very good but he thought he was bloody Buddy Rich.'

I was sure that Peg had a lot of showbiz stories but this wasn't the time; she was starting to nod off again. I found her coat where she'd dropped it, covered her over and left.

Chapter Eight

I stayed with Peg and the boys for most of that summer, against my mother's better judgement, I might add. Dad, on the other hand, was glad to get me from under his feet.

'Peg seems to have a good heart,' he schmoozed, putting on his best soft-soaping voice. 'The boy needs some friends his own age, Merle.'

It was true – until now I'd never had any real friends my own age; I hadn't been in a school long enough to make any. My friends were grownups, the musicians, showgirls and performers that Dad had worked with. Playing with kids my own age was a new experience for me, not to mention the adventures I was about to have with Pip.

My mother wasn't convinced that I should get involved with this feral family, but she was working all hours in the pub and she knew it would be impossible to keep her eyes on me twenty-four seven. She'd caught me trying to sneak out when she wasn't looking, so she accepted the inevitable and I was left mainly to my own devices for most of the time.

It was a revelation living with Peg. She had two distinct personalities; she was a cross between Auntie Mame and Cruella de Vil. When she was sober she was kind and loving, cramming all three of us boys in bed with her and telling us stories till the sun came up. But when she had the boozers' gloom, which was often, she would turn in a minute, lose her temper and beat the shit out of Pip and Frankie with the aforementioned stick she kept by the fireplace.

She never washed our clothes, we had to forage for sticks in the woods to light the fire and there was hardly ever any food in the house. Peg spent all her money on booze, so there was little left for any essentials. The kids were survivors though; they had to be. I couldn't understand how they could care so much for her but they thought the sun shone out of her arse. Apart from Pip and Frankie she had two other kids, Pip's two older sisters. The girls, being older, were rarely in evidence; they'd moved out as soon as they'd got jobs.

Susie, who I had a secret crush on, worked in the bank and Carina was a nurse at the local hospital. All four of them looked different; my mother was convinced they had different fathers. Peg would never say who Pip's dad was but there was a picture on the mantelpiece of a Catholic priest who was the image of him. Whenever Pip would broach the subject she would spin him some line about his father being a German prince and he'd swallowed it. What did he know? He was only a kid.

Pip was Peg's favourite and Frankie knew it. Whenever we got into trouble it was Frankie who got it in the neck even though it was Pip that had usually committed the crime. I felt sorry for Frankie, even though I felt he resented my closeness to his brother. He was a stolid tacit sort of kid. A deep thinker, Peg said. The difference between him and Pip was tangible, but what do you expect? They had different fathers.

The only partner of Peg's that anyone knew anything about was Frankie's father. Sean, a piss artist and coke-head who'd introduced Peg to the seedier side of life, had been the lead guitar player in Peg's band, 'The Playmates', but he'd run out on them when the gigs had dried up. Peg told me she was glad to get rid of him; he was a cruel bastard who would beat Frankie and the girls and abuse her when he was pissed, especially when he was snorting a few lines. The abuse had a profound effect on Frankie who was still wetting the bed, which was unfortunate for me as I had to share a bed with him on occasion.

These scenes of my childhood come back to me sharp and clear through my old faded eyes. Like most memories they come in no particular sequence, jumbled up like a child's pop-up book that had been ripped up and stuck back together in no particular order.

Everything seemed bigger back then, from the big blue skies to the view from the top of Garn Wen Mountain. I can still remember the resinous scent of the pine trees, peat, moss and bracken but above all I remember the silence. I'll never forget that silence, broken only by the tinkling sound of the crystal clear waters of a stream that tumbled from the summit, meandering like a silver snake towards the sea, and the cries of skylarks hovering so high above us that they could hardly be seen. I remember too the buzzing of insects and the sound of the wind amongst the sun-dried couch grass where whinberries nestled. We would pick these small purple berries till our fingers and tongues were stained from their juice and what was left we took home to our mothers to make tarts.

I can still recall with longing roaming the mountains with the boys, sliding down the grassy slopes on tin trays and pieces of cardboard, riding bareback on the horses that Roy the gypsy kept in the garden of his prefab that backed onto the mountain and riding Patch, my favourite – a half broken-in skewbald that went like the wind.

Pip, for all his bravado, wasn't a lover of horses but, goaded on by Frankie and me, he reluctantly joined us as we rode the mountain tracks. All was well until a farm dog spooked his horse and it took off. Pip was gripping on for grim death, ashen-faced, head lolling from side to side like some tailor's dummy that had been strapped on the back of a packhorse.

I gave chase, encouraging him to hold on then, nearing a fence, his horse reared up and threw him and took off, reins dangling, stirrups jangling. Roy was going to kill us. We needn't have worried; the horse knew its way home. When we arrived, expecting the full force of Roy's wrath, the horse was stood peacefully munching on some hay, back leg cocked in the camp position favoured by the milkman's horse.

I was scrubbing Patch down, who was dripping with sweat, when I noticed Roy eyeballing me from the doorway.

'You like riding fast, then, Jono?'

'Yes,' I said nervously, thinking I was in for a bollocking for over riding his horse.

'Do you want to learn to ride point to point, kid?'

'Point to what?'

'Racing. Real racehorses, not like these bags of old bones,' he said, indicating his scruffy skewbalds.

I looked at him in wonder. Did he mean it?

'I'll…have to ask my dad,' I said.

'Go on, then. Ask him.'

I ran all the way home and stood panting in front of my father, too out of breath and excited to speak.

'What is it, Jono?'

The words came tumbling out like a river. 'Dad, Dad, can I ride a racehorse, Dad? Can I, Dad…please, Dad?'

'Calm down, will you; you're not making any bloody sense.'

'Roy said he can fix it.'

'Fix what? What are you talking about?'

'For me to ride point to point. He said he's got connections.'

'I don't know…ask your mother.' He was trying to evade the question.

'She won't let me, Dad, I know she won't. Can I, Dad? Please can I?'

'Shut up, will you. You're like a bloody dripping tap.'

I kept on at him all that day until the dripping tap wore him down. Eventually, exhausted by me constantly banging on about it, he gave in and took me to Eddy Jones' racing stable the next day.

I couldn't sleep that night. I was too excited. I lay in my bed, tossing and turning, waiting for the sun to come up. I got up at six; the pub was silent, no sign of life. I made myself some toast and settled down to read a book but I couldn't concentrate; my thoughts were consumed by visions of me galloping across the countryside on a racehorse.

Chapter Nine

The thoroughbred was led out of its stall, nostrils flaring, eyes blazing, his beautiful dish-shaped face evidence of his Arab blood. I'd never seen anything like him. His skin gleamed with health, veins were standing out like knots on cotton through his black shiny coat; this was a blood horse. I was helped up onto his back by the stable boy and led to the adjoining field. Eddy, a rough unshaven man in riding boots and duffle jacket, was waiting for us.

'How much riding have you done, boy?' he grunted, chewing on a thin cheroot clenched between his teeth. 'And I don't mean those nags of Roy's either.'

'I've done a bit,' I said, not too convincingly.

He slowly shook his head. 'I'm going to have to retrain you. I'll walk him around in a circle on a lunge rein until he gets used to you and be sure not to touch him with your heels or he'll take off. This is a racehorse, remember, so take it easy.'

He fixed the lunge rein onto the bridle and helped me to adjust my stirrups. I was trotting quite comfortably when a leg of my jeans started to rumple up. I bent over to pull it down and accidentally touched the horse with my heel. Big mistake. The stallion went berserk, rearing up and bucking, fighting against the lunge rein. Eddy was struggling to hold on to him but he was too strong; he couldn't control him and the lunge rein came away in his hand, bridle and all. The horse took off up the field like a bat out of hell, leaving Eddy still holding the reins, yelling for me to hang on. The horse's mane had been platted so there was nothing to hang on *to*. I had no way of controlling the stallion. I put my arms around his huge neck and with the sound of the wind rushing past my ears and the sweet smell of his sweat filling my nostrils, I held on for dear life.

As he raced towards the railway line that skirted the field, my only thought was to get off the galloping horse. I released my feet from the stirrups and leapt from his back. I felt like I was falling. There was a sensation of incredible speed and the sound of pounding hooves in my head. I don't remember what happened next; it's all a bit of a haze. I came around with my father's face swimming into view and his distant reassuring voice in my ear.

'You're alright, Jono…take it easy; you're alright…you're alright.'

I was aware of a voice saying, 'No, I'm not… No, I'm not.' Then I realised it was *my* voice. I ran my hand over my head. There was a lump the size of a golf ball forcing my ear to stick out at right angles.

I don't know how long I'd been unconscious but Eddy had had time to catch the horse that was now standing agitatedly chomping on his reinstated bridle, his bit jangling as he bit on it.

'Come on, Jono,' he said. 'Get back up.'

I got unsteadily to my feet. I looked at the powerful horse with trepidation.

'Come on, Jon bach,' he said again, softening. 'Get back on or you'll never ride again.'

I did ride again but not a bloody racehorse. Patch was fast enough for me.

Chapter Ten

The summer, which had seemed endless with its long warm days and sultry nights, came to an end at last and it was time for me to enrol in a new school and I wasn't looking forward to it. As I approached the intimidating Victorian building, the sound of hobnailed boots sparking on the stone pavements and the hullabaloo of children's voices filled the air. Autumn had come early that year and frost glistened on the school yard. Kids were skating on the ice-covered playground. The frost had hardened from the many hobnailed boots that had compacted it, making slides that shimmered like black glass.

A teacher, bell in hand, rang furiously. It was time. I entered the brown stone building, stomach churning. The familiar smell of chalk, pencils, wet raincoats and dirty kids filled my nostrils. I'd been to too many schools already and they all smelt the same. I was always the new kid and the thought of yet another one was filling me with dread. I'd even escaped from infant school when I was five. When my mother found me, I was wandering down the high street.

'I've gone over the wall,' I said. 'I've escaped. The teacher made me drink someone else's milk. It wasn't mine, Mam, honest. It was warm, it tasted horrible and the end of the straw was all chewed up and soggy.'

I still remember that teacher and the foul-tasting liquid she made me drink and I've hated injustice ever since.

I looked for Pip for moral support amongst the pack of jostling kids but there was no sign of him; he was six months younger than me so he'd gone to a different classroom. I was put into Mr Powell's class and told to sit at a two seater desk next to a boy called Islwyn who ponged a bit. His dirty daps, or plimsolls, to give them their proper name, stunk to high heaven. I inspected the ancient, ink-stained desk made of cast iron and dark oak that was going to be my place for the foreseeable future. It had a multitude of initials that previous bored kids had carved into it. A wooden penholder with a bent nib lay next to a new exercise book. There was a space for me to write my name. I picked up the pen and contemplated the battered sharp end. How could I be expected to write with this? I dipped it into an inkwell that had been filled with black ink made from powder and scrawled my name as best I could. Islwyn noticed me struggling.

'The boys have been playing darts with it when Viper wasn't looking,' he said.

'Who's Viper?'

'Who'd you think?' he said nodding towards Mr Powell.

The large man with a red face and balding pate had a V-shaped vein on his forehead that was throbbing in time with his pulse. It made him look quite intimidating but the connotation of the name Viper and his menacing appearance was a misnomer; my new teacher was a nice man and the boys took advantage of his good nature. When he caught Islwyn chewing gum, or pepsin as we called it, he told him to spit it out. Islwyn burst into tears.

'It's for my jaw, sir,' he protested. 'My mam said I must chew it for my jaw.'

'I didn't know it was for your jaw, Islwyn bach,' he said, softening, and gave him sixpence to go and buy some more.

Islwyn had an answer for everything. When he fancied a day off he'd say he had a touch of whooping cough or 'I've got measles but the spots haven't come out yet.' Viper swallowed it; he was a real pushover as far as the kids were concerned.

Mr Powell always started the morning with prayers. 'Okay, boys,' he announced in his loud booming voice, 'The Lord's Prayer.'

This at least was something I knew but when they started to recite it in Welsh I wanted to escape; home time couldn't come quick enough.

The end-of-school bell rang and I went looking for Pip. In the far corner of the yard there was a group of kids in a circle chanting something I couldn't quite hear. As I came closer I realised Pip was being picked on by a boy about his own age.

'Oy! What do you think you're doing?' I yelled.

'Why...wot *you* gonna do about it?' sneered the boy, turning his aggression towards me.

The kids made a circle and, with the chant of 'Fight, fight, fight' ringing in my ears, we squared up. Always being the new kid on the block, I was a target for school bullies and had learnt how to defend myself but this time I was in for a rude awakening. Lenny, that was his name, laid me out in two minutes flat. The punch came from nowhere. It uncoiled like a snake, slamming into my face with the force of a mule kick and I went down gushing blood from my flattened nose. The gang, seeing Philpots the janitor approaching, quickly legged it leaving me humiliated and bleeding on the floor.

'Don't upset yourself, Jono,' said Pip, helping me up. 'His father was a bare-knuckle mountain fighter – he taught him all the tricks; you didn't stand a chance.'

'Why was he threatening you, Pip?' I said, wiping the blood away with my sleeve.

'He was calling Peg a slut. Said I didn't know who my father was. I told him to watch his mouth and shot at him with my sling; then

Lefty walked in. We both had the cane and Lefty confiscated the sling.'

Pip would defend Peg to the end. Everybody in town had her tagged as a bit of a tart but to Pip and Frankie she was a star singer.

'Come on, Jono,' he said. 'Let's break into Lefty's office. I want my sling back. If we double back now we can get in before old Philpots locks up.'

Why I went along with it I don't know. I knew it was wrong to break into the headmaster's office and I was about to find out that by following blindly in Pip's footsteps I would get into all sorts of trouble.

'I don't know about this, Pip,' I said. 'What if we get caught?'

'Come on, Jono, don't be a chicken. All the kids have gone now. Nobody will see us.'

I had a gnawing pain in the pit of my stomach and my heart was pumping like a steam hammer. I felt like it would burst out of my chest but Pip seemed to have the nerves of a bank robber. He started rifling through the draws, pocketing all sorts of things: potato guns, catapults, conkers, pen knives – then Lefty walked in. He swished his cane menacingly in his left hand as if testing the air, took a seat behind his large desk and fixed us with an icy stare. We stood there shivering in our shoes. I was terrified. What was he going to do? He peered at us over his glasses. There was a long pause then he spoke.

'Do you want six of the best or do you want to come with me?'

'Six of the best,' we whimpered. '*Come with me*' conjured up all sorts of hideous visions. He paused again, a hint of a smile playing about his lips then...

'Go on, get lost and don't let me catch you doing anything like this again.'

On reflection, Lefty was okay, even if he was a little insensitive. Having been to so many schools, my education was sadly lacking and, coupled with the fact that I suffered with what's now recognised as Attention deficit hyperactivity disorder, the only thing I excelled at was swimming. So, when Lefty, unfeelingly announced to the packed assembly hall, as he presented me with my certificate for winning a swimming gala, that 'Even Jono Griffiths can do something,' I felt like shit.

Lucky to have been let off our heinous crime we escaped, laughing hysterically with relief.

'Come on, Jono,' yelled Pip. 'Let's go home the river way.'

I followed him as he ran towards the polluted river that oozed through the industrial wasteland to the centre of the town. We clambered down the river bank and followed the surge of brown water until it disappeared into a brick-lined culvert. Pip disappeared into the dank, slimy tunnel. It didn't look too inviting to me but I had no option but to tag along. The water was rushing past my feet just inches away. Being careful not to fall in, I kept close to the moss-covered wall, feeling my way along until the water emptied out into a deep swirling pool below. We clambered down some rusty iron rungs and continued to follow the river. On the river bank, lying on its side next to a rotting makeshift quay was what remained of an old rusty boat. Tied up to it was a makeshift raft cobbled together from some old oil drums and planks of wood. I followed blindly as Pip entered the wreck through a hole in its side.

'What is this, Pip?'

'You'll see.'

The wreck didn't look safe. Shafts of sunlight filtered through the gaping timbers of the rotting deck, illuminating the interior of the hull that was sprayed with graffiti. Litter was strewn everywhere: cigarette packets, match boxes, empty cider flagons. Why was I letting this kid lead me into danger again? Was he crazy or was I crazy to follow him? I stumbled on a pile of old seventy-eight records next to a battered 'Dansette' record player that had been wired up to an old car battery. I picked up a scratched seventy-eight of 'Great Balls of Fire' and put it on the turntable.

'I wonder if this works, Pip,' I said, placing the needle on the scratched vinyl. The voice of Jerry Lee Lewis and his percussive piano rocked into life, proclaiming that she shook his nerves and rattled his brain.

'Come and listen to this, Pip,' I yelled. No answer. 'Pip… Pip… where are you?'

I smelt him before I saw him. I turned. Standing there was a tough-looking older kid. His clothes were filthy and his hair matted.

He opened his mouth to speak, revealing a mouthful of rotten teeth.

'Wot you doin' messing with our stuff?'

The sour smell of alcohol on his breath hit me. He made a grab for me, ripping my shirt. Terrified, I pulled myself free and ran for my life. I leapt from the boat and sprinted to where I could see Pip already boarding the raft. The big kid was gaining on me. Pip was screaming for me to jump but my legs were turning to jelly. I leapt onto the raft just as he punted away from the quay side, leaving the big kid yelling abuse. A shower of stones hailed down on us followed by yells of 'When I catch you little bastards I'll break your fucking legs.'

I was shivering like a dog shitting razor blades. 'What the hell are we doing, Pip? Who was that kid?'

'One of the Jones boys. If he catches us it'll be our arse. He's one of the roughest kids on the Park Estate. Together we could probably beat the shit out of him, that is if Frankie sat on him. But the fat bugger would have to get off him sooner or later to go for a piss and then he'd beat the shit out of *us*.'

'Does he go to our school?'

'Na, he goes to the Catholic school. He's not a Catholic but it was the only school that would take him.'

The river was running quite fast by now so we crossed to the opposite side and dumped the raft. The river bank had widened considerably, becoming almost like a shingle beach. A row of terraced miners' cottages backed onto the river. Their gardens leading down to the water weren't fenced off, which allowed the chickens and geese that the miners bred for some extra income to forage for food along the banks of the river.

'Come on, Jono. Let's make these buggers fly,' yelled Pip.

My narrow escape forgotten, I joined him as he chased the geese, much to their indignation, until they took off and sailed across the water. An irate local, seeing his beloved birds being tormented, ran after us with a stick. Pip, enjoying the crack, made his escape across the shallow part of the river. I watched in amazement as he jumped from stone to slippery stone as sure-footed as a goat. I was woefully inexperienced at crossing rivers; there hadn't been much call for it in Ruislip Manor.

Following Pip across the river wasn't the best idea I'd ever had but it beat being caught by our angry pursuer. The stones being wet and slippery made it doubly difficult and I fell headlong into the foul-smelling water. Apart from being dripping wet I was now covered in slimy weed. What would my mother say? She'd warned me not to play near the river. 'It's infested with rats,' she'd said. 'You'll catch Weil's disease.' Very dramatic, my mother.

We squelched down the high street towards my old man's pub. I hoped I could creep in unnoticed to dry my clothes before my mother found out what we'd been up to but Pip had other ideas. There were ten pubs in the high street. A few doors up from the Collier's Arms was the King Alfred Hotel. It had large double doors leading to a coach house. Pip said he knew the landlord kept the apples from his orchard in there and he was going to get some. It was obvious to me by now that he was a delinquent in the making and I refused point-blank to be drawn in to yet another of his hare-brained adventures. He called me a chicken and went in anyway. I was hovering nervously outside when he appeared. Not only had he stolen the apples but he'd nicked two bags to carry them in. I cracked up. He might have been a delinquent but he was a character.

It was almost dark by the time we squelched towards my father's pub. What would my old man say? I should have been home hours ago. I was about to creep in when Pip spotted a drunk having a piss against the old iron door that led to the back entrance. He pulled out the sling that he'd nicked from Lefty's office and shot a ball bearing hitting the metal door with an almighty clang. The guy nearly had a heart attack and pissed his pants. We took off down the road with 'When I catch you little bastards...' ringing in our ears for the second time that day. Pip had the feel for it now and shot out one of the street lights.

'You mad bastard,' I said. 'You've bloody done it now.'

Pip, convulsing with laughter, stuffed the sling up his bomber jacket and ran like hell down a back alley.

'Come on, Jono. Let's go up the Forge,' he yelled and jumped over a wall. I followed and found myself on a quiet backstreet. I slowed down to a walk not to look too suspicious and breathed a sigh of relief.

I thought I'd got away with it but my relief was short lived. A large hand grasped me by the shoulder. It was Sergeant Lewis, or Fatty as we called him. I managed to wriggle free and ran after Pip who was halfway down the road by now, running towards the Old Forge. Fatty gave chase but with his flat feet and big belly he was no match for us fleet-footed kids.

Chapter Eleven

The Forge, a disused iron foundry on the outskirts of the town, was now owned by the National Coal Board. It was a great place to play, if somewhat dangerous. Where once heavy machinery had lain there were stagnant pools where we hunted for crested newts and frogs and a crumbling furnace chimney tower that echoed with the croaking sounds of rooks.

The pong of the old nests and bird droppings that littered the floor didn't deter us. We would climb inside the tower to try to scale the walls and crawl through the old brick-lined culvert – the end of which was blocked up – that led from the now abandoned furnace to where we would store all the stuff we collected throughout the year for bonfire night: tyres, wood, cardboard, and oil that we would nick from the bus depot, and anything else we could scavenge from the local shops. We would guard this flotsam with our lives. Other gangs would try to raid our stash but they never found our hiding place. We would watch as one by one the waiting beacons resembling funeral pyres were ignited on the surrounding mountains. Our aim was to have the biggest bonfire in the valley and be the last to set it alight.

Water dripped from the ceiling of the dark, dank tunnel, gathering in pools on the floor. Earlier generations of kids, who like us had hidden their bounty there, had placed planks over the water to walk on. The blocked-up end of the tunnel was dry enough to store our stuff. It was also a secret place; a place where we could steal our first innocent kisses from the girls in the gang.

Adjacent to the tunnel, decaying old railway trucks stacked with disused wooden pit props lay abandoned. We would take these unwanted logs to build makeshift log cabins and pretended to be cowboys just like Dan the Yank.

I was following Pip as he headed for one of these home-made dens when we noticed, between two of the old railway trucks, a red Ford Consul Convertible gleaming softly in the moonlight. The hood was closed and its windows were shut. Because the interior light was on I could see that it was Liz, Dan's girlfriend, and a man we didn't recognise in the back seat. The man leant forward, cupped her tit through her sweater and ran his tongue across her lips. Liz seemed to put up with this but by the bored look on her chops I don't think she was enjoying it much.

The man's hands were everywhere; buttons popped, zips tugged and clothes removed until Liz was down to her bottom layer. The man rolled on top of her and started to thrust, his white bare bum shining in the moonlight. She was moaning and writhing for all she was worth. I didn't know what was happening. I'd never seen anything like it. Was she in pain?

'I don't like this, Pip,' I said. 'Is the man hurting her? Should we run to tell Dan?'

'Don't be a twat, Jono. Don't you know anything? It's sex; she's on the bloody game, mun.'

The man's breath was coming in short, sharp pants. Suddenly, he jerked in an uncontrollable spasm and flopped back onto the seat. He opened the steamed-up window, lit a cigarette, flicked the dead match out and puffed smoke into the air with a long, satisfied sigh.

'How much, love?' he asked taking out his wallet.

'Five bob alright?' she ventured.

The man pulled out a ten-shilling note.

'Sorry, mate,' she said. 'I got no change.'

'Don't worry, love,' he said. 'Keep the change; buy yourself a bit of cake.'

Pip clasped his hand over his mouth but his strangled laugh escaping through his fingers sounded like an old car starting up.

'Shut your gob,' I said. 'The last thing we want is for Dan to find out we've been spying on Liz.'

It seemed that not only was the Forge a great place to play it was an ideal location for romantic appointments, a thought which had also crossed Sergeant Lewis' mind. He'd been staking out the place for weeks in the hope of clamping down on the girls who used the secret place to turn their tricks.

I crawled out of the den only to be recaptured by a stern-faced Fatty Lewis. Pip, needless to say, made a bolt for it, leaving me to face the music. I was hauled back to the pub where Fatty presented my shivering wet and slimy self to my father. He wasn't too pleased.

'Get upstairs before your mother sees you. I'll sort you out later.'

'Is that you, Jono?' It was my mother from the kitchen.

'Yes, Mam.'

Fortunately for me she was engrossed in her daily fix, listening to *The Archers*, and I was able to creep past without her noticing my soggy state.

I knew I was in for it but fortunately for me, my old man had a good relationship with the local plod. They often popped in for a clandestine pint while on duty and Dad used his influence to get me off the heinous crime of trespassing on NCB property.

The next time I called to see Pip, there was no sign of Peg. The door was never locked so I pushed it open and went in. The house was silent.

'Pip, it's me.' No answer. I ventured as far as the staircase. I could hear someone crying. When I found him he was crouching in a corner of the kitchen clutching a piece of paper.

'What's the matter, Pip?'

'She's not my mother,' he sobbed, screwing up the paper and throwing it on the floor. 'She lied to me. I hate her.'

'What you talking about? Who?'

I picked up the crumpled paper and opened it up.

'What's this, Pip?'

'My birth certificate.'

I shot him an enquiring look. 'I don't understand. It says here that your mother's name is Amelia.'

Pip shook his head, a look of complete desolation on his face. Tears were coursing down his cheeks.

'Who am I, Jono? Was everything she told me a lie? She promised me we would get away one of these days and find him...my father. She told me I had to believe to make it happen. She told me he was a German prince.'

'Why are you crying?' I reasoned. 'Peg...or...Amelia or whatever her name is loves you doesn't she?' I tried my best to pacify him but Pip was inconsolable. For all his bravado, he was still only a kid.

'I'm going to ask my granny. She'll tell me the truth,' he sobbed.

'Look, Pip, if Peg's not your mother then your granny's not your granny, is she?'

'No, stupid, I mean Benny's mother. She'll know.'

'Where does she live?'

'Over there.' He pointed vaguely in the direction of the mountain at the back of his house. 'Cardiff. Are you coming?'

'How are we going to get there?'

'I don't know – p'raps we can walk.'

Chapter Twelve

The Journey

When Frankie turned up, Pip was rifling through Peg's handbag.

'If you're looking for fags, there's none left,' he said. 'I've already looked.'

'I'm not looking for fags. I'm looking for some money; me and Jono are walking to Cardiff. You comin'?'

'Are you nuts? Peg'll kill us if she finds out.'

'Suit yourself,' he said, grabbed a handful of change, stuffed it in his pocket and made for the door.

'Wait a minute – why you going to Cardiff?'

'I'm going to find Benny's mother.'

Frankie noticed the screwed-up birth certificate, picked it up and read it.

'What does this mean...?' But Pip was already out of earshot. 'Hey, wait for me.'

Although Pip was younger than Frankie and me, he was the most daring of us all; he was the natural leader. Perhaps it was because he'd always had to fend for himself. We knew we shouldn't be doing half the things that he led us into, but we followed him anyway. We hadn't gone far when Frankie started complaining.

'I don't suppose anyone thought of bringing any food. I'm bloody starving. How much money you got, Pip?'

'I only got 3s 6p – that's all Peg had in her purse.' They looked at me.

'It's no good looking at me; I didn't even know we were going to bloody Cardiff. My old man's gonna kill me.'

Mrs Flannigan, a skinny be-turbaned woman, sold everything in her emporium: soap flakes, potato guns, gob stoppers that changed colour when you sucked them, liquorice root, which looked like twigs until you chewed them, black bubble gum called Samba which exploded and stuck all over your face, sherbet dips that turned your fingers yellow and cigarettes called 'Craven A', which she sold individually for tuppence each and for an extra penny she would chuck in the collectable cigarette card as well.

'Can I help you, boys?' It was Mrs Flannigan from behind her counter, a cigarette dangling from the corner of her mouth as usual. The smoke from her non-stop chain-smoking, which had stained the front of her white hair a dirty yellow, filled the air. Pip rummaged in his pocket and slapped a handful of change on the counter.

'Three sausage rolls and three cigarettes, please, Mrs Flannigan.' She raised an eyebrow.

'The ciggies are for Peg, honest,' he lied.

She laid the cigarettes on the counter. 'You sure they're for your mother?'

'On my honour, Mrs Flannigan,' he said crossing his fingers behind his back.

She wrapped the sausage rolls in greaseproof paper, put them in a bag and gave them to Pip.

'I hope you're telling the truth; you're too young to be smoking,' she said, squinting as the smoke curled upwards from the end of her dangling fag, stinging her eyes.

'When did *you* start, Mrs Flannigan?'

'When I was twelve,' she said. 'And don't be so bloody cheeky; those were different days.'

Pip grabbed the paper bag, handed Frankie and me a sausage roll each, stuck one in his mouth and headed for the mountain. Our adventure had started.

Chapter Thirteen

We climbed steadily until we came upon Echo Valley Pond. The large crater, made by a stray World War II bomb, had been filled from mountain streams over time and the water was freezing. Pip ran towards the water, stripping off his clothes as he went. Pip was like a water spaniel, as soon as he saw any water, no matter how polluted it looked, he had to swim in it.

'Come on in, Jono,' he yelled.

'My old man says it's stagnant and full of rats – you'll catch something.'

'Don't listen to him; I swim in it all the time,' he said and plunged headlong into the murky water.

Nothing could persuade me to join him. The sight of the bird-sized multi-coloured dragon flies buzzing above him like helicopters gave me the willies and I refused to budge. Frankie, thinking it a great joke, pushed me in. Wham! I hit the water and went under in a swirl of bubbles. Water was filling my nostrils; I couldn't breathe. Which way was up? My waterlogged clothes were dragging me down and my legs were tangled in water weeds. I started to panic. Frankie, realising he'd gone too far, ran down the steep muddy bank, jumped in and managed to drag me out, leaving me choking and coughing, covered in pond weed and stinking of the muddy stagnant water.

'I can't feel my hands and my balls have shrunk,' I spluttered. 'What will my mam say? She's only just bought me this jumper. How am I going to dry my clothes?' Pip joined us, rummaged through his stuff, found what he was looking for and tossed Frankie a box of Swan Vestas.

'See that gorse bush, Frankie? Light it up – they burn like hell.'

Pip always carried matches. Amongst other things he was a pyro-maniac; he was always starting mountain fires by lighting the gorse bushes. He told me he was doing the farmer a favour because new grass would grow for his sheep. It backfired on him when the fire spread to the forestry commission and he had to run to tell the fire brigade. He didn't tell them he'd been the culprit and ironically was congratulated by the fire chief for letting him know. Pip got away with bloody murder.

I peeled off my wet clothes and hung them on sticks around the fire. Frankie was complaining that he knew this was a bad idea from the start and proceeded to beat his wet socks against a flat rock. Pip mischievously told him to put rocks in them because they would dry quicker. After he got through bashing them on a rock they had more holes in them than a Swiss cheese.

'You rotten sod,' he yelled. 'You knew that would happen. What am I going to do now? My socks are fucked.'

Pip cracked up. 'You fucked your own socks up, you twat.'

He pulled out some unsavoury-looking sausages from his pocket that looked like they'd been through a mangle, picked the fluff off them, impaled them on a stick and plunged them into the fire.

'I thought you said you didn't have any food,' said Frankie accusingly.

'I nicked them from Alwyn Jones' butcher shop yesterday when Phyllis wasn't looking.'

Phyllis the Fish, the butcher's wife who also ran a chip shop in the market square, was a formidable figure. Her bleached blonde hair with its beehive and marcel wave made her look much taller than her five foot five, and the white eye patch she wore over one eye, on account of an accident she'd had in the munitions factory during the war, made her look quite menacing. Pip took advantage of this and when he was on her blind side he'd nicked the sausages.

'I almost got caught though,' he continued. 'Jim Collins came in just as I was swiping the bangers.'

Jim Collins, the eighty-year-old errand boy, who worked for Alwyn, looked like a Toby jug in his gaiters and fancy waistcoat. In a previous life, Jim had been a stone mason lured from his native Cornwall by the offer of work that followed the industrial revolution. Jim couldn't read, write or tell the time, but this didn't deter him from wearing a wristwatch on each arm and a fob watch on a chain. If anyone asked him the time he would quip as quick as a flash, 'The same time as it was this time yesterday.' There were no flies on Jim, which is more than could be said for his cottage by the river; it swarmed with blue-arsed flies because of all the leftover meat he'd nicked and hoarded under the stairs.

Frankie looked at the already charring chipolatas with disdain. 'They don't look too tricky to me, Pip. You'll get sick.'

'They'll be okay when I've cooked 'em, you wimp.'

We huddled, teeth-chatteringly cold around the fire, savouring the smell of the sausages as they spat and sizzled. When they were cooked we fell on them like vultures; I hadn't eaten since I'd wolfed down the stale sausage roll from Mrs Flannigan's and I was sure the boys hadn't had anything, since Peg hadn't been at home when we left.

Pip wiped the grease from his mouth with his sleeve, pulled out a dog-end and lit it with a burning stick. He took a drag, let out a satisfied sigh and proclaimed in a pretentious voice that there was nothing like a fag after a good meal then passed the soggy ciggie to me. Frankie called him a pompous prat and threw a wet sock at him. Pip jumped on him and they rolled about, kicking and punching in the mud. After I managed to break them up, we dressed in our clothes that were still damp and reeking of smoke, and continued to climb steadily up the mountainside. The sky had darkened somewhat by now; the glowering clouds were threatening rain and there was no shelter to be seen anywhere on the barren mountain.

A sockless Frankie, his shoes squelching, was lagging behind, limping badly and complaining like hell.

'I gotta stop, boys,' he said. 'I got blisters. There must be a quicker way than this.'

Pip pointed towards a railway tunnel. 'We can take a short cut through there if you like,' he said.

'I'm not going in there,' protested Frankie. 'You're bloody mad. What if a train comes?'

'You're fuckin' chicken; I've done it loads of times. All we have to do is wait for the next one then we know we've got time to get through, see?'

Pip spotted a discarded six-inch nail by the track, picked it up and put it on the line. A train belching steam came roaring into view and disappeared into the tunnel. Pip ran to retrieve his nail that was now as flat as a pancake and razor sharp.

'See! I got a knife now,' he said, sticking it into his belt. He placed his hand on the rail track. 'Nothing comin' boys. Come on.'

Frankie gave him a withering look. 'He thinks he's a fuckin Red Indian. Come on, Jono. I'm going over the top.'

'Don't be a twat, Frankie,' said Pip. 'It's at least five miles; it'll be bloody dark by the time you see Cardiff. We can do it in fifteen minutes this way. We got time; the train's gone already.'

'What if you're wrong?'

'Dare you.'

'Dare you first.'

'Okay, go over the top if you want to; I don't give a shit. See you on the other side.'

Pip plunged into the tunnel and vanished from sight. With my stomach churning, I followed him into the pitch-black void.

Jumping from sleeper to sleeper, I went deeper into the blackness, straining my eyes, searching for the pin prick of light that would signal the end of the tunnel. As it became visible, I ran towards the welcoming light. Frankie, who had thought it better to join us than go it alone, was lagging behind. We were halfway through when I was aware of a distant rumble and felt a vibration under my feet. The rumble was getting louder. Frankie screamed '*Train*' and broke into a shambling run. Pip started running for his life but my legs had turned to jelly; I couldn't keep up. Frankie, his blistered feet forgotten, ran past me in a panic. The boys reached the end of the tunnel, jumped off the rails and rolled down the embankment. The train was bearing down on me, the rumble of grooved wheels turning heavily on the rails was deafening but all I could hear was Pip and Frankie screaming for me to jump. Sweat was running down my face burning my eyes and I could feel the thump, thump, thump of my heart in my chest. I reached the opening, jumped and plunged headfirst down the bank just as the train roared past.

I lay face down, motionless in the wet grass, listening to the metallic clickety-clack of the diminishing locomotive as it disappeared into the distance. I felt Pip's hand on my shoulder. He was hunched over me. His whole body was shaking. It took me a minute to realise that he wasn't shaking with fear – it was hysterical silent laughter. I don't know if he was laughing with relief or if he was fucking nuts and enjoyed the danger. The boy was insane.

'Come on, was. Let's go,' he said, hauling me up.

'You mad bastard,' I said turning on him. 'We could have all been killed.'

'Fuck off. We made it, didn't we?'

It was getting dark by now and a fine drizzle was coming down. Through the mist I could just make out what looked like a large prefabricated building with a corrugated tin roof. As we got closer I could see that it was an old bus depot. It was deserted save for a few buses that had been parked up for the night. Pip, ever the resourceful one, pressed a button and the door of a bus hissed open.

'You got any of those fags left, Frankie?'

'I only got a few dog-ends.'

'They'll do,' said Pip, lighting up. 'Come on, boys. Let's play with our willies.'

Pip started puffing on his dog-end and playing with his dick. I started puffing, pretending to inhale just to keep face; I didn't want to choke like the last time.

Everything I knew about smoking and sex I learnt from Pip. He'd learnt all about it from his elder sister and showed me how if I rubbed my cock I would get, in his words, 'On the itch.' We were far too young to ejaculate but it was a nice feeling all the same. None of us had developed properly yet; okay, Frankie had a few hairs but my pubic area was as bald as a coot.

'Do girls do this too, Pip?'

'Do what?'

'Wank.'

'Of course they do; twice as much as us, but they never own up to it.'

'How do they do it? They haven't got willies.'

'I dunno, I've never seen it. I heard my sister in the bathroom once but she'd plugged up the keyhole with toilet paper so I couldn't see anything.'

'You heard her?'

'Yeh, she was moanin' and groanin' and yelling, "Oh, Trevor."'

'Who's Trevor?'

'How the fuck should I know? Some pop singer, I expect.'

Pip noticed that Frankie was sitting at the back of the bus just staring into space.

'Hey, Frankie, why aren't you wanking?'

'I'm trying to give it up.'

A dog barked in the distance. Someone was whistling.

'Shut up, you two,' I whispered. 'I think someone's coming.'

Frankie and Pip's heads shot up like two meerkats, straining their ears in painful attention for any sound. Another whistle, then… 'Here, boy!'

'Shit, it's Dyfrig.'

'Who the hell's Dyfrig?' I asked.

'The nightwatchman and he's a mean bastard.'

Pip jumped out of the bus, doing up his flies as he went. Frankie scrambled over the seats to join him with me following up the rear. Dyfrig spotted us and gave chase. He was fast; he'd played wing forward for the local rugby team and he was gaining on me. I saw what looked like a big puddle of water blocking my escape route. My socks were still wet, so what the hell. I ran towards the water but instead of the expected splash I felt myself falling headlong into a void. What was happening to me? I landed with a thump. Dazed and disorientated, I lay still, listening to the barking of the dog as it got fainter. I looked up and saw Pip peering down at me from the blackness.

'What happened?'

'You've fallen down the service pit, you twat,' he said, offering his hand.

'Where's Dyfrig?'

'Chasing Frankie.'

'Where's Frankie?'

'Still running. I gave Dyfrig the slip. Come on. Let's go before he comes back.'

He hauled me out and we made a run for it. Frankie, who'd been hiding behind some oil drums, joined us and we made for the top of the hill.

Chapter Fourteen

The Big City

As we came over the ridge the big city was spread out before us like a living map. The twinkling lights below stretched as far as the eye could see. The moon shining on the River Taff reminded me of some great silver highway as it meandered towards Cardiff docks and the Bristol Channel beyond. I gazed silently at the daunting prospect. I looked at Pip for reassurance.

'So where does the old girl live?'

'Down there,' he said, pointing vaguely in the direction of the city. 'Come on. Let's go.'

Frankie shook his head. 'I can't go any further, boys; my feet are bloody killing me.'

'What about you, Jono?'

I hesitated.

'You pair of pussies. It's easier to go on now than to turn back.'

We didn't answer.

'Please yourselves,' he said and with a determined look on his face, he plunged down the hill towards the distant metropolis.

I watched as he ran down the hillside then gave in as usual and followed. I reasoned that he must know where he was going. Frankie followed on grudgingly, mumbling and bad-mouthing Pip under his breath. His blistered feet had started to bleed by now but not wanting to be left alone he gritted his teeth and doggedly soldiered on. As we approached the city, the traffic, honking of horns and the sound of the tram cars clanking on their rails assaulted our ears.

We stood gawping at the relentless commotion. A driver got out of his tram with a long pole with a hook on the end. We watched as he struggled to put back the antennae that had come off the overhead cables. We gazed in awe at the tall buildings, debating which way to go. Frankie and I, well…we were feeling completely lost. But Pip had the instincts of a homing pigeon; he'd only been to old Ma Joseph's house once. How he remembered where it was was a mystery to me.

Footsore and weary, we stood gazing across a green recreation ground towards some grand Victorian villas with gabled roofs and bay windows that were standing majestically on the other side of the park. Pip pointed to the grandest.

'It's that one,' he said. 'Just like I remember it.'

'You liar!' accused Frankie. 'If Benny's mother owns a house like that how come Peg is always skint?'

'Okay, you suckers, I'll prove it,' he said and strode off across the green with me and Frankie following nervously behind. He mounted the steps that led to a double-panelled front door, looked around at Frankie and me, grinned, then gripped the brass knocker and knocked. No answer. He knocked again – still no answer.

'Come on, Pip. There's nobody there,' I said nervously.

Frankie tried to pull him away. 'You've got the wrong house, Pip.'

He knocked again and this time the porch light came on. The door creaked open to reveal a smart middle-aged lady dressed in black.

'Can I help you?' she enquired, a disdainful look on her face as she took in the three scruffy kids on the doorstep.

'I've come to see my grandmother,' announced Pip in a grand voice.

'You've clearly come to the wrong address, then, my boy,' she said and started to close the door.

Another woman's voice came from behind. 'Who is it, Trudy?'

'It's three little boys, looking for their grandmother.'

An elderly lady wearing gold-rimmed pince-nez spectacles peered around the door.

'What do you want?' she asked, squinting at us over her unusual eye-wear.

'It's me, Pip… Pip and Frankie.'

She paused, squinted at us again then, as it dawned on her who we were, said, 'It's Peg's Boys, is it?'

Whenever I pass that house now I think of the time we stood on the doorstep of that grand house, Pip, Frankie, and me, and the way that Benny's mother had called us Peg's boys. She took it for granted that I was one of Peg's boys too. Well…I suppose I was in a way.

'You'd better come in,' she said reluctantly and led us through a grand black and white tiled hallway to the dining room where the remains of what could only be called a banquet had been laid out.

'Wait here,' she said and left, closing the door behind her.

We could hear what sounded like a party in full swing coming from the next room. Pip, curious to find out what had been going on, opened the door and crept out into the hallway. He pushed the door open a crack.

'Come and see this, boys,' he whispered.

We could see through the crack that Benny was kissing a woman. She was about Peg's age. She wasn't flashy like Peg but good looking in a grown-up sort of way in her twin set and pearls. A group of well-dressed people were toasting the couple and shouting mazel tov. We didn't understand what was going on. Who was this woman?

We were spotted peeping around the door by one of the party and a hush fell over the crowd. One by one they all turned and stared at the strange sight of us three dishevelled kids standing before them like

81

orphans of the storm. Benny, embarrassed, quickly bundled us back into the dining room. He noticed us gazing hungrily at the food left on the table and gestured for us to help ourselves. We waded in like we hadn't seen food for a month.

'What's going on, boys? Why are you here?' He looked around nervously. 'Where's Peg?'

Between mouthfuls, Pip explained that he had found his birth certificate. He looked at Benny expectantly.

Benny shrugged. 'So what?'

'Do you know who my mother is?'

'What do you mean? *Peg* is your mother.'

'No she isn't. It's some woman called Amelia.'

Benny smiled. There was an awkward pause then…

'You'll have to ask her, Pip.'

'But I thought you would know.'

'Her real name *is* Amelia; Peg is a stage name. It's an old showbiz trick, if your name is short it looks bigger on the bill so she chose Peg. Everybody calls her Peg.'

'I thought I was adopted.'

Benny's face broke into a benevolent smile.

'No, Pip. You're not adopted but if you want to know who your father is you'll have to ask Peg.'

Benny's mother burst into the room.

'Are you coming back to your guests, Benny?' she snapped, annoyed at her party being interrupted by these three waifs. 'Stella is waiting for you.'

Pip was confused. 'Who are all those people, Benny? Who's Stella? Is it your birthday or something?'

'No, Pip,' he said, avoiding his eyes. 'I've just got engaged.'

'What? But you're with Peg!'

Benny seemed at a loss for words. 'Sorry, Pip, your mother and I well…it's over. I couldn't take it anymore, and Stella and me, we've been friends for years and it seemed the most sensible thing to do. I tried my best, Pip, I really did. I thought the world of Peg but her constant demands and drinking…well you know how it is.'

There was guilt written all over his face. I'd seen that look before when my mother had caught my old man flirting with a chorus girl and this was the same look. Benny dug into his pocket, pulled out a wad of notes and pressed them into Pip's hand.

'Give this to your mother. Tell her… Tell her I'm sorry.'

Pip looked up at Benny. His eyes, as big as saucers, were filling up.

'Does this mean you won't be coming back?'

Benny shook his head. 'Sorry, Pip, I wish it could have been different.'

Pip wiped the tears from his eyes with the back of his hand. 'Come on, boys,' he said. 'Let's go. We'll get the train home.'

Chapter Fifteen

Eviction and Flight

When we arrived, Peg was pacing the floor like a cat wagging its tail.

'Where the bloody hell have you little buggers been? I've been worried sick.'

'We've been to Cardiff, Mam,' said Pip.

'Cardiff? What the hell for?'

'We saw Benny.'

'Where is he? I've had that bastard Congo around here threatening me with eviction. It seems that Benny, the little shit, hasn't been paying the rent.'

'I don't think he's coming back, Mam... He...well, he's just got engaged.'

'What do you mean he's just got engaged? Who the hell to?'

'Some woman called Stella. We've just seen them.'

'Is this true?' she said, turning to Frankie.

'Yes, Mam, it's true.'

Pip pushed the bunch of notes into Peg's hand. 'He told me to give you this.'

'I don't want his fucking blood money,' she screamed and threw the crumpled notes into the fire. Pip grabbed the burning notes out of the grate and stamped them out on the floor.

'What you doing, Mam? You need this money.'

'If he thinks he can pay me off with that measly sum he can fucking forget it. This is all down to his mother, this is. She's been trying to get him married off to Stella for years. He doesn't love her. The creep is just frightened of losing his bloody inheritance.'

Peg seemed to notice me for the first time. 'Sorry, Jono, you shouldn't have to hear all this,' she said, trying to hold back the tears. 'You'd better get home. Your old man's been here looking for you and he's not too happy.'

A frantic hammering on the door stopped me in my tracks. The huge shape of a man could be seen through the frosted-glass door. Peg opened it to be confronted by an unsavoury-looking character with a tattoo of a tarantula on his shaven head and a scorpion on his neck. He was leaning up against the door jamb, his bulky figure blocking out the light. Over his shoulder, I could see his van rocking back and forth. The culprit was a huge German shepherd, barking fit to burst a blood vessel. It was hurling itself at the window, trying to bite its way through the glass, smearing it with saliva.

'What the hell do you want, Congo?'

'Deakin wants his money.'

Peg thrust the wad of notes into his hand. 'There's your money, now piss off.'

'That'll do for this month,' he said, counting the notes, 'but what about the last two years?'

'I don't owe two years. Deakin waved it for services rendered.'

He fixed her with a menacing stare. 'Yeh, but you ain't shaggin' him no more and he wants his money.'

Peg was bravely facing him down but for all her bravado I could see she was terrified but she wasn't about to show it to this thug.

'If Deakin wants his blood money tell him to come and get it himself.'

'I'll tell him but he won't be too pleased,' he sneered. 'And next time it'll be no more Mr Nice Guy; you'll be out on your fuckin' arse and your snotty sprogs will be back in care.'

'You don't frighten me,' she spat and slammed the door in his face.

She was visibly shaking. We stood there not knowing what to say. It was Pip who spoke first.

'Is it true, Mam? Will we be taken back into care?'

She looked down at Pip's little concerned face streaked with dirt and broke down. 'Never,' she sobbed. 'We've been in bigger fixes than this and I'll fix this one. Come on, Jono. Let's get you home.'

When we entered the pub the last few stragglers were leaving and Dad was about to close up for the night.

'Where the hell have you been, Jono?' he fumed. 'Your grandfather's been waiting to see you all day. He's gone home now.'

'Sorry, Dad,' I said and relayed the story of my adventure, emitting of course the fags, and the wanking, and cut to the part about Pip looking for his grandmother.

Peg looked decidedly uncomfortable. My father shot her a concerned look then turned to me.

'Get up those stairs, Jono,' he said. 'I'll see to you later.'

I was halfway up when I heard Peg say, 'I need a favour, Bert.'

'What kind of favour?'

'Benny's gone and I can't pay the rent.'

'How much do you need?'

'Two grand...'

'Two bleedin' grand? Are you nuts? Where do you think I can get that kind of money?'

'I'm being evicted, Bert,' she said, holding back the tears. 'That bastard Benny has deserted me and the rent hasn't been paid for two years. You're the only one I can turn to... You owe me.'

I was intrigued; what did she want? What did she mean he owed her? I crouched on the creaking stairway, not moving a muscle for fear of being heard.

'Look… I'd like to help, Peg, but I'm skint. I'm not in the money like when I was in show business. This bloody job only pays fifteen quid a week plus rent, coal and light.'

'Why did you give the business up, then?'

'I think we both know the answer to that one.'

'I won't tell her if you won't.' The sentence hung in the air like a threat. It had the desired effect. Dad punched the keys of the till, grabbed a bunch of notes and thrust them into Peg's hand.

'Sorry I can't do more, Peg,' he said, pushing his glasses up his nose with his forefinger. 'But you know how it is.'

'Yes, I know how it is…you're all bastards.'

'Why don't you sing again, Peg? That's what you do.'

'Deakin wants me to work it off in his club but I don't think he means singing somehow. Anyway, they don't want singers here anymore. It's all bloody strippers now. I've got to get back to Wiesbaden; the American bases, that's where the money is. This fuckin' country's had it.'

I couldn't wait to tell Pip what I'd heard but, after being stupid enough to follow him on his mad mission to find his grandmother, I was grounded. Pip and Frankie hadn't turned up for school either. I didn't see the boys for some time after that. The next weekend came and went then the next and the next. I was eventually allowed out with strict instruction from my mother not to go near Peg or the boys.

'They're a bloody bad influence. She's a slag and they're bloody tearaways. Now promise me.'

'I promise I won't, Mam,' I lied.

As I approached Peg's house I was surprised to see the Dormobile parked on the road in front of the house. The wheels were back on and it was sporting a new paint job. Frankie was standing next to it, paint brush in hand, looking decidedly pleased with himself and Pip was pinning a home-made banner on the van, announcing *'Peg on Tour!'*

I was about to call out when a red Jaguar with wire wheels and white wall tyres pulled up. I held back to see who it was. Peg got out first followed by a man with slicked-back hair, a camel-hair coat slung over his shoulders and a heavy gold identity bracelet glinting on his wrist. I couldn't quite hear what they were saying but it was obvious by the body language they were arguing. Keeping a low profile, I crept closer. The man approached the boys.

'You kids get lost,' he said. 'Me and your mam got business.'

'We haven't finished painting yet,' Pip muttered.

'You have now,' he said, raising a hand crammed with sovereign rings.

Pip had been on the receiving end too many times so he didn't hang around to argue. He made a speedy exit into the house followed closely by Frankie.

Keeping out of sight, I continued to listen. The man was berating Peg.

'I set you up in this house. No sex, no house. You owe me.'

'You got to give me time, Deakin,' she pleaded. 'I'll find it.'

'You've had too much fucking time already; you'll have to work it off in the club like all the other girls.'

'You can piss off! I'm not doing that again.'

'Consummation. It's easy money.'

'"Consummation"? Is that what you call it? That's a bleedin' laugh – I've been there, remember.'

'Whatever you want to call it, Peg, you're sitting on the best commodity… You got it, you sell it. You still got it.'

Cackling at his own joke, he got into his car and roared off up the street with the horn playing 'Dixie'.

Peg slumped down. She looked vulnerable and sick with fear. She pulled out a half bottle of Scotch from her bag and took a swig. Not wanting to intrude on Peg's grief, I turned and went home. My news could wait.

Chapter Sixteen

The Circus

The following week a small travelling circus came to town with its various side shows and boxing booth. It came every year and as always, pitched its tent in Bates' Field. Dan the Yank, whose caravan was parked in Bates' Field, was always glad to see them; he could always get some work helping the show people, which would save him from having to go totting for junk on the nearby tip for a change.

The circus was a magnet to the local kids who wanted to see the animals, clowns and the ladies in their white tights on the high wire but to Pip it was an opportunity he'd been waiting for. With Dan busy with the circus, Pip reckoned he could nick an old battery he'd seen amongst Dan's heap of junk stacked next to his caravan. The battery of Peg's Dormobile was as flat as the tyres and she had no money for a new one. Pip's goal was to get the old wagon on the road again so Peg could escape from Deakin. I didn't like the idea of stealing from Dan and I told him so.

'I'm sure if you ask him he'll give it to you, Pip. He's a nice bloke; I like him.'

'I like him, too, but Peg is my mam; she comes first.'

Frankie refused to have anything to do with it.

'Come on, Jono,' he said. 'Pip can do what he likes. I'm going to see the show. You coming?'

A swarthy-looking boy not much older than us, carrying a bunch of leaflets and tickets, approached us.

'You want to buy some tickets, boys?' he said, flashing the leaflets at me.

'We got no money,' I said.

'No hay problema,' he said.

'Where you from, butty?' I asked.

'That depends. I was born in a wagon in Spain. My mother's Russian and my father's English.'

An irate voice came from the entrance to the tent.

'Hey, hombre, déjà de perder el tiempo con esos niños. Vende algunas billetes.'

'Lo siento, boss.'

'What language were you speaking?' I asked.

'Spanish.'

'I thought you said your mother was Russian.'

'She is. I speak Russian as well. I don't care which language I speak – I just pick it up. We travel a lot.'

It struck me that this kid had the same kind of upbringing as me, always travelling, different town every week, different country even. He'd probably had the same shit education as me but at least he could speak three languages and those were only the ones he'd demonstrated. I was jealous; I couldn't even speak Welsh.

'Sure you don't want tickets, boys?'

Frankie piped up. 'He told you, butty, we're skint, brassic. No bloody dosh. Capish?'

'That's Italian, you twat,' I said.

'How the fuck do *you* know?'

'Saw it in a film.'

'Look, if you want to go in, boys, just crawl in under the canvas, but don't let *him* catch you,' he said, nodding in the direction of the boss.

Ignoring the disapproving stares from the paying customers we crawled under the canvas, through the sawdust and came up behind the bleachers. The ringmaster announced the next act as Billy the Kid Cody, trick rider and sharp shooter. An out-of-tune band consisting of an organ, drum, and trumpet struck up 'The Man from Laramie' and a dog raced into the ring with a monkey on its back dressed in chaps and a sombrero. We laughed till we were sick. After the performance we emerged blinkingly into the bright sunlight to be confronted by Dan. He was tamping mad.

'That mate of yours has pinched stuff from my stash and had the bloody audacity to nick my wheelbarrow to take it in.'

I tried hard to stifle a laugh. 'What you going to do about it, Dan?' I spluttered.

'He can have the bloody battery – it's not much good anyway – but you tell that little bastard I want my bleedin' barrow back. He'll come to a bad end that kid, you mark my words.'

Frankie protested that it was nothing to do with him and bolted towards the exit.

Dan turned on me. 'Does your old man know you hang about with those bloody tearaways?'

I didn't answer. I just stood there, shamefaced.

'Go on, get home,' he said. 'And don't let me catch you sniffing about my stuff again.'

I gave Peg's house a wide berth for a while after that. I hadn't seen the boys for a few weeks when I decided to call. As I approached the house I realised there was something different about it. There was no sign of life. The Dormobile had gone and Dan the Yank's wheelbarrow lay abandoned on its side where the van had been. My first thought was that the van had been re-possessed. I tried the door. It was locked. Peg's door was never locked. I went around the back of the house. There were flies buzzing around bags of abandoned rubbish that had been left next to the bin. I tried the back door. It was open. The kitchen was a mess; there were dirty dishes and the remains of a meal left in the sink and cupboard doors left open.

'Anyone home?' I yelled.

No answer. I went into the lounge. Most of Peg's stuff had gone, save for a few of her half-finished mobiles that still littered the table. I couldn't believe it; they'd gone. My best friend had gone without a bloody word.

Chapter Seventeen

It was strange walking to school the next day. I didn't even have Pip to soften the blow. I'd made other friends of course but I never forgot Peg and her boys. The weeks turned into months, months turned into years without a word. Birthdays came and went; no cards came. I had to admit it: they weren't coming back.

'Get up, Jono.' It was my mother from the kitchen. 'There's snow on Garn Wen Mountain.'

It was winter. Wind was blowing in from the north with ice on its breath. The inside of my window was frosted over from the condensation, making pretty star-like patterns on the glass. They looked like paper doilies. I breathed on the glass and rubbed it; the warmth of my hand melted the ice, making a clear circle. Flakes of snow were swirling on the wind but the wind was having little effect on my mother's bed sheets on the washing line; they were as stiff as boards with frost.

I could see the mountain in the distance. It looked like a sugar loaf with its dusting of snow on the summit. My gaze fell on the dressing table and the snow scene that Peg had given me. Where had they gone? I was lost in thought when my mother called again.

'Come on, Jono. You'll be late for school.'

My new school, number eleven by my calculation, was a mile and a half away and I couldn't afford to be late. My old man had threatened me with all sorts if I didn't work hard this time. I'd failed my eleven plus not once but twice. No surprise there; I hadn't done any work. The questions on the English paper were all on *The Hound of the Baskervilles*. I hadn't even bothered to read it; I just made something up. Goodness knows what the examiners thought when they read the crap I'd written. It was no wonder that I'd been relegated to Llwynderw, the dreaded secondary modern.

The crachach (the snobs of the town) looked down their noses at the secondary modern boys, inferring that in some way that the kids who went there were second class, but they were wrong. The standard was every bit as high as the grammar school. Cadwalader Jenkins, the history teacher, brought the past alive with his stories of Owain Glyndwr, the last native Welshman to hold the title Prince of Wales, and Dic Penderyn, the coal miner hero of the Merthyr Rising.

At last *this* was a school I enjoyed. My biggest inspiration was the English teacher who read passages from *Shaka Zulu* and *Nada the Lily* by Rider Haggard. The first period of the day was English and I couldn't wait to get to his class for the next instalment.

'Coming, Mam,' I yelled. The oil cloth under my feet was freezing. I grabbed my shirt and jumper together with the rest of my clothes, got back into bed and struggled to dress under the warm bedclothes. I jumped out of bed, forgot to wash, brushed my hair and rushed down stairs. My mother had prepared porridge but I had no to time to eat; I was going to be late. I grabbed a piece of toast and ran to school. I caught up with Islwyn who was trying to make snowballs from the smattering of snow on the pavement but he wasn't having much luck.

'Not enough snow yet, Islwyn,' I said.

'Fancy going up Garn Wen later, Jono? There'll be plenty up there. P'raps Echo Valley pond will be frozen over – we could skate on it.'

'It'll be dark after school,' I said.

'Let's mitch off after lunch; nobody will cleck on us.'

Mitch? Cleck? These kids had their own language.

The bell rang. 'Okay, Islwyn, see you lunch time. Bring your sledge with you.'

Echo Valley Pond *was* frozen over. Islwyn ran onto the ice, skidding along with glee.

'Come on, Jono. This is crackin' fun.'

I followed him as he ran. The ice was cracking but not in the way he meant; it was cracking behind him. He made it across but I wasn't so lucky; his weight had weakened the ice and it gave way under me. For the second time in my life I fell into Echo Valley Pond. This time it was much more dangerous.

With Islwyn's help I grappled my way up the bank and lay there, shivering uncontrollably. There were icicles forming on my eyelashes; I looked like a character out of a Walt Disney cartoon. I couldn't feel my hands or feet and I was finding it hard to walk. Islwyn loaded me onto his sledge and somehow dragged me home then made a run for it before my father made an appearance. I squelched my way through the pub, leaving a trail of mud behind me, much to the amusement of the punters. Wisecracks were coming thick and fast.

'Bit early in the year for swimming, isn't it, Jono?' quipped Dan the Yank.

'I think he's trying to pinch my *Cruel Sea* act,' joked Victor.

Hearing the laughter coming from the punters, my mother appeared from behind the bar, tea towel in hand. To say she wasn't pleased would be an understatement.

'What the hell have you been up to, Jono? Bert, come and see to this boy, will you? I'm up to my arse in dishes.'

My father yelled from the landing. 'Jono, get up here.'

I climbed the stairs, following the sound of running water, to find my father filling the bath.

'Come on, get undressed. I don't know what's got into you, Jono,' he scolded. 'I gave up the business to give you some grounding and all you do is get into trouble.'

I stripped off with difficulty; my hands were so cold I could hardly undo the buttons of my shirt. I dropped my sodden clothes in a heap on the floor then dipped my foot in the water.

'Ow! It's flippin' scalding, Dad.'

'Don't be a wimp. How old are you, six? Act your age. Get in. It's only because you're so cold it feels hot.'

'What's been going on, Bert?' It was my mother from the hallway.

'The bugger's fallen in Echo Valley Pond again.'

'You stupid boy,' she yelled. 'You could have drowned. Those bloody kids you knock about with are delinquents. You wouldn't have known about the filthy place if that tearaway Pip hadn't taken you there.'

'Pip's gone, Mam.'

'I know, and his slag of a mother and a bloody good riddance too.'

Chapter Eighteen

That was the last time I fell in Echo Valley Pond. I was thirteen and growing up fast. My hormones were raging. Rock 'n' roll, drainpipe trousers and girls with breasts on their chests were taking over from falling in stagnant water.

My first romantic experience with the opposite sex, however innocent, was with Jennifer Jones. Our eyes first met at the local swimming pool, where a bunch of us teenagers would meet every day during the summer break. Even bad weather didn't deter us; diving in and looking upwards to watch the rain making patterns on the surface of the water above was fun.

The leader of the gang, Colin, a blonde, good looking and physically more mature boy than the rest of us, was horsing around with a beautiful girl with long black hair and deep violet eyes. I couldn't take my eyes off her. She noticed me staring and smiled. My stomach flipped. She held my gaze until, feeling self-conscious, I turned away. The horseplay continued with the giggling girls trying to get into the boys' changing rooms till the lifeguard, a barrel-chested bruiser you didn't argue with, slung them all out.

I couldn't stop thinking about Jennifer. Colin was egging me on to ask her for a date but I was too shy; I didn't think me, a seven stone weakling, stood a chance. I'd sent for a Charles Atlas course but his 'dynamic tension' bullshit hadn't bloody worked.

'Go on, Jono,' he said. 'Ask her out. We're all going to the Regal. *Boy on a Dolphin* is on. Sophia Loren's in it. She comes out of the water with her blouse stuck to her chest; you can see everything.'

The Regal cinema was the local flea pit. It burnt down in suspicious circumstances a few months later; the wags in the pub said you could hear the bugs cracking in Cardiff. During the interval I went to get the ice-cream. It's funny how songs can stir the memory. Between the double feature – you got a lot for your one shilling and nine pence in 1957– they played 'Wake up Little Suzie' by the Everly Brothers. Every time I hear the line *the movie's over, it's four o'clock, and we're in trouble deep*, I think of sitting next to Jennifer Jones, trying to pluck up courage to put my arm around her shoulder.

Sophia Loren rose from the water like Venus rising from the waves. Colin wasn't joking; her wet shirt clung to her ample breasts like fine tissue paper that goes transparent when it gets wet. The image sent a message from my brain to the trouser department. I could feel a stirring. Embarrassed that Jennifer would see the bulge I stuck my unoccupied hand in my pocket. I looked across at Colin. He wasn't looking at the screen. He had ideas of his own. Colin, who boasted he'd copped a feel from most of the girls in the gang, had *his* arm around Velma. My first impression of her was that her exotic name matched her appearance. She was the most developed of all the girls in the gang. With her red lipstick, pencil skirt, cinched in by a patent leather belt that accentuated her twenty-one-inch waist, and her tight sweater, she looked like her idol, Lana Turner.

I watched Colin as he manoeuvred; perhaps I could learn something. He slowly slid his right arm behind Velma's back and over her right shoulder. His hand, fingers moving like a tarantula after its prey, moved slowly towards its target. But Velma had been here before and slapped the creeping hand, which recoiled as quickly as it had approached. If Colin couldn't get away with it, I was sure I couldn't, so reluctantly I left my arm, which was now getting cramp, in the same position till the film ended.

The house-lights came up. We all stood for the national anthem then filed out in an orderly fashion. Colin passed arm in arm with the sexy Velma.

'We're going up the Forge,' he said with a wink. 'You coming?'

Jennifer, sensing my nervousness, took my hand and we followed on. I can't tell you what it felt like; the butterflies in my stomach were having a field day – what would happen next? As I hesitated, she kissed me. Her kiss tasted slightly of garlic, which added to her Italianate exoticness. She was in fact as Welsh as the hills but to me she was Sophia Loren. My heart raced as her knee moved up the inside of my leg towards my underdeveloped nether region and bald pubic area. I pulled away; I was too shy to let her go any further. I wished I was like Colin; he would know what to do. I had to admit it; I'd blown it. I thought she'd never kiss me again even though I wanted her to more than anything I'd ever wanted in my life.

From that day on I was besotted. I would take the long way home from school just to pass her house in the hope of catching a glimpse of her. I would watch on the side lines of the rugby pitch as she rehearsed with the Cwm Teg Tigers – one of the kazoo jazz bands that most mining districts had back then. I would watch as she paraded in her short cheerleader skirt, pill-box hat and sash, marching with the band as they competed against the Tondu Turks, Abergwynfi Arabs and other such colourful-sounding bands. I would look at her smiling eyes glowing as she twirled her baton and blew her kazoo. I watched as she flirted with older, more mature, boys in the band and wished it were me but I knew I would never be able to pluck up the courage to do anything about it.

The last time I saw her I was standing outside Campanini's Italian cafe, or the Bracchi's as we called it, after the first Italians that had arrived from Bardi. Even though the Italian cafes that seemed to be in every valley town were called different names – Malvisi, Rabbiotti, Ferrari, Carpannini, Fulgonni and the like – to us they were all Bracchi's.

It was Sunday and the ritual we called the Monkey Run was in full swing. I watched as the parade of young people passed by. It was an amazing spectacle. The high street was alive with teenagers dressed in their finery just parading up and down, interacting, making dates and drinking frothy coffee from the gleaming hissing Gaggia machines. It was up close and personal then.

Chico, the village lothario, passed by. Suited, booted, Brylcreemed and quaffed in his best black suit, white socks and penny loafers. He looked the business and he knew it. All the boys wanted to be him and all the girls wanted to be with him and Jennifer was with him.

As they passed she turned and looked at me. My stomach turned over. The butterflies I felt was the same feeling I'd felt when she'd kissed me.

'Hello,' she said, flashing me a flirtatious, if somewhat coy, smile.

Did she fancy me after all? Did I stand a chance against the charismatic Chico? I wanted to say something but my mouth was too dry and my teeth were sticking to my lip. I started to raise my hand in recognition but she'd already turned away and with a toss of her head she was gone. I didn't think that I would ever see her again but the memory of the look in that lovely girl's eyes is etched indelibly on my memory to this day.

Part Two

Chapter Nineteen

Peg

I watched Deakin as he roared off up the road. I was shivering like a kid who'd stayed too long in the sea.

'You alright, Mam?'

'I will be, Pip, but we have to get out of here. Get what stuff you need. Tell Frankie to do the same and go to bed. We've got an early start. I want to put as many miles between us and that sleazy bastard as possible.'

My guts were churning. I couldn't sleep. My head was filled with mixed emotions; it was obvious what Deakin wanted me to do. What was the name he'd used? Consummation? I looked it up. The bringing of something to a satisfying conclusion? My arse. *His* version wasn't that kosher. My head was swimming. I heard the town hall clock strike midnight then one then two. I eventually dozed off, dreaming of Congo whistling for his dog. The whistle penetrated my dream. I became conscious to the sound of a kettle whistling in the scullery. Somebody was in there. I checked the clock. It was six o'clock. I slid out of bed as quietly as I could but Pip heard me.

'Mam, if you're making tea I'll have one.'

I poked my head through the door and put my finger to my lips then crept down the stairs. Pip followed. I slowly pushed the scullery door open. Deakin was warming the teapot.

'Fancy a cuppa, Peg?' he said with a sneer. 'I was a bit disappointed you didn't show last night.'

'How the hell did you get in?'

'I've got a key, remember?' he said with a malevolent smile.

'You'll get your money, you bastard. I just need a little more time.'

'Time's the one thing we're all running out of.' He looked me up and down. 'Time's been good to you though, Peg; you're wearing well – still got your figure, I see. Perhaps we'll see it in action tonight.'

'If you think I'm going to work for you in that cesspit you call a club, you can go to hell.'

'You don't like the Why Not Club?' he mocked.

'It's a fucking den of iniquity. A bloody front for your drug and prostitution business and you know it, you bastard.'

'I'm sorry for Congo's overzealous behaviour before,' he said, changing the subject. 'He's seen too many movies… He's got this thing about playing the heavy, see. Still two lumps?' he said, plopping the cubes into my cup. 'I think I might abstain myself – I'm trying to give it up. See you tonight, then.' He sneered and dropped a paper bag into my hand, and left.

I opened it. It was a dead bird. I felt the bile rising in my throat.

'What's that, Mam?'

'Nothing, Pip. He thinks he's bloody Al Capone. He'll be kissing a guy on the lips next. Get dressed. Call Frankie. We're leaving.'

Frankie and Pip managed to get the Dormobile going and we hit the road. I was high on adrenaline. I was singing something from *Calamity Jane* and driving faster than was necessary in my boneshaker.

I hated leaving without saying goodbye to Bert but I had no option; after Deakin's sinister overtures the only thing to do was to get as far away from Cwm Teg and his clutches as possible.

I had the money Bert had given me, which was just enough to fill the tank and buy some provisions for the trip but not much else. I'd decided to go back to Germany but for all my promises I knew I couldn't take the boys with me. I pulled up outside Benny's mother's house.

'Jump out, boys,' I said. 'Benny's got something for you.'

Pip and Frankie climbed the steps and stood looking at the imposing door for the second time. When Benny answered, I revved the van's engine and took off.

'Sorry, boys,' I yelled. 'Don't hate me. It's for your own good.'

I stepped on the gas and pushed the rear-view mirror to one side – there was no time for fucking tears. I convinced myself that I was doing it because I cared. Who was I kidding? There was no way I could support them; I was desperate. I had to get back to Germany. My only hope was if I could pick up some of my old contacts I could earn big bucks again – then maybe, just maybe, I could make a home for me and the boys.

My wreck of a Dormobile coughed and spluttered all the way towards the ferry that would take me to Hook of Holland. The battery wasn't the only thing that was knackered; I was only halfway towards Harwich when the accelerator cable snapped. I managed to coast into a local garage but they didn't have a part for my ancient wagon. It was imperative I catch the ferry that day so I employed all my acting skills to schmooze the young mechanic. It's amazing what a flutter of the eyelashes can achieve. Flattered by the fact that he thought I was remotely interested in his grease monkey persona, he rigged up a Heath Robinson contraption that would take me on my way and I limped the next sixty miles by pulling on a string attached to the carburettor. I just made the ferry in time. As I creaked up the gangway I was half expecting to be turned back. But luckily nobody noticed and I was on my way.

Chapter Twenty

Wiesbaden

The Weisses Ross Hotel, on the opposite corner to the more salubrious Schwarzer Bock, was just as I remembered it but it looked a little sad now. The brown stain running down the wall from the sulphated water spewing from an ornate lion's head, and the tin cup on a chain to drink the so-called healing water from, was still there and so was the smell. It didn't look too inviting but it was cheap and I was too tired to look anywhere else; the crisp white duvet was calling me. The first time I'd stayed there I thought someone hadn't made the bed. I'd never seen a duvet before – it was sheets and blankets at home; duvets were continental. I hit the pillow and fell into a deep sleep. The next morning, I went to my old agent's office. It was closed. The sign above the door, announcing 'German American Agency', was hanging on at a crooked angle. I looked through the grimy window. The room was empty, save for the big leather-top desk where Charlie Klopp, my agent, had sat wheeling and dealing while smoking his Cuban cigars.

Charlie, a half German half Cherokee guy, had been booking the American bases during the glory days. It was a licence to print money back then and he'd cleaned up. The money he'd earned from American and British acts must have been colossal. He'd agree a price with the act then sell the act to the American bases for twice the price. Buying and selling, he called it. I know what I'd call it: a fucking rip-off. He was charging commission as well as buying and selling, which was illegal. But that was then and this was now and I needed a gig but it looked like Charlie had gone. Fuck it!

I hadn't eaten in forty-eight hours, I was starting to get the shakes and I needed a drink badly. Benny always told me not to make important decisions on an empty stomach so, heeding his advice, I went to the Cafe Europa on the Wilhelm Strasse. The Europa had been a favoured meeting place for the acts in the old days. I expected the place to be alive with musicians, performers and GIs but it was all but empty now. I ordered my Frühstück and a double brandy. A bored waitress plonked eggs and coffee in front of me.

'It's quiet today?' I said, trying to make polite conversation.

'Most of the American forces have moved out,' she said in her strong Bavarian accent. 'The halcyon days are over.'

'Do you know if Charlie Klopp's still around?'

'Haven't seen him in years. He married a Japanese dancer called Mika and moved back to the States, I think.'

I had to own up; it's true – you can never go back. I picked up my brandy and considered pouring it into my coffee. Fuck it. I downed it in one and made my way to where I remembered the Vagabonds Club to be. It was a magical scene in the old days. Everyone congregated in the Vagabonds after their gigs. Perhaps I could fix a gig there until I found another agent, or at least get enough money to get me back to England.

A flickering neon sign on a semi-derelict building announced 'The Valhalla Night Club and Disco.' My eyes were drawn higher to an earlier sign bleeding through the peeling paint-work. A logo in day-glow that said 'The Vagabonds Club' was still just visible. The memories came flooding back: Rex Roper doing his shooting and roping act, Chalky White with his musical saw, and Whiplash Willie, the black American tap dancer, jumping over three chairs and landing in the splits…great days. Where had they all gone? I opened the boot of the van and dragged out my suitcase and sound gear.

I entered the club. There were a few men hanging around the bar chatting to some dubious-looking girls; this wasn't a disco. A sleazy-looking guy came towards me. He eyeballed my sound equipment.

'Vos ist los, Schnuckiputzi?' he said with a leer.

'No sprechen Deutsch,' I said. 'Do you need a singer?'

'We don't have singers no more but you can join the girls if you like,' he said with a sleazy smile.

I'd met his type; I knew what he was thinking. I'd been here before and eaten the bratwurst; it wasn't that tasty. But I was skint. It seemed my only option was to go along with what this sleazy bastard wanted. I might as well have taken up Deakin's offer in the first place; at least he was a sleazy bastard I could handle. I was about to tell him to go fuck himself when, seeing I was close to tears, his manner softened.

'Put your stuff in there,' he said, nodding towards the dressing room.

I gazed around the drab room. There were still dog-eared posters and photos of performers from the old days plastered around the walls. My eyes were drawn to a photo of a smiling man at the piano. I could feel the tears welling up in my eyes. The first time I'd met Bert was here.

It was eight years ago. I had just finished my gig and I was high on adrenaline. I didn't feel like sleep so I decided to call in at the Vagabonds for a nightcap. The place was smoky, up-beat and jammed as usual. The GIs were dancing with the local fräuleins to a jazz trio playing on the small stage in the corner of the room. The only ones who had anything after the war were the GIs and the girls knew it. It was the first time some of them had seen silk stockings. They weren't drawing lines up the back of their legs anymore; they had the real thing now, all silk and swanky. I sashayed in, in my usual fashion. Traps, the drummer spotted me and yelled over.

'Hey, Peg. You gonna give us a song?'

'The boys in my band have got all my charts,' I yelled back.

'It don't matter. Bert can play anything.'

I knew the guys in the band but the pianist was a new one on me. He shot me a disarming smile. He was short, skinny, and wore glasses. He wasn't the best-looking guy in the world but for some reason he intrigued me.

'What do you want to sing, love?' he asked, pushing his glasses up his nose with his middle finger.

'"I Can't Give You Anything but Love",' I said. 'B flat.'

It was his talent I fell for; he sounded like an orchestra when he played. After some of the crap pianists I'd had to battle with this was more like it. I finished the song, thanked him and gave him a peck on the cheek.

'Not like that,' he said grabbing my arm. 'Give me a lingerer.'

I felt my colour rising as he pulled me towards him. Why was I acting so girlish? I'd snogged guys before; I had the kids to prove it. What was it about this guy?

'Go on, Peg. Give him a kiss,' goaded Traps. 'You know you want to.'

I can't explain what it was like. It was the best kiss I'd ever had and I'd had a few; it was like surrendering all my emotions in that one kiss.

I didn't see Bert for a while after that. Charlie Klopp had booked me into the NATO base in Naples but I never forgot that kiss.

The distance from Wiesbaden to Naples was almost a thousand miles and Charlie, the cheapskate bastard, sent me by train. It was bad enough spending two days in a couchette with a stranger snoring in the next bunk but the dining car went on strike as we passed through Switzerland and I was bloody starving. And just to put the tin hat on it, I got ripped off by the taxi driver in Naples.

The hotel on the Via Domitiana, a none-too-salubrious area where prostitutes plied their trade, was no picnic either. A fat hooker nicknamed Humpty Dumpty sat on the wall outside. There was a railway track at the back and a fun fair opposite. If I wasn't being rattled out of bed by the trains thundering past till all hours, or hit on by the manager, I was woken up by a trumpet that kicked off every five minutes when someone in the fair won a prize. I couldn't wait to get back to Wiesbaden and Bert. I couldn't stop thinking about that kiss.

The train pulled into Wiesbaden Hauptbahnhof late that night. I left my luggage at the station and walked up the Wilhelm Strasser towards the Vagabonds Club.

The last of the customers had left, the barman was clearing up and the band was just packing away their gear. Bert was busy checking the band parts when I walked in.

'Who do I have to shag to get a drink around here?'

He dropped the music all over the floor.

'I thought you were in Naples,' he said, struggling to retrieve his band's charts.

I knelt down to help him gather them. Our eyes met. I could see his cheeks colouring up.

'Am I in time for a drink or what?'

'I'm sure we can do something. Verner…a nightcap for the lady?'

'For you, Peg, anything,' said the bar tender with a smile. 'What'll it be?'

'Scotch on the rocks.'

Verner hit me with a single malt and I sat talking to Bert till the small hours. I felt so comfortable with him. My life up till then had been a bit of a train-wreck. I'd been let down by so many men and their false promises that I found it hard to trust anyone but I felt I could trust Bert; I could tell him anything. I was rabbiting on about the trip to Naples when he leaned over and kissed me. That kiss, how did he do it? Why did it affect me like that? I felt like a teenager on a first date. He slid off his stool, said goodnight to the long-suffering barman, took my hand and we walked to the Weisses Ross Hotel.

The sex was even better than I expected. No… I'll rephrase that. It wasn't sex; it was making love. I fell in love with him big time that night and I think he fell in love with me too. The last few weeks of my tour were the happiest I can remember. We breakfasted al fresco on the Wilhelm Strasse, swam in the Opelbad and picnicked by the Rhine. I'd never been treated like this before; the bastards I'd been out with just wanted to shag me, but this time, I told myself, was going to be different.

'Will I see you again, Bert…when we get back, I mean? We can't just let it end like this.'

'I'd love to see you, Peg, you know that, but, well…you know how it is.'

'Yeh… I know how it is. You got to go back to the wife. It's the story of my fucking life.'

I spent the next year schlepping around the workingmen's clubs in the North of England. It was no joke struggling against hostile concert secretaries, crap musicians and rowdy audiences, who were only quiet when the bingo was on, but what choice did I have?

I found the exotically named Flamingo Club in a Liverpool back-street. The place was jammed. The only musical backing as far as I could see was a solitary organist set up in the middle of the room. There was no drummer. I pushed my way through the crowd that consisted of mainly hookers and pissed drunk Norwegian sailors and handed the organist my music. There was no way we could rehearse; I just counted him in and hoped for the best. He was good but it made no impression on the crowd. I finished my opening song and, for the first and only time in my life, there was no applause, just the hubbub of the mob. A woman in a dress too short for her age and scuffed white shoes noticed me and yelled, 'It's Dusty,' then resumed snogging the guy she was with.

I looked at the organist. He shrugged. 'Don't worry, love. It's always like this,' he said. 'The girl last week left in tears.'

'Did she? Well, they don't frighten me; I've faced the fucking Japs.'

Halfway through my set there was an almighty crash. A guy who'd hidden in the loft, with the intention of robbing the place when it closed, fell through the ceiling onto the bar. The owner, a middle-aged woman wearing a fur coat and slippers, yelled the immortal words, 'Lock the doors. Don't let anyone out.' I'd played some dumps in my time but this one took the bleedin' biscuit.

I made my way back to London and did the rounds of auditions. I heard 'Thank you and next' so many times I thought I was in a post office line up. Then I got lucky. I saw an advert for singers for a new revue opening at the Pigalle in Piccadilly.

I arrived for the audition at ten sharp. The room was full. All the usual suspects were there: girls in leotards and leg warmers, singers going through their audition pieces and musicians setting up. Then I saw him, the rehearsal pianist.

'Hello, Peg,' he said.

My heart flipped. 'I thought you were on tour, Bert,' I spluttered.

'I was but I've cancelled it. I've taken this job in town.'

'When you're quite ready.' It was the director's voice from the floor.

'What you going to sing, Peg?'

'"I Can't Give You Anything But Love", what else?'

He shot me a wry smile. 'B flat?'

I was waiting for 'Thank you, next', but it didn't come. I opened two weeks later.

The opening night was a glitzy affair. The director arrived wearing a cloak and top hat and sat at a front table drinking champagne. This was more like it; it was definitely an improvement on the crap gigs I'd been used to. The icing on the cake was I could see Bert every night.

The stage door of the Pigalle was in Jermyn Street. Opposite was Harry's Bar where, during the interval, we would dine on rare-beef sandwiches with horseradish, washed down with Chateauneuf du Pape. We'd meet at Lyons Corner House for tea or Olivelli's Italian Restaurant in Soho for romantic dinners. But I knew it couldn't last; Bert was getting home later and later after work and his wife was getting suspicious. Our succession of romantic assignations became less and less frequent. I didn't see him for a couple of weeks. When he eventually turned up, I could tell there was something wrong.

'She's pregnant, Peg,' he said.

I was stunned; he'd promised me his marriage was over. 'How long?'

'Couple of weeks...a month.'

'What you gonna do?'

'I'm going to have to go back on tour, aren't I? The poxy money I earn as a rehearsal pianist isn't going to support a family.'

Bert sold his nice semi-detached in the leafy suburb of Ruislip Manor and told his wife he was going back on the road. I didn't believe it was because he needed the money. That was an excuse; it was because Bert and I had history. I still loved him but he'd made his choice. When he left that day it was the last time I saw him till I rocked up at his pub in South Wales eight years later.

I was still staring at Bert's photo when the sleazy guy dragged me back to reality.

'I've just spoken with Otto Gunter in Frankfurt. He says he can get you a gig in the EM club in Mainz if you want it. It's not great money but it'll be cash in hand.'

I'd worked this club in the old days. Enlisted men's clubs were murder. I wasn't looking forward to repeating the experience but I had no option; I was skint. The cab pulled up outside an austere marshal-esque building. I was looking at it with foreboding when a huge black guy met me at the door. He informed me he was the custodian. A poncy name for a doorman, I thought.

'Okay, buddy,' I said. 'Let's get this fucking show on the road.'

I followed him into the club. The large concert hall was full to bursting, but the only sound was the drone of the bingo being called by the MC. Someone yelled 'Bingo!' and the place erupted into life. Orders were called, bottles clinked, tills rang.

The atmosphere was intimidating. The enlisted men didn't want to be there in the first place and there was segregation. The white guys standing on one side of the auditorium were hurling insults, along with the odd Coke can, at the black guys on the other side, and vice versa. The EM club in Mainz wasn't nicknamed the Snake Pit for nothing.

'Where's the band?' I asked, scanning the room.

The custodian nodded towards an area in front of a square stage. It was covered in chicken wire. I raised an eyebrow.

'It's to safeguard the boys in the band when the guys throw bottles and cans at each other.'

'Classy!' I said. 'Can they read music…the band, I mean?'

'No idea. Ask the girl. She speaks English.'

The band members were all Italian. Not only could they not speak English, they couldn't read music either. How the hell was I going to do my show with these guys? The girl singer noticed my look of apprehension and approached me.

'The boys don't read this music – they only read tonic sol-fa,' she said in her broken English.

'What? Doh, Ray, fucking Me? How the hell can I do my show like that?'

'Don't worry. I will translate.' I handed her my music. 'You can put your stuff in there with mine,' she said, pointing to a room at the side of the stage.

I changed into my one beautiful gown in the cold unwelcoming dressing room. The photos of some of the previous acts, stuck on the nicotine-stained walls, were the only decoration. As I listened to the hullabaloo going on around me – people ordering drinks, going to the toilet, etc. – I reflected that this was a far cry from the old days when I would have been backed by the Ivy Benson All Girl Band or even Count Basie.

I peeped through the curtain. There were four white caps standing on the stage, one at each corner. The MC came in.

'You ready, babe?'

'They'll have to move before I go on,' I said, pointing to the four MPs. He shook his head.

'They have to stay on otherwise the guys get overexcited and try to grab the acts, especially the good-looking chicks,' he said with a grin and left.

I could hear him trying to get order. It was futile but he announced me anyway. I made my entrance. The audience was tough but somehow with the girl singer yelling out the notes to the guys in the band I got through the show. I was sitting half dressed, head in hands, physically and mentally exhausted, when the custodian barged in unannounced.

'I got your money, lady,' he said, ignoring my semi-naked state, and started to slowly count the dollars into my hand. It was obvious by the look on his face that he didn't think I was worth the paltry fifty bucks I'd been promised. I was demoralised but I soldiered on just to keep body and soul together. The only gigs I could get were in enlisted men's clubs. They didn't want to be there and neither did I; the well-aimed Coke cans weren't meant just for the black guys now.

I'd been schlepping my arse from Frankfurt to Heidelberg for six months when things came to a head. A skinny black guy, seeing me struggling in with my sound gear, stopped me at the door of the Rocker Club.

'You ain't thinking of putting that on stage, are you?' he said in his southern drawl.

'How else do you think they're going to hear me?'

I nodded towards two huge TV sets on stage. They were showing back-to-back *I Love Lucy* shows.

'I'm going to have to turn them off,' I said.

'Lady, you really don't; there'll be a fucking riot.'

'How am I supposed to do my show with those still on?'

'That's up to you, lady, but if you don't sing you don't get paid.'

Competing with two TV sets at full volume with no microphone wasn't my idea of a fun gig but I had no option. It was either that or end up fifty bucks short. It was difficult enough trying to keep in tune with the crap band, but with the sound of the TV sets blasting in my ear I had no chance. Some smart arse yelled, 'Sing up, babe. We can't hear you.' I gave him the finger and soldiered on. Fuck it, I thought, they're not listening anyway.

My act had never felt so long. I finished to sparse applause and started to de-rig; I couldn't get out of the place quick enough. One of the GIs, seeing me struggling, helped me dismantle my sound gear and I made for the door. The atmosphere was threatening. I was pushing my way through the drunken crowd when a guy stuck his hand up my skirt. I smacked him in the face. He made a grab for my tits, the custodian intervened and all hell broke loose. I'd never felt so demoralised…is this what it had come to?

The party was well and truly over and I knew it. The only thing to do was to sell everything and get back to the boys. It broke my heart to sell my old Dormobile; it made everything seem so final somehow. Show business had been my life; was this how it was all going to end?

But sentiment doesn't pay the bills. The only door open to me now was to work for Deakin and I knew what that meant. But if it was the only way I could get my kids back, so be it.

Chapter Twenty-One

The Why Not

.

I dumped my bag on the bed, pulled out my only good dress and some sexy underwear that I'd saved for such an occasion, and started to make up. The clientele of the cheap boarding house on the Taff embankment consisted of mainly long-distance lorry drivers and hookers. I'd had the wolf at the door before but this time it had been inside and had pups.

The place was a shit hole. The only illumination in the tawdry room was a shade-less low watt light-bulb. A solitary fly circled the forlorn, occupied fly-paper that dangled from the ceiling. The single divan bed looked like it had been slept in, the threadbare low-pile carpet looked sticky and the whole place smelt of damp. The dripping shower in the corner sported the kind of plastic curtain that attacked you as you showered, the soap looked used, the shampoo looked cheap and the not-too-clean towel on the rail was thin.

'Going somewhere nice?' It was the fat landlady, rollers in hair, watching from the doorway.

'I'm working for Deakin tonight.'

'I know what that means,' she said with a smirk and left.

I put the finishing touches to my make-up, put on my false eyelashes and made my way to the Why Not Bar and Disco.

I walked past the front door and made for the side entrance.

'Fancy a quickie, luv?' he said, giving me a seductive wink. It was one of the bouncers on the door.

'You couldn't afford me, mate.'

'What's with the get-up?' said the other, eying up my glittery dress.

'I wore it just to get you going.'

'Anything gets him going,' quipped his mate.

'It's a bloody good job I'm not wearing my liberty bodice with the rubber buttons, then, init?'

I left the bouncers cracking up and went around to the side entrance. A dirty chef came out with a grubby tea cloth in his hand, lit a roll-up, looked furtively around and, not seeing me, decided to have a piss. I watched as he stood pissing up against the alley wall, enjoying the relief, and the cool night air. He gave himself a few shakes and wiped his hands on the tea cloth.

'Classy,' I said.

He gave me a sour look, flicked his dog-end at me and went back inside. I followed him into what was to be my place of employment for the foreseeable future. I felt sick.

The club was full to bursting. A fan was slowly turning, moving the stale smoky air about the room. Lounging against the bar were a few of Deakin's heavies. They had a dangerous, if somewhat charismatic, air about them with their large muscles and goodness knows what else bulging beneath their shiny Italian-cut suits. A smell of stale sweat mingling with the scent of Old Spice and Californian Poppy filled the air. The pretty, if somewhat tarty, mini-skirted hostesses with their beehive hairdos, and winkle-picker stiletto-heeled shoes, were hustling the punters and a third-rate comedian was on stage struggling with a series of tired one-liners. He wasn't having much luck commanding the rowdy audience; they were more interested in the vintage porn being beamed onto a large screen on an adjacent wall.

Ensconced in booths around the stage were some seedy-looking guys being plied with over-priced champagne substitute by the bored-looking hostesses. It wasn't even cava. Deakin always was a bloody chintzy bastard. He was sitting at his own special table, next to a very young blonde dressed in expensive bad taste. As I approached him he glanced up at me from under his eyebrows.

'You're looking good, Peg.' He sneered, giving me the once-over. 'Even if you are the wrong side of thirty.' I felt the heat of anger rising.

'I see you like 'em young these days, Deakin,' I countered, eyeballing his girlfriend. 'There's a name for men like you. You'd better get going, love,' I said, turning to the girl. 'You'll be late for school.'

Deakin ignored my remark but I could see he was stung by my comeback.

'Fancy a turn in the Jacuzzi, Peg?' he said, nodding towards a door with the words 'Cuddle Puddle' emblazoned across it.

'No, thanks. I don't know what I might catch!'

'It's as clean as a whistle.'

'I wasn't talking about the Jacuzzi.'

He couldn't compete with my one-liners; I was the professional. He changed the subject.

'You've done this before, Peg, so I'll make it brief. Admission is free for the punters but the first drink is ten quid and no punter gets to talk to you without buying a drink. You get a quid commission on each drink, and if things progress, it's twenty-five quid for the room upstairs, and you get to keep anything extra. But don't make a meal of it – I like a quick turnover,' he said, giving his blonde a nudge. She was too thick to get the joke but she laughed anyway. 'Get to work, Peg. Your first punter's over there.'

He gestured towards an adjacent table. I could just see the back of a bald head. Another old fucker, I thought. I shot Deakin a look that could curdle milk and walked over to the booth.

'Hello, Peg.' I was gobsmacked. It was Benny!

'You bastard, Deakin,' I mouthed. 'What you fucking playing at?'

'He's a regular,' he said with a wink. 'Treat him right but no freebies, mind. This is business.'

I slid into the booth. 'What the hell are you doing here, Benny?' He looked uneasy.

'I heard you were back. I just had to see you.'

'What happened to the love of your life? You remember *her*, don't you? The one you abandoned me and the kids for?'

'Look, I didn't want it to come to this, Peg.'

'What? You mean shagging hookers? You left me for this? You abandoned me and the kids for *this*?'

'What? Like you did, you mean? You just dumped the boys on my doorstep like a couple of unwanted orphans and buggered off.'

I didn't answer; he was right, of course, and the jibe had hit the spot.

'Look, the kids are fine,' he said, softening. 'They're being well looked after. It hasn't been easy since you left. Stella wasn't over the moon about taking them in, as you can imagine. I decided the best thing was for them to go to my sister, Hannah in London.'

Deakin, enjoying my discomfort, yelled over. 'Stop stalling, Peg. I've got a business to run, a profit to make.'

I led Benny upstairs, found an unoccupied room and started to undress. I avoided his eyes. The situation sickened me.

'No kissing, mind,' I said.

Benny was nervous, like a schoolboy on his first date. I watched him fumbling with his fly. I couldn't help feeling sorry for the poor bastard. I went through the motions with no emotion. I reminded myself that it was just a job and I wanted it over as quickly as possible. My coldness towards him had the desired effect; he climbed off muttering that it must be the booze.

'Sure it's not the guilt?'

'It's just I've never paid for it before,' he said, offering me the money.

'Yes, you have. You just didn't realise it.'

I regretted my crass remark as soon as I'd said it; he'd been kind to me in the past and I'd used him.

'Sorry, Peg… Sorry for everything,' he mumbled.

He fumbled in his pocket, pulled out a notebook, scribbled something down, then ripped the page out and gave it to me.

'What's this?' I said, looking at the torn piece of paper.

'It's the address of the boys' school…in case you want to get in touch,' he said. He kissed me on the cheek and left.

I took a taxi back to the flop house I'd booked into earlier. I emerged from the cab blinking in the stale cold light of morning.

The driver held his hand out. 'Twenty quid, okay.'

'You taking the piss? For a ten-minute ride?'

'That's the rate, Flossie.'

'How do you know? Your meter's not even working, you thieving bastard. And don't call me Flossie.'

I flung a handful of crumpled notes in his face and he drove off giving me the finger.

'You only need a bleedin' balaclava and shot gun,' I yelled.

I stood in that deserted street still in my slinky dress and tattered stockings. I slumped to the floor in the porch of the flop house, pulled out a half bottle of Scotch from my bag and took solace the only way I knew how.

The next day I woke up with the shakes and the mother of all hangovers. I felt like shit. I fumbled in my bag for the whisky bottle; it was empty. I reflected on my sad life. I'd abandoned my kids; I had no money, no work. I certainly wasn't going back to Deakin; just the thought of it set my teeth on edge. I'd tried my best but my best hadn't been good enough. The only thing that stopped me from ending it all was the thought of the boys. I thought of Bert. I must find him; he was the only person I'd ever loved and I think he loved me too. If only things had been different but he'd made his choice. I didn't want to make trouble for him but he was the only one left I could turn to.

Chapter Twenty-Two

My cheap raincoat and down-at-heel shoes were no protection against the fine drizzle coming down. My hair was hanging lank and sticking to my face. The locals, some of whom I recognised, were staring with disdain at my dishevelled appearance. These were proud people; even the poorest polished their shoes. I arrived outside the Collier's Arms. I stood there trembling. Was I doing the right thing? What if Merle was there? How would I explain why I was turning to her husband for help? But desperate times call for desperate measures and I was desperate. There was nothing else for it. I took a deep breath and entered.

Heads turned in recognition and calls of 'Hiya, Peg. Long time, no see,' welcomed me back. I gazed around. Everything looked the same: Dan the Yank was in his usual seat, his faithful dog at his side, the sound of the old girls singing to Liberhumphrey's crap accompaniment was filtering through from the smoke room and Victor the theatrical barman was behind the bar. I scanned the room; there was no sign of Bert. Dan noticed me looking.

'Victor's the manager now,' he drawled. 'He took over from Bert when he left.'

'He left?'

'Yeh, he's gone to Cardiff, a new pub on the outskirts. It's called the Celtic Castle, I think.'

'I think he's left there now,' said Victor, cutting in. 'Gone back into showbiz, I heard.'

He pushed a Scotch towards me. 'Where've you been, Peg, Hollywood?'

'No, Vic, Wormwood.'

'I thought Wormwood Scrubs was for men only.'

'What do you think this is for,' I said, slapping my arse.

The wisecracks were coming thick and fast.

'He thinks he's a star comedian,' yelled a punter.

'He's a comedian alright – the prices he charges in here,' yelled another.

Victor stuck out a limp hand. 'Bert's told me a lot about you, Peg,' he said with a glint in his eye.

His grip was slithery; he wasn't my kind of guy.

'Obviously not enough,' I said, pushing the Scotch back. 'I like the single malt.'

There was nothing for me here now. My thoughts of finding Bert had been a mistake. He'd made his choices years ago – why should he change now? I took a last look around, grabbed the Scotch, sank it in one, said adios to Dan the Yank and left.

I caught the train back to Cardiff. My mind was in turmoil. I thought of the boys. Would they want to see me? I asked myself. I didn't want to intrude on their new lives but I just had to see them.

The next day I went to Cardiff General and took the train to Paddington. The guy at the ticket office said the nearest station to my destination was Golders Green. I knew where that was. I took the Bakerloo line to Charing Cross then changed on to the Northern line. I joined the crowd of commuters, pushing and shoving as if they were late for a life or death appointment, and exited the tube station into the light.

The high street was buzzing – people all getting on with their lives: white, black, Asian, and Hasidic Jews in their long coats, trilby hats and beards. I stopped one of the bearded guys, pulled out the piece of paper with the address of the boys' school on it and asked if he knew how I could get there. He took the crumpled paper, looked me up and down, paused for a moment then pointed me in the right direction.

It had only been a thirteen-minute walk from Golders Green with its kosher restaurants, delicatessens and synagogues, but the difference was hard to believe. Hampstead Garden Suburb, with its imposing red brick and white stucco houses, beautifully manicured lawns and hedges, was another world. No wonder the Jewish guy had looked at me strangely.

Expensive cars were arriving outside the posh school, dropping off the well-dressed pupils then driving away. I pulled out the crumpled note again to check if it was the right address. Satisfied, I hovered nervously on the opposite side of the road. A large limousine pulled up. I can't explain how I felt as the boys got out. My emotions overwhelmed me; it was an odd diversity of remorse and joy at seeing them again. They looked so clean and tidy in their pristine uniforms. I reflected on how my own down-at-heel appearance was in stark contrast to these now smart young boys.

They entered the school gates and waved goodbye, to whom I took to be Benny's sister. I'd never met her but the resemblance was remarkable. She looked like Benny in drag. I wanted to call out to the boys, to see them turn, to see them smile, to hear 'Hello, Peg.' But how could I encroach on their new lives? Better that they should forget me; I'd only ruin their future with my false hopes and promises. I watched, choking back the tears, unable to speak. I watched until the last child had entered the school gates, then I turned and walked out of their lives forever.

I didn't know what to do or where to go. I rummaged in my bag for the train fare to God knows where but it was empty. So, swallowing what little pride I had left, I asked a passing stranger if he could spare any change for a cup of coffee. I started to walk, not knowing or caring where I was destined. I had no one to turn to. I was desperate so I made my way to Soho and sold the only thing I had left to sell.

Chapter Twenty-Three

Jono

Snow was falling, insulating every sound, sentencing the half-built council estate to an eerie silence. In contrast, the Celtic Castle Hotel was a hive of activity. There were builders everywhere. It was still under construction and some of our furniture was still on the van. My only thought, as I saw the removal men struggling with my old man's piano, was to escape to the haven of my grandmother's house. I pulled my bike out of the van and announced in a grand voice that I was off to see my nan. I peddled off into the snow. It was freezing; only the thought of the coal fire in Nan's black-leaded grate kept me going. My mother accused me of being a rat leaving the sinking ship but secretly she was glad to get me from under her feet; she needed to get the pub ready for the grand opening.

After Peg and the boys had left Cwm Teg, my dad, cajoled by my mother, decided to move back to Cardiff. It was a new adventure, he said, but I had mixed feelings; the thought of yet another school filled me with dread. My mother, on the other hand, couldn't wait; she'd hated being dragged away from her family and was determined, as she put it, to get back to civilisation which, to my shame, I reiterated to Mr Powell, my old teacher.

'I hear you're leaving us, then, Griffiths,' he said.

'Yes, sir. Back to Cardiff and civilisation.'

There was an awkward silence. The V-like vein pulsated on his forehead. What was I thinking? That valley people weren't civilised? I cringe when I think of that insensitive remark. These were hard-working people I was disrespecting who'd toiled at the coal face from morning till night. These were the people who had paid for my education by paying three old pence a week out of their meagre wages towards the miners' institutes that had educated so many. I was starting to feel uncomfortable then he smiled a knowing smile, shook my hand and wished me luck. Viper was a gent. I wish I could take it all back, apologise for my unfeeling comment, but Viper is long gone by now.

Opening day and the pub was rammed with an incongruous mix of people. The old man's cronies from the world of showbiz had turned up and were mingling with brewery officials, builders, musicians and BBC producers. Dad was tinkling a white grand piano in the background. It could have been a scene from a Hollywood movie, not the opening of a provincial pub on a Cardiff council estate. Dad was in his element holding court with all his mates. This was more like it. My mother, on the other hand, was wondering if she'd done the right thing. It had been her idea to return to Cardiff. Had it been a big mistake? Was Bert getting nostalgic for the 'smell of the greasepaint'?

I had mixed feelings about going back. Despite what I'd said to Viper, I loved Cwm Teg. I missed my friends. Moving back to Cardiff seemed like a grand adventure at the time but I was homesick for the little valley town and the thought of enrolling in another school made my stomach churn; I couldn't wait till my sixteenth birthday to leave.

My mind was in turmoil. I was going through what was dismissed by my parents as just teenage angst. 'It's just your hormones,' they said. 'It's all in your head.' But it seemed very real to me. I was going through a dark period in my life. My head was consumed with thoughts of my mortality and dying. Every song, every film I saw, reminded me of it. After seeing John Wayne in *The Alamo* when everyone got slaughtered, I can still remember the gnawing pain in my stomach, reminding me of my inevitable demise and it filled me with dread.

It was showbiz that saved me from my teenage torment. It gave me something to strive for. It gave me purpose. I was mingling with my dad's showbiz friends, listening to their stories and loving it.

I noticed a lean, wiry man walking towards me. He moved like a cat.

'It's Jono, isn't it?' he said holding out his hand. 'I'm Ron. I worked with your old man at the Windmill Theatre back in the day. You dance, don't you?'

'How'd you know?'

'I could tell by the way you walk,' he said.

I was a bit wary; I didn't know how to respond. What were this guy's motives?

'What do you think, Bert?' he yelled. 'How about we get the act back together? The boy can dance, you can play the piano and we could do three-part harmony.'

My mother looked on with apprehension. Was this history repeating itself? 'I don't think so, Ron,' she yelled over the hubbub. 'I think those days are over.'

'It's only an idea, Merle, for the boy, I mean. It's in his blood.'

My father was trying to make light of it but there was a look on his face that belied his true feelings. The lure of what had been his life for so long was still strong. Merle shrugged. She'd been here before; she knew once Bert made his mind up about something there was no point arguing.

The next period of my life was magical. The following months were the happiest I can remember, rehearsing and honing the act, Dad on piano and Ron choreographing the routines. Ron had great style. I was fascinated by his easy low to the ground technique reminiscent of the black American street dancers. He'd been taught by Buddy Bradley, a famous American tap dancer who'd choreographed routines for Astaire, and passed it on to Ron who, I'm grateful to say, passed it on to me. I looked forward to learning each new step like a kid looks forward to a present at Christmas. I knew then that this was what I wanted to be. I was on cloud nine – stage struck wasn't in it. I was on Broadway already.

The longing for the little valley town seemed to have faded into a distant memory. I was back there, in the theatre. I'd been brought up in it. It was in my blood. I looked forward to hearing again the sound of the tinny bands striking up, bleeding into the dressing room through the antiquated tannoy systems, the smell of the dust on the tabs, the smell of the canvas flats painted with size, the sound of tap shoes on the stairs as the pretty chorus girls made their way to the stage and the excitement as the tabs flew out to reveal the smiling faces of the expectant audiences. I had hoped that one day I'd be back there, performing as my father had once done, and it looked as though my wish was about to come true.

Then it happened. Dad told the boss of the brewery to stick the pub up his arse, and whether my mother liked it or not we were out of work, out of house and home, and moving back in with my long-suffering but ever-welcoming nan, dog and all. Dad contacted his old agent and we were back in show business. But we were in for a rude awakening; the show business my old man had been used to no longer existed. TV had killed the music halls and all that was left were the clubs.

Chapter Twenty-Four

November the fifth wasn't the best time to be in Manchester. The freezing fog, mingling with acrid smoke that belched from the myriad coal-fired chimneys, hung in the damp evening air, enveloping the town, condemning it to premature dusk. The meagre fire in the grate of the digs looked half out and the wind was howling through the window frames. Adding to the already depressing atmosphere, the wallpaper was hanging off the wall, some of which had been stuck back on with drawing pins. Ron, wearing his suit over his pyjamas, quipped 'I suppose there are walls behind this wallpaper.'

It got worse. The Southern Sporting Club wasn't what I'd expected. The entrance hall looked like it hadn't seen a lick of paint for years. Adorning the smoke-stained walls were sepia photos of the club's past heroes, eerily staring at us from their dusty frames. Vying for position with paintings of Longhorn Scottish cattle up to their fetlocks in soggy marshes were posters of the next pigeon fanciers' dinners, hot pot suppers and the forthcoming wrestling match starring Giant Haystacks and El Bandito.

We fought our way past the horde of none-too-salubrious-looking punters who were buying their tote tickets from the doorman. He was sitting behind his desk, wearing the uniform of all such doormen: a cloth cap, three-piece suit, a little shiny around the edges, trousers held up by belt and bracers, and well-polished best black boots. He looked us up and down.

'You members?'

Ron glanced at the straw boater and a silver-top cane he was carrying then back to the doorman. 'What the hell do you think?'

'Oh…the turns, is it?' he said and waved us through.

The night was well underway. We struggled up the stairs with our props, trying to avoid the trickle of less-continent members making their way to the gents, and entered the huge auditorium.

The room was full to bursting. The drone of bingo being called by a dapper MC in a too tight tuxedo to the hushed audience was all that could be heard. Someone yelled 'House!' and the place erupted into life. Orders were called, bottles clinked, tills rang and the metallic sound of the resident organist and drummer struck up the latest pop song of the day.

There was a boxing ring incongruously plonked in front of the stage. I wondered how we were expected to perform in that. This wasn't the glamorous profession I thought it was going to be. The master of ceremonies left the stage and came over to us.

'You must be the turns for tonight?' he said, giving us the once-over. He nodded towards the door at the side of the stage. 'The dressing room's through there.'

This wasn't what I was used to either. I'd been brought up in the theatre where everyone had a dressing room that had mirrors with lights around them. This room had a stack of old chairs piled up in the corner, boxes of bingo and tote tickets piled on a table that doubled as a dressing table, an old cracked mirror that had an assortment of yellowing dog-eared publicity photographs jammed into its frame, and posters for forthcoming attractions stuck haphazardly on the dirty walls with sticky tape.

It was an experience I'll never forget. Changing in a dressing room with two strippers, four wrestlers, a girl vocalist and a comic, all jostling for position, wasn't easy. The strippers went on first dressed as tramps and did a routine to 'We're a Couple of Swells'. To all intents and purposes they were fully dressed but when they turned around one had a tit hanging out and the other had the arse out of her trousers, drawing laughs and wolf whistles from the mostly male audience. The girls returned to the dressing room stark naked. One of them had a plaster on her foot.

'You didn't go on stage like that, did you?' the comic said, alluding to the dirty plaster.

'You don't think they were looking at my fucking feet, do you?' she countered.

The comic went on next. He died on his arse. The audience had only come to see the strippers and El Bandito kicking shit out of Giant Haystacks. Then it was our turn. I don't remember how it went; I was still traumatised from my first close encounter with two naked women but I'm sure we didn't fare any better than the comic. The concert secretary, holding a couple of envelopes in his hand, burst into the room without knocking.

He addressed Ron. 'How much do I owe you?'

'Twenty-five quid,' he said.

He didn't look happy. He opened the envelope and started to count the money into Ron's hand. 'Five... Ten... Fifteen...' He paused, looked up at us, slowly shook his head in disbelief, let out a long disdainful breath, then continued counting as if it were the worst deal he'd ever done in his life.

After this disastrous outing which lasted all of two weeks, my old man decided that his days as a performer were over and we returned to Cardiff. All our furniture was in store; we didn't have a pot to piss in, so it was back to my grandmother again.

My old man, for all his irresponsible ways, was nothing if not resourceful. A few weeks later he made a grand entrance and announced that our troubles were over. We were all moving to Port Talbot. My mother lost it.

'I bloody hate Port Talbot. Where are we going to live? You've got no money to buy a place. We left the pub with the £100 bond we went in with. You spent all the profits on your bloody cronies, you waster.'

'Don't worry. George has got connections. He's promised to find us somewhere.'

'Who the hell's George?'

'Georgie Tobin. He's opening the first casino in Wales and he's asked me to be the manager. You can run the bar, Merle, and Ron and the boy can do the cabaret.'

George was the local Mafia and did indeed have connections, some of them not quite kosher. He had the council housing officer in his pocket. We moved into a council flat overlooking the sea two weeks later.

Chapter Twenty-Five

The half-finished casino was a hive of activity. There were carpenters, plumbers, electricians et al., all getting the place ready for opening night. I was rehearsing my tap routines amongst the mayhem when a workman dropped a hammer on George's pride and joy – a glass dance floor that was lit from underneath. It smashed one of the panels and all the lights went out. George went ballistic. Amongst all this chaos, Ron was busy trying to choreograph some not very good local chorus girls accompanied by my old man on the piano.

'Which one of you can kick up to here?' he said, holding his hand shoulder high. A red-headed girl, with big knickers protruding from below her high-cut leotard, put her hand up. Ron looked at her mismatched apparel and shook his head in despair.

'It's a bastard being a choreographer,' he muttered.

'Okay, which one of you kicks the lowest?' Another girl tried her best but could only reach waist high.

'Right, you lot,' he said. 'All kick the same height as her or it will look fucking awful.'

Opening night was looming but the casino was nowhere near ready. The place was still full of workmen and the brewery was refusing to deliver the booze until the money was paid up front; they'd had dealings with George before. My old man, ever the showman, assured us it would be all right on the night. He pulled in a few favours from the brewery, got some TV coverage from the BBC, and two weeks later we opened to a full house.

Everything was looking rosy; we were all getting paid, we had a flat on the sea front and George's wife had invited us to spend Christmas with them. Then the shit hit the fan. The old man caught George's son taking bottles of Scotch from the bar and plying his mates with generous doubles. When he confronted him he said he was the owner's son and he could do what the fucking hell he liked. Bert told him that *he* was the manager and it was his arse if the stock was down. George was called, a fight broke out between father and son, and my old man told George to stick his fucking casino up his arse, and like it or not we were out of work again. This was becoming a bit of a habit.

Needless to say Christmas was going to be a meagre affair. We were expecting to go to George's for Christmas dinner but that was out of the question now. My mother was at breaking point.

'You've done it to me again. I left a lovely pub with everything I needed and now we're stuck in a poxy council flat with no Christmas dinner.'

'Don't worry, love,' he schmoozed. 'I'll fix it.'

'Yeh…you're always going to bloody fix it,' she said.

Dad was gone for most of the day. When he came back he had a chicken and a Christmas pudding; he was nothing if not creative. My mother was suspicious.

'Where the hell did you get that from?'

'From Bryn Beynon.'

Bryn owned the only other club in the town and was George's arch-enemy.

'Bryn said he could use me playing the piano in his club from time to time.'

'From time to time? What the hell good is that? We've got no bloody money; I've been looking down the back of the couch for any loose coins just to buy bread and milk.'

She was right; the money from my old man's ad-hoc gigs didn't go far and the future was looking grim. I had to do something to keep body and soul together. The next week I got a job in a gents' outfitters that paid five quid a week.

Chapter Twenty-Six

The Haberdasher

A large man of about sixty, with huge feet, pockmarked skin and a bulbous nose that would have given Rudolph a run for his money, was counting the petty cash with his gloves on and still wearing his hat and overcoat.

I'd entered the pretentiously named Paris House on the Monday morning wearing my best suit, white shirt and tie, all pressed to perfection. I waited until he'd finished counting.

'I'm your new assistant,' I said.

'Ah... Griffiths, is it? I've been expecting you. This,' he said, gesturing with hands as big as hams towards the fancy department, 'will be your sole responsibility: hats, ties, handkerchiefs, socks, underwear, etc. etc. On this side you will find boy's rugbys – that's boy's suits with short trousers to you. From now on I don't want to see any of it. It will be your responsibility to keep it tidy and well stocked. But first you must start the boiler. Over there,' he said, pointing towards the back of the shop, 'you will find an overall and some gloves. Then, down there,' another gesture, 'is the cellar. There you will find the boiler. It will be your job as the junior assistant to light the said boiler every morning to heat the central heating system. You will find paper, sticks, steam coal and anthracite,' he continued. 'You will start with the paper, three sticks and two lumps of steam coal – no more no less. When it is well ignited you will place the anthracite on top. Is that clear? Mr Jones here will show you the ropes,' he said, dismissing me, and he returned to his office.

I didn't know what to say. What had I let myself in for? The rumours I'd heard about this heinous haberdasher were true. I'd been warned that he was a bloody tyrant but nothing could have prepared me for this. I felt like I was in some Dickensian play. I came here to sell clothes not light bloody boilers. If he wanted a stoker he should have rung the bloody steelworks.

Mr Jones, the first salesman, a man not much older than me, had been observing my induction with interest, a hint of a smile on his face.

'Don't worry about Tom,' he said. 'You just have to learn how to handle him.'

It was like good cop, bad cop. Mr Jones or Jeff, as he asked me to call him, lived in Cwm Teg. I'm not a great believer in coincidences but in this case it turned out to be true. He knew most of the characters of the village that I did. When Tom wasn't cracking the whip we would reminisce about the place and the mutual friends we had. He knew Pip and Frankie. Being a year older than me, he'd been in the same class as Frankie. He knew Jennifer Jones – every boy in the school knew Jennifer Jones. I pumped him as to what had happened to her. He wasn't sure but he'd heard she'd got married to a local boy and moved away.

Jeff became a good friend and mentor during my brief career as a fancy hand, as Tom insisted on calling me. He patiently showed me how to sleeve the stock so that the rows of suits on rails were aligned as perfectly as soldiers. He taught me how to press a suit with the huge 'goose iron' for the window display, fold and pack a suit in sheets of brown paper so they wouldn't crease then tie them with string. My lessons were interrupted by Tom bellowing from the office.

'Mr Griffiths, put the kettle on. I fancy an attractive cup of tea. You'll find the makings in the staff room. Oh, and after you've done that,' he yelled as an afterthought. 'You can get me a middle cutlet and chips from the chip shop and a custard slice. I'm nuts on custard slices.'

My first day as a shop assistant was turning out to be a nightmare, but I had to suck it up. I was trapped; we needed the money. I had to bite my tongue and get on with it as best I could. It was very busy that first day. Apart from my cleaning and boiler duties there'd been a run on the fancy department and most of the stock was running low. It was ten minutes before closing. I was tidying the stock ready for the next day when a customer entered in search of a tie.

'That line, Mr Griffiths,' yelled Tom, gesturing for me to go forward.

'I've only got six ties left, sir,' I said, nodding towards my depleted stock. 'But you're welcome to look.'

The man hovered, not knowing quite what to do, then…

'Okay, I'll try the Co-op,' he said and left.

Tom exploded. 'What do you mean we *only* have six ties? We *have* six attractive ties,' he yelled. 'Which one would you like? Negativity will get you nowhere, Griffiths.'

If nothing else Tom had taught me a valuable lesson that I would remember for the rest of my life – negativity gets you nowhere.

Tom donned his hat and coat and made for the door.

'Jeff, I'm going to the Chinese laundry *on paper*,' he yelled.

'What does he mean *on paper*?' I asked.

'He means, if his wife calls he's gone to the Chinese laundry. He's having an affair with the cashier at the other branch.'

'How could anyone fancy him?'

'You haven't seen the cashier, have you?' he said with a smirk.

Apart from the obvious drawbacks of working for a tyrant my time as a shop assistant wasn't all that bad. Jeff and I became firm friends and the laughs we had at Tom's expense were many. I was pressing a suit with the goose iron when Jeff yelled, 'It's the cockle woman,' and dashed out to buy a bag of cockles from the pinafored lady carrying her basket of wares, fresh from Penclawdd. I followed, forgetting the suit and the iron that was resting on it. I returned, clutching my bag of cockles, to find the iron had burnt a hole in the brand new jacket, much to Jeff's amusement.

'Stick it back into stock, Jono. Tom will never notice.'

I don't know if he ever did; I left before my heinous crime could be discovered. I'd decided that shop life wasn't for me. I thought of Peg and her words for me to follow my dreams and this wasn't it. I made the decision there and then to embark upon a solo career in show business.

My father wasn't happy. 'Are you crazy? You'll starve to death as a hoofer.'

'I'm going into the business, Dad, whether you like it or not.'

'Look what it's done to your mother and me... The family... Look at us? We're like a bunch of broken-down gypsies living in a one-bedroom flat.'

'Whose fault is that?' I asked accusingly.

'The rat race, that's what; the dog-eat-dog existence. Okay the rewards were great but the temptations were greater. I gave it up for that reason. Do you think I wanted to throw away a career where I was earning sixty quid a week to run a poxy pub for a measly fifteen quid plus house, coal and light? Well do you?' I didn't answer. 'But it was either show business or the family and the family had to come first. Do you honestly want to take the risk?'

'It's all I've dreamed of, Dad. You don't realise – all the time I spent backstage when you were on tour, listening to tin pot bands tuning up, the crackly announcement on the tannoy, the smell of the size on the scenery flats, even the smell of the dust as the tabs flew out. I loved it all, Dad. It's in my blood.'

He shot a look at my mother, looking for some back-up but it wasn't forthcoming. She sighed and shook her head in resignation. He knew he was beaten.

I soldiered on working at the menswear shop for another six months, but all I could think of was how soon I could leave. This nine to five existence was driving me nuts.

I came home from a particularly hard day; Tom had bollocked me for losing a sale and I'd burnt my hand on the fucking boiler. Dad met me at the door, brandishing a letter.

'I've got you an audition,' he said.

'What do you mean, dancing?'

'It's no good just being a fucking tap dancer; you'll be out of work by the time you're thirty.'

I grabbed the letter. The heading on the paper announced 'The Debonair's Concert Party. Shows for all Occasions.'

'When's the audition?'

'Two weeks' time.'

'Two weeks! I haven't got a bloody act yet. I've never even sung on my own.'

'You've never tried.'

From that day on the hard work began. 'If you're determined to do it,' he said, 'you're going in with both feet. No point being half-hearted about it.'

Every day after work Dad would coach me, drill me, with songs, impressions, gags, until my act was honed. What the people in the adjoining flats thought of him hammering the piano till all hours and me singing at the top of my voice I dread to think. At last I was ready but it wasn't going to be a walk in the park. I'd had a taste of club life, however brief, with my old man and Ron but now I was going to have to face the hostile audiences alone.

'I don't know about this, Dad,' I said. 'I've never ever performed solo.'

'You won't be alone. Jack and Gwyn will be there and I'll be there to play for you.'

Chapter Twenty-Seven

Being part of 'The Debonair's Concert Party' was an education I'll never forget. It was run by Jack and Gwyn, a double act who played guitars, sang and told racist jokes. This wasn't what I'd dreamed of. Life, in the shape of stone-faced concert secretaries, hostile audiences, jealous husbands and us all trying to change in the same lavatory, soon jerked me back to reality.

Jack, the leader of the party, fancied himself as a bit of a lothario. Moustachioed and Brylcreemed, he looked like one of those forties film stars. When he wasn't on stage, he could usually be found under Ruby the soprano's crinolines, copping a feel. The cramped backstage areas of the clubs weren't the most favourable ambiances for romantic assignations but it didn't seem to worry Jack. Ruby's ill-fitting dentures weren't very conducive to French kissing either; she never went anywhere without her dental fixative since her false teeth fell out in the middle of her rendition of 'The Chocolate Soldier'.

Ruby wasn't a particularly good singer but she was the only one with a car – a pink Vauxhall Cresta with white wall tyres. I, alongside Cyril the puppeteer, Dai the mime act (whose records were so cracked he decided to put them on tape, scratches and all), and Sid the tenor and compère (or 'compact', as he called it), would cram into Ruby's passion wagon. Dressed in our black tuxedos and wing collars we looked like the bloody Mafia. I soon found out that touring the South Wales clubs wasn't going to make me rich. We got twenty quid for the whole show; two pound for each performer, two pound for the petrol and Jack got the extra two quid on account that it was his concert party.

My first outing was at the Ty Nant Labour club. Cledwyn, the camp concert chairman, or the Maid of the Mountains as he was known to the locals, met us at the door. He eyeballed Jack. 'What do you call yourselves?'

Jack shot a look at his case with The Debonair's Concert Party plastered on it then back at Cledwyn. 'Lock, Stock and Barrel,' he said.

'You trying to be funny?'

'We did think of "Hook, Line and Sinker",' said Gwyn, 'but we think this sounds classier.'

'I hope you're as funny as you think you are. You'll need to be with this lot,' he said indicating a bunch of yobs bawling out 'Men of Harlech'.

'Give your music to madam over there,' he said, indicating a skinny guy in an ill-fitting wig sat at an organ.

Jack handed our music to the organist – I use the term loosely; it would have been more fitting if he'd had a handle on his bloody organ and a monkey on the top. He peered at the manuscript.

'Don't you have any music with the pictures on the front?' he said. 'I can't read this handwritten stuff.'

'What d'you mean? It's the same bloody notes, init.'

'I follow the words.'

'In other words you're a bloody busker.' Jack let out a resigned sigh. 'Okay…just do your best.'

The gig was a nightmare. The members of the audience who weren't reading newspapers were singing rugby songs and heckling.

Jack, trying to calm the situation, asked if they had any requests.

'Yeh… Piss off,' yelled the ring leader.

'Think you're funny, do you, mate?'

'Funnier than you, you twat, and you're getting paid for it.'

Jack came back with, 'When they circumcised you they threw away the wrong piece.'

The heckler hurled his meat pie at Jack. Jack threw it back, hitting him smack in the face, and a riot broke out. Bouncers were called and the culprits were thrown out. The second half of the show went relatively well. The Maid of the Mountains paid us; we packed our props, and left. The angry mob who'd been turfed out was lying in wait for us. A large barrel-chested man with muscles in his spit was bearing down on me. He looked like he could fight to the death just for fun.

'You're not so funny now, are you, mate?' he sneered.

I was surrounded; there was no escape. I knew what was coming so I swung my case full of props as hard as I could and caught my looming attacker full in the face. He just shook his head and came back at me, like some heavy in a B movie. Cyril the mime act jumped on his back followed by Jack. Bouncers from the club joined in and all hell broke loose. Ruby was screaming for help when Cledwyn appeared at the door. 'I've called the police,' he yelled. The crowd of revellers dispersed as quickly as they came and boarded the bus back to Merthyr Tydfil.

From schlepping around the clubs I gained valuable experience and a veneer so tough I could face any hostile audience. But it was time to move on. I couldn't wait to get my first solo gig. I had to find an agent.

Tony Miles' backstreet agency above a chip shop in Cardiff wasn't what I had in mind but Barry, a camp tailor known to his friends as Naughty Bar, who was measuring me for a stage suit at the time, insisted I check it out.

'You've got a bit of a lazy there,' he said, measuring my inside leg.

'You need to get a manager and stop handling yourself,' he added, giving me a suggestive wink.

'Is Tony any good?' I said, trying to deflect his attention away from my crotch.

'I don't think he's even booking a dog fight but his auditions are worth seeing. I saw a bus conductor in one of those raincoats the lower classes always seem to acquire carrying his bag of money and doing a tap dance. Top of the bill was a group he called the Mountain Men with hair down to their cobblers belting out a rock 'n' roll number.'

'I think I'll pass on that one, Barry.'

'What have you got to lose? Come on. I'll take you over. It'll be good for a laugh.'

The agency was above a chip shop. Oil paintings adorned the walls, Bukhara rugs covered the floor. Antique vases and Tiffany lamps were strategically placed on mahogany tables. It could have been some swish office in Bond Street not some backstreet gaff in downtown Cardiff. The flamboyant Tony was sat in a Victorian spoon back chair. In his skin-tight leather trousers, blouson shirt, floppy bow tie and immaculately trimmed beard, he looked more like a poncy hairdresser than an agent.

I shot Barry a what-the-fuck look.

'His wife is an antiques dealer,' he said from the corner of his mouth. 'She's older than him. He was going out with the daughter, saw the mother was loaded and married her instead.'

Tony eyed me up and down. 'Hi, Barry. Who's this?'

'This is Jono, a customer of mine.'

Tony clicked his fingers. 'Garcon! Champagne for my guests.'

The girl hovering behind him handed Barry a cut glass flute.

'Things are looking up I see,' he said, caressing the Stuart Crystal.

'Not bad but I've had a bit of bother with the tax man lately. The twat said I owed him ten grand. I offered it to him in readies. He said he'd see me in court, the bastard. Anyhow, to what do I owe this visit?'

'My friend here is a song and dance man. I thought perhaps you could put a few gigs his way?'

'Not much doing around here, Barry. I'm booking more gigs abroad these days. I booked a great act into Malta – an Elvis tribute.

He looked just like him; his sideburns met under his fucking chin. I got him a grand for the night. Then I get this call from the club saying the band can't read his music. So I thought I'd better get over there – I've had the money up front, see – what an impresario, me! Anyhow...they said they had this army band on Gozo. "Can they read music?" I said. "Read music?" he said. "Only fourteen anthems at bleedin' sight, that's all." They turn up; the bass player picks up the music and starts to shake. I said, "What's wrong with him?" He said, "He's nervous." "I'll give him fucking nervous," I said. So they get this doctor to give him an injection – fuck me if he didn't throw up in the middle of "Blue Suede Shoes".'

He waited for the laugh. 'I used to be a comedian, you know.'

'Were you any good?'

'I'll tell you how good I was, son; the bloody dog act got the standing ovation. I was what you might call a footsteps comedian – I walked off stage to the sound of my own bleedin' footsteps.'

Is this guy for real? I thought. His story was very funny but I'm sure he'd made half of it up.

'Anyhow, about you, son – do you mind travelling?'

'No problem,' I said. 'Done it all my life.'

'I got a gig in Liverpool if you want it. It pays a hundred quid. Interested?'

A hundred quid? It sounded like a fortune. Was this guy kosher? I looked at Barry who tipped me a reassuring wink. Tony pushed a contract at me and told me he'd be on twenty percent commission.

I thought the commission was a bit steep, most agents only took ten, but I had nothing else so I signed the contract and caught the next train to Lime Street.

I entered the Temple Club on Liverpool's pier head full of enthusiasm. I was greeted, by a man whom I took to be the manager.

'Are you a blue comic?'

'No,' I said.

'Oh Christ, they like it blue here, lad.'

I scanned the room. 'Where's the band?'

'We haven't got a band. We got a group.'

'Can they read music?'

'They can't read the fucking *Echo*.'

I picked a pop song the group knew and asked them to play me on. I sailed into a string of blue jokes. I was doing okay with the mainly male audience until the only woman in the place stood swaying in front of me. She was holding a tray of drinks.

'He got everything.' She slurred, 'He can have me after.'

'Go on, kid,' yelled a punter. 'Throw one up it.'

'It would be like chucking a sausage up the Mersey tunnel,' came another.

The manager jumped on stage, snatched the microphone from my hand and told her to fuck off, she was ruining my act, then handed the mic back to me. I finished with 'Delilah'. I was packing up when the manager approached with my fee.

'You coming back tonight?' he asked.

'What the hell do you think?' I said, counting my money.

I gathered up my props and headed for the exit.

'That's the trouble with you woolly backs,' he mocked. 'No bleedin' guts.'

After this baptism of fire I thought I'd give Tony and his wacky agency a miss. I spent the next three months tramping around London, looking up my dad's contacts, getting publicity photos done, doing auditions and looking for a proper agent to take me on.

One of Dad's old agents, Harry Lewis, had connections. He arranged an audition for me at Max Silva's rehearsal rooms. Accompanied by Dad, I entered the seedy-looking building in Soho. Max, a fat guy in shirt sleeves with sweat patches under the arms, was sitting behind his desk. He looked like a James Bond villain. He even had a white cat sitting on his lap, albeit a dirty one.

'Hello, Max. Still got the cat, I see. My boy's got an audition.'

'It's for a summer show,' I chipped in.

Max nodded us towards the stairs.

'Room six, Bert,' he mumbled. 'You remember the rules, don't you? No tap dancing – it disturbs the other clients.'

I nodded in agreement but I was determined to show my full range of talents and if that meant tap dancing then so be it. This was my one and only chance to get into a proper professional show and I wasn't about to blow it now.

We entered the room. Three people were sitting at a table illuminated by a single light. There was no other light in the room except for an angle poise lamp on top of an upright piano. My father sat down, spread my music out on the stand and waited for instructions.

'When you're ready,' came a voice from the semi-darkness.

I counted my Dad in and sailed into my song and dance routine. I was halfway through the tap dance when a loud warning bell started to ring with ear-splitting volume. It stopped me in my tracks. I didn't know what was going on. Fortunately for me they'd seen enough. I couldn't stop grinning like some bloody halfwit; I'd just got my first real job in show business and I couldn't wait.

Chapter Twenty-Eight

Summer Season, 1963

The train pulled into Skegness station at nine forty-five on a grey, windswept Monday morning in May. I stepped onto the platform to be confronted by a poster of a jolly fisherman announcing, 'Welcome to Skegness; it's so Bracing.' Bracing? It was bloody Baltic. I looked at the mud flats that masqueraded as a beach and the distant grey uninviting sea being whipped into white horses by the prevailing wind and wished I were back in Wales.

The holiday camp where I was to perform, looked more like an army camp than a place of entertainment. I made my way past the rows and rows of what were grandly described as chalets. The only similarity to a chalet of the Alpine region was the wood. They looked more like Nissen huts to me.

In contrast, the beautiful auditorium had two grand marble horses standing majestically each side of the proscenium arch and the rows of raked seats were upholstered in red velvet.

The band was already in the orchestra pit tuning up. The members of the cast were getting ready for the first day of rehearsal and a line of beautiful chorus girls in leotards and legwarmers were being put through their paces by the choreographer.

'You're late.' It was the producer sitting in the stalls.

'I've just come from Cardiff. The train…'

He cut me dead. 'Rehearsal starts at ten sharp; that's not five past.'

'Sorry… I…'

'No excuses. You should have been here ready to start at ten.'

The girls were all staring at me now. The rest of the cast – a three-piece close harmony group, a speciality act and a comedian – were all looking at me with disdain. My stomach was churning. That familiar first day at school feeling was back. I was the new kid on the block again and I was going to have to prove myself.

'Right, well you're here now,' he snapped. 'So let's get on with it, shall we.' He indicated the band. 'Give your music to the musical director. You'll be first to do your band call.'

I placed my musical arrangements that my father had done for me in front of the band and handed the lead sheets to the musical director. He'd been a band master in the Royal Marines; he was a sound musician but Duke Ellington he wasn't. I counted them in. They weren't as bad as I'd expected and the sound of the ten-piece band striking up lifted my spirits. For all the years I'd spend in show business the sound of a band striking up would never cease to excite me, that feeling of euphoria. I can't explain what it's like. It just takes me to a different place somehow. I can't stop myself laughing out loud, like some kid who's been given a new toy.

As I sang, I was aware of a girl with blonde hair and legs all the way to the airport smiling at me. I tried not to make eye contact but every time I looked she was still looking. I finished the band call and was collecting my music when she came over.

'Have you got any digs yet?'

'No,' I said. 'I've only just arrived.'

'There's room going where I'm staying.'

Was this lovely girl flirting with me? I could feel my colour rising.

'I could introduce you to the landlady if you like. She's a bit of a nosey parker but the rooms are clean and she's not a bad cook.'

The three-storey red brick house on the windswept sea front was full of acts and an assortment of dancers and ice skaters from another show in town. I had to share with Eddy, one of the ice skaters. My new-found friend, Julie, was sharing with Christine, another of the girls from the ice show. Eddy fancied Christine and tried to blag me to go up to Julie's room so Christine could join him in ours.

'I've only just met her,' I protested.

'But she likes you,' he said, flashing me a soft-soaping smile. 'I can tell by the way she looks at you.'

It wasn't the best decision I'd ever made; under normal circumstances I wouldn't have done it but Eddy got me drunk. The drink must have given me Dutch courage and off I went like a lamb to the bloody slaughter.

Julie was already in bed. It was a hot night. Only a sheet covered her; I could see the outline of her naked body through the sheet that gaped and clung to her glistening skin. I stood gawping at her lying there, like some village idiot.

'I'm sorry,' I stuttered. 'I…shouldn't be here but…Eddy…'

'Are you getting in or what?' she said with a naughty smile and drew back the sheet.

I self-consciously stripped down to my underpants and slid into the bed next to her. A shiver went through me as I felt the warmth of her body. I was as stiff as a flagpole. I didn't know what to do. I'd never been all the way before and it showed.

'Don't worry,' she said, sensing my nervousness. 'I'll show you.'

She kissed me gently then guided me until I entered her. It was all over in a shuddering minute. Embarrassed, I turned away from her.

'Don't be embarrassed, Jono,' she said, pulling me back. 'It happens to everyone at some time or other.' Then she wrapped herself around me and held me until I was ready and I was in for the first and most wonderful experience of my life.

Afterwards I couldn't sleep a wink; I just lay there, listening to her breathing and thinking how I could escape before she woke up. The early morning sun came over the horizon and bled through the thin unlined curtains. She was snoring now and I couldn't wait to leave but my arm was trapped beneath her; if I'd been a coyote I would have chewed it off. I tried to ease my arm from under her but it wouldn't budge. I prodded her gently but got no response; she just lay there motionless. I poked her again, nothing. I listened. She didn't seem to be breathing anymore. I started to panic – was she dead? Then she made one of those funny snorting noises like she was choking, turned over, releasing my arm, and then went on snoring. Relieved, I slipped out of bed. I'd better get back to my own room, I thought; if the nosey landlady finds out I've been having sex with another of her guests she'll tell my mother.

I gathered my clothes in one hand and my shoes in the other and left, quietly closing the door behind me. I stood motionless listening for any sound. All was quiet save for the muffled sounds of snoring coming from the other guest rooms. Satisfied, I tiptoed towards the stairs.

I didn't see the round brass-top table nestling in a dark corner at the top of the staircase. I bumped into it and it bounced down the stairs with an almighty crash. I froze, standing motionless in my nakedness, expecting lights to go on all over the house like in some West End farce. I stood there, rooted to the spot, listening for anyone approaching but nothing stirred. I crept down the rest of the stairs and made my way to Eddy's room. I tried the door. It was locked. I tapped gently. No answer. What was I to do? Fortunately, the room was on the ground floor. I quietly opened the back door and climbed onto the window ledge and tapped the window. Eddy was fast asleep with his arm around his girlfriend. He opened one eye, saw me, half naked, precariously balancing on the window ledge, and burst out laughing.

'What the fuck are you doing out there?'

'Shut up, Eddy. You'll wake everyone up. Let me in.'

After that night I couldn't shake Julie off. I wasn't ready for a full-time relationship and told her so but she wouldn't be dissuaded. She bought me all kinds of gifts. When she gave me a gold identity bracelet with my monogram engraved on it, alarm bells rang. This was getting serious.

Two weeks later she cornered me. 'I'm pregnant, Jono,' she said. I freaked out. How long did it take? Surely she couldn't have known after just two weeks.

I knew I hadn't used anything. In the heat of the moment it hadn't crossed my mind that I could get her pregnant. The last thing I wanted to do was to get a girl pregnant; my Catholic mother would have a bloody fit. I don't remember doing the show that night; all I could think of was how I would get out of this one. I stood in the wings, lost in my thoughts.

'You okay, Jono?' It was Reg, the Camp comic, with an assortment of wigs for every occasion. He'd taken a shine to me from day one and taken me under his wing. He'd been a big star back in the day, earning a thousand quid a week in the West End. But he'd fallen out with the biggest agent in the country, been black-balled and relegated to working holiday camps, Mason's dinners and bar mitzvahs. I learnt a lot from Reg and valued his advice. 'Never swear on stage,' he said. 'Because once you say shit you've got to follow it with fuck and then you've got nowhere to go.'

He listened, a concerned look on his face as I told him the whole story of my first full sexual experience. When I got to the part where she said she was pregnant after two weeks, he started to smile.

'You can't have that,' he said, tongue in cheek. 'Tell her it's defamation of character. Tell her to write you a letter explaining it's nothing to do with you. Oh. Yes…and get her to sign it over a sixpenny stamp to make it legal.'

He must have been laughing up his sleeve as he pulled the leg of this fresh-faced, wet-behind-the-ears new kid. Julie must have been more gullible than me because she did it. I kept the letter for years as a reminder of how green I was.

I left Skegness like a thief in the night. The season had ended but Julie was still stalking me. Every time I got back to the digs she would be in my room crying. What was I to do? I wasn't ready for a commitment.

There was nothing for it but to go back to South Wales and keep a low profile.

The thought of working for the tyrannical Tom in the menswear department again, not to mention stoking the furnace, didn't fill me with enthusiasm but with no work in the pipeline I had to do something. I decided that doing the odd shift at Paris House was the lesser of two evils and at least Jeff would still be there to soften the blow.

Chapter Twenty-Nine

The winter of 1963 was the coldest for more than two hundred years. It brought the whole of South Wales to a standstill. Temperatures were so cold the sea froze over. Blizzards, snow drifts and blocks of ice, in temperatures lower than minus twenty Fahrenheit, blocked many of the roads. The main road from Port Talbot to Cardiff was only just passable. Where a channel had been ploughed through the snow drifts it looked like someone had sliced through a huge wedding cake.

'Do you know any nice girls in Cardiff, Jono?' Jeff asked.

'A few,' I said, shooting him a suspicious glance. I wasn't quite sure what he was getting at.

'No, not like that,' he said, noticing my look of concern. 'I just fancied a night out in Cardiff, that's all. I thought it would be nice to have some company. You know, like a blind date or something.'

'I dunno, Jeff,' I said. 'I'll think about it.'

Because of the freezing temperatures I wasn't really up for a trip to Cardiff and after my narrow escape in Skegness, I hadn't planned on getting involved with the opposite sex for a while either.

'Go on, Jono. It'll be fun,' he wheedled.

It was the first time I'd been on a blind date, albeit somebody else's. I rang an old girlfriend of mine who worked in a hairdressing salon. I didn't know what kind of reception I'd get; it had been a while since I'd seen her. We'd split up when I'd left for Skegness. I told her I had to follow my dreams. The truth was I couldn't take commitment.

'Hello, Joan.' There was silence at the other end of the phone. 'Joan?'

'Is that you, Jono?'

'Yes. How are you?'

'Okay I suppose… You back home now?'

'Yes, for a while.' I dipped my toe in the water. 'It would be nice to see you again.'

There was another long pause. 'Joan? Are you still there?'

'Yes… I'd like that.'

Not to be denied what promised to be a very romantic appointment, I ignored my old man's protestations that we'd never make it through the harsh conditions and set off full of anticipation, sliding and skidding the thirty or so miles in convoy; Jeff in his clapped-out Triumph sports car and me trailing behind in my Mini Van.

The girls met us in front of a provincial hairdressing salon called Angelini's of Rome; it was above a greengrocer's. Hovering behind Joan was a beautifully quaffed mini-skirted girl who she introduced as Penny. She eyed up Jeff's sports car, didn't wait to be invited and jumped in the front seat. Joan joined me in my Mini Van.

The Homestead restaurant on the high street was nothing special but it was all we could afford. Thinking we were the height of sophistication, in our best Italian-style bumfreezer suits and highly polished winkle-picker shoes, we ordered steak pizzaiola and a bottle of Mateus Rosé.

I was getting stuck into my not-very-tender steak when I felt someone playing footsie with me under the table. My initial thought was it was Joan. I looked up. It was Penny who was making eye contact. There was something about her that I couldn't put my finger on. Then it dawned on me; with her black hair and blue eyes she reminded me a little of Jennifer Jones. She flirted unashamedly with me for most of that evening, much to the annoyance of Joan who thought we were rekindling our romance.

It was a year later when I saw her. She was standing at a bus stop, holding a suitcase. I pulled over and rolled down my window.

'Hi, Penny…it is Penny, isn't it?'

'Yes, that's me.'

'Still working for Angelini?'

'No, he did a bunk. He was done for tax evasion and did a runner with all the takings.'

'What happened to him?'

'Don't know. He hasn't been seen since. He abandoned his sports car on the dock at Southampton, by all accounts, and hopped on a ship.'

'Where you going? Can I give you a lift?'

'I've just finished with my boyfriend. I'm going to collect my things from his flat.'

After a rather embarrassing confrontation with her now ex-boyfriend, she invited me back to her place and seduced me with her good looks and culinary skills; roast duck with plum sauce followed by strawberries and cream would turn anyone's head. And for better or worse that was the start of it, a relationship that was to last many stormy years.

I should have heeded the warning signs. They weren't hard to spot. Penny would turn on a sixpence. She threw her engagement ring into the road in a fit of pique, which had me dodging oncoming cars to retrieve it. She ripped up the marriage licence the day before the wedding then stuck it back together with sticky tape. She locked herself in the car when I had the audacity to wear a leek to celebrate St David's Day. She jumped out of my car while it was still going, leaving the door wide open, resulting in a passing bus ripping it from its hinges. What the hell had I let myself in for!

She wasn't the most trusting of women either; in fact she was downright jealous. If any of my previous romantic attachments came up in conversation she would go ballistic. She ripped up the letter I'd kept as a momentum from Julie and accused me of having affairs with every leading lady I worked with. I, in my stupidity, confessed to an affair I'd had on a cruise ship and she never let me forget it. It wasn't her fault; showbiz was another world to her. I shouldn't have married her. I shouldn't have married anyone. I wasn't the marrying type. It seemed I was a chip off the old block. And me being in close proximity to beautiful long-limbed showgirls was a recipe for disaster. The fights were epic. During a particularly acrimonious altercation my agent called offering me a Caribbean cruise. Penny hit the roof.

'If you think you're going on another ship after what happened last time, you can think again,' she screamed.

'There are girls everywhere,' I reasoned. 'I don't have to go on a ship to find one.'

'Tell your agent you're not going.'

'I can't. He's signed the contract on my behalf...I can't let him down now!'

'Do what you bloody well like, then,' she yelled, 'but don't expect me to be here when you come back.'

No amount of cajoling would change her mind. My agent tried to persuade her, even his wife tried to persuade her but she was having none of it. I offered to take her with me but that didn't work either. Her mind was made up.

The next few weeks were strained to say the least. As the day of my departure loomed communication between us hit an all-time low and I left with a heavy heart. At every port I would call her and leave messages. She wouldn't return my calls or answer my letters. When I returned home my worst fears were realised; the house was empty. She'd gone to her mother's and taken the kids with her. She came back but it was never the same; every time I went away she made my life hell. I tried to reason that it was the only life I knew but it had little impact. She'd married the wrong man and I had definitely married the wrong woman.

Looking for the Stars, that was the name of it, the TV show that started it all. I'd been doing odd gigs around the country but I didn't seem to be getting anywhere, then my old man rang Raul, an old friend, who ran a ballet school in London, and Raul had connections.

'I can get the boy an audition. Can he get to Liverpool by next week, Bert? The auditions are at the Jacob's Biscuit factory.'

The factory club was like any other workman's club: bar at one end, stage at the other and a load of tables and chairs in between. Hughie, the producer of the show, was sitting with his entourage at a long table in front of the stage. A woman sitting at a piano was the only visual accompaniment. The first to step on stage was a middle-aged guy in a shiny suit, grey shoes and a dodgy haircut. He handed his well-thumbed copy to the pianist.

'Go on, Norman,' said Hughie. 'Let's hear it, "Born Free"!' It seemed Norman was a regular.

'Next,' he said, and a woman of dubious age dressed in a white lace dance frock tottered on stage and sang 'Nobody Loves a Fairy When She's Forty' – it had been a long time since she'd seen forty. Then it was my turn.

'What are you going to do for us, old son?'

'"Let Me Sing and I'm Happy",' I said.

My old man took over from the pianist and I sailed into my song and dance routine. Hughie thanked me for coming and I exited stage right. A very excited secretary followed me into the wings.

'Don't you go anywhere,' she whispered. 'Hughie wants to see you.'

I don't think Penny realised how important getting a spot on a network TV show was or what it would lead to. She was a home girl and seeing my picture splashed across all the newspapers, contracts that took me all over the world and a husband starring in West End shows wasn't what she'd bargained for.

It had been a long, hard road to the top but, for want of a better phrase, I'd made it. Posters announcing the opening of my show were everywhere: on buses, on hoardings, on tube stations. I would even go up and down the escalators just to see the poster with my name on it. I couldn't believe my luck.

Chapter Thirty

London, West End

It was summer. London was full of tourists. Driving in the city was a nightmare, and parking in the West End was even worse. I caught the Routemaster, from Dolphin Square to the Strand, got off the bus and walked the rest of the way to Covent Garden. I arrived at the theatre an hour before curtain-up. The playbill out front with my photo on it shouted: *Johnny Fontane staring in 'Cindy the Musical'*.

I'd been staying with a friend of mine, when he'd called. Eddie, the producer of the show, was an East German Jew, who'd escaped the Nazi death camps by swimming down the River Spree to safety. He'd made a fortune in publishing and he'd kept it; you'd have to sue him for your royalties.

'Jono,' he said in his thick German accent. 'I saw you on a TV talent show last night. I'm looking for a male singer to record for me and I think you might fit the bill. Are you interested?'

Eddie's publishing house in Tin Pan Alley was above the La Giaconda, a coffee shop where all the musicians and wannabe pop stars congregated. I climbed the rickety stairs that led to his office. Sitting behind the reception desk was a pretty blonde girl with a skirt so short you could see what she'd had for breakfast. I thought about chatting her up but this was not the time.

'I've got an appointment with Mr Kerzner,' I explained.

She smiled and nodded me towards Eddie's office. I smiled back. Later, I thought.

Eddie, a short fat guy with a cigar protruding from the side of his mouth, was sitting behind an enormous leather-topped desk; he looked like he'd been sent from Central Casting. Standing next to him was a beautiful German girl half his age who he euphemistically referred to as his girlfriend. Next to her was a record producer he'd poached from EMI and Lenny Schwartz, a New Yorker with a Bronx accent who looked like Humphrey Bogart. It felt like I'd entered a scene from a gangster movie.

'Lenny is over from the States,' Eddie informed me. 'He's my associate producer on *Cindy* – a musical I'm publishing. There's a song in the score that will do for you what "Portrait of My Love" did for Matt Monro. But first things first, you have to audition for the director. I've made an appointment for you to see him tomorrow, ten o'clock, Fortune Theatre, okay?'

Alexander De Beaumont, not his real name, was sitting in semi-darkness halfway up the auditorium. I walked nervously on stage, presented my music to the house pianist and waited. A voice came from the stalls.

'When you're ready.'

He stopped me halfway through my number.

'Okay, okay… I can see that you can sing, but can you act?'

'I don't know,' I said. 'I've never tried.'

'No matter. I'll teach you. Take your shirt off.'

I felt uneasy; what was it with this guy?

'Do you want this fucking job or what?' he said, sensing my hesitation.

I'd heard about Monsieur De Beaumont. He was well known in the business for auditioning boys with their shirts off. I pulled my shirt over my head and stood there feeling more than a little exposed. What the hell was I doing? I wasn't auditioning for a porn movie, for Christ sake!

'Okay, you'll do,' he said. 'Rehearsal starts at ten sharp tomorrow.'

Being in the company of hardened West End professionals was intimidating to say the least. I'd never acted before and wasn't sure if I could hack it but Alexander was true to his word. He taught me a lot and I was grateful for it.

'Don't flap your arms about – you're not singing a fucking song,' he barked from the stalls. 'And stand still; the hardest thing to do on a stage is to stand still. You're bopping about like a fucking cork. You have to have repose to command your audience, Johnny.'

Johnny he called me; Jono wasn't showbiz enough for the flamboyant Monsieur De Beaumont.

'You'll never make it with a fucking name like Jono,' he said.

I worked hard, learning my lines and choreographing the dance routines, but somehow I didn't feel as if I fitted in. It didn't help that my confidence was being undermined by the West End luvvies. They obviously resented me. I'd been parachuted in because Eddie was the producer and they knew it. 'Where did you train, darling?' they would goad, knowing full well I'd had no classical training. It planted the seed of doubt in my mind. Perhaps I should have gone to a drama school. I'd learnt on the job. I'd begged my old man to send me to a stage school as a kid but it fell on deaf ears. 'You can't be taught how to perform,' he'd said. 'You can either do it or you can't.'

A week before we were due to open, Monsieur De Beaumont called me into the office.

'Johnny, there's no easy way to say this,' he said avoiding my eyes. 'But it's not working out. I'm afraid I'm going to have to replace you.'

'What do you mean replace me? We open on Monday.'

He just shrugged. 'Sorry, I just don't think you're right for the part.'

I was gobsmacked. Okay, I wasn't the best actor in the world but I could sing and dance and I'd choreographed all the routines. The bastard had bloody used me. I'd seen this kid skulking around the theatre all week watching me, taking notes as I went through my routines. I didn't give it much thought at the time but it was starting to add up now. I called my agent but he wasn't much help so I called Eddie.

'He says I'm not right for the part, Eddie, says he wants to replace me.'

'Who with?'

'Don't know. Some am-dram kid he knows, I think.'

'It's his bloody boyfriend. Leave it to me. I'll fix it, or I'll pull the fucking show.'

The show was about to open and I was shitting myself. My old man was more nervous than me. He got so pissed drunk that he spewed out his false teeth in the interval. This is what we'd both worked for. For five years I'd played clubs pubs and taverns up and down the country, punctuated with the odd summer show, cruises and pantomimes. But my name up in lights on a West End theatre! This was more like it.

Salina Star, the friend I'd been staying with, insisted on coming to the opening night. I didn't really want her to. She was well known in the business as being a bit of a diva. I knew how outspoken she was and I was worried in case she would upset someone. She sat in the circle with my father. When I did my big number she started yelling 'Encore' at the top of her voice and whistling. Oh Christ! What is she doing? I thought. I needn't have worried – she knew full well what she was doing; the audience picked up on it and I got a standing ovation.

We were all sitting in the stalls when De Beaumont arrived, a sheaf of papers in hand. I knew what was coming: the customary after-show notes. I was nervous. I'd proved him and his up-their-arse luvvies wrong and they weren't going to like it.

'Ladies and gentlemen, there must be a pause here,' he said, alluding to my number. 'It's a potential showstopper.'

So much for his view that I wasn't right for the part; I'd stopped the show and he'd had to admit it. Champagne was flowing backstage as we waited till the small hours for the early morning papers to come out. The notices weren't good. One sarcastic bastard wrote, *'when the curtain finally fell I thought it was the best piece of material I'd seen all night.'*

De Beaumont hurled his glass at the wall. 'Those felt-tipped fucking assassins wouldn't know a good show from a fucking dog fight,' he screamed.

His reaction was understandable, especially as my performance had been singled out as the one thing that had been any good.

I was still basking in the plaudits from the first-night audience as we drove back to Salina's place. She lived in a mansion in Kent. Hadley Hall was open house to any lame duck that needed a bed for the night. Salina was very hospitable; when she found out I was opening at the Fortune Theatre, she insisted I stay with her. Her grand house became my home whenever I was in London. I couldn't believe my luck. My last des res was a council flat in Port Talbot. The twenty-two-roomed mansion with a swimming pool was something with which I very soon become accustomed…and it had fringe benefits.

'Right, Johnny,' she said, 'am I making up two beds, or are you going to be crawling across the landing all fucking night?' I didn't know how to respond; how do you reply to a question like that? She indicated the bar. 'Pour me a brandy, will you? And get whatever you want. I'll be back in a minute.'

She came out of the bathroom stark naked. I'd never seen her without her wig before; I didn't even know she wore one. I stood staring at her bleached blond bitten-off hair, not knowing quite how to react.

'What you looking at?' she said. 'Let's go.'

I hesitated. Should I go there? Apart from Salina being married to a gangster called Mickey, I didn't know what she was expecting. I'd had a few affairs but she'd been round the block. Would I come up to her expectations?

'You coming or what? Or are you going to stand there like a spare prick?'

She's not going to tell Mickey, I reasoned. My marriage is on the rocks, so what the hell. So, I followed her like a sacrificial lamb into the biggest bedroom I'd ever seen.

When I entered the stage door the next day I was still on cloud nine, not only from the previous night's sexual fireworks but I was still high on adrenaline from my first-night triumph. I picked up my post, sifted through it, discarded the obvious junk mail, picked up the local paper from the stage door man and made for my dressing room.

I went through my usual ritual, putting on my make-up and doing my warm up, as I did before every performance. I looked at myself in the mirror, inspected the crow's feet around my eyes; they were getting deeper. I glanced at a photo of myself outside the Palladium posing with some smiling showgirls. I'd made it in show business alright but it hadn't been a walk in the park.

With some time before curtain-up, I made a cup of coffee, pulled out a half full bottle of Scotch, unscrewed the top and poured a generous measure into my cup. I picked up the paper and scanned it. It was full of the usual crap: what was the government doing about crime on the street, Enoch Powell was warning of dire disaster if we joined the Common Market and Harold Wilson was going on about Progress. 'He who rejects change is the architect of decay,' he said. 'The only person that rejects progress is in the cemetery.' The pompous twat!

I was about to throw the paper in the bin when I noticed a small article in the corner.

Local bag lady found dead

A woman found dead inside a burning building in Whitechapel has been identified as Peg, 50, a local bag lady. According to neighbours, Peg was believed to be squatting in the derelict building. At around 7 a.m. the police received reports of a fire at the house. Members of the Whitechapel Fire Department responded and found the property fully engulfed in flames. While extinguishing the fire, fire-fighters located what appeared to be a charred body. There has not yet been a determination on the cause of the fire or whether foul play was involved. The investigation surrounding the incident is ongoing so if anyone has information regarding this investigation they are urged to contact the police.

Was this her? *My* Peg? The Peg I'd seen squatting in a bus stop all that time ago? I hadn't seen her since although I'd been looking all the time. Over the years the memories of her and the boys had faded but never completely and seeing this brought it all back to me. The questions remained unanswered. Why had they left without a word? What had happened to them and most of all why had Peg ended up begging in a bus shelter? I glanced at the collage of the Bavarian Castle on my dressing table that she'd given me all those years ago. I was still clutching the paper when the tannoy system crackled into life.

'*Overture and beginners, please, ladies and gentlemen. Members of the chorus and Mister Fontane to the stage please.*'

I stood in the wings. My head was in turmoil. All I could see was Peg in her iridescent dress, her Celtic eyes flashing, plonking eggs Benedict in front of us scruffy kids and the vision of what she'd become: a down-and-out begging in a bus stop. I was a big star now. I had money. I could have helped her. Why hadn't I gone back?

The music struck up but I didn't hear it. I stood motionless in the wings. The stage manager prompted me to go on. I made my entrance. I don't remember doing the performance; I was consumed with a mixture of grief and guilt. The vision of that pitiful look on Peg's face, willing me to remember her, haunted me. Until it dawned on me who she was I'd thought she was just some random punter who'd seen me on TV. It happens all the time, I reasoned; people recognise me; they're not sure from where but think they know me. I was just making excuses. I should have gone back.

Chapter Thirty-One

Heavy summer rain was bouncing off the steaming bonnet of my taxi. The wipers were flopping back and forth, trying to clear the rain-streaked windscreen. Through the diffused window I could see an old church standing alone, propped up on one side by a huge timber brace; the adjacent buildings had been demolished. A handful of mourners, a man and woman in Salvation Army uniform and some old dossers, were standing huddled against the wind and rain in the unkempt graveyard.

I paid the cab driver and walked towards the graveside. The drone of a priest, soullessly chanting a prayer as if he had no faith in what he was saying, was the only thing that could be heard.

One man stood alone. He was about my age but smaller. I noticed that he was wearing expensive trainers, designer jeans and an expensive looking leather coat, which was in sharp contrast to the bunch of down-at-heel dossers next to him.

As I walked towards him he turned to face me.

'Hello, was,' he said.

He hadn't changed much even though it had been about fifteen years since the day he'd left. I hadn't been aware of it as a kid but I was struck by how much like Peg he was. He had the same black hair, same eyes, but his voice was different; the lisp that we'd teased him about as a kid had gone and there was a slight cockney twang mingling with his Welsh accent.

'This is Spider, my bodyguard,' he said, indicating a man with a tattoo of a spider's web on his neck peeking out from under his collar. I shot him an enquiring glance. 'I'll explain later,' he said.

The plain wooden coffin was lowered into the grave. The priest chanted his final ashes to ashes routine, Pip threw a single rose on top of the coffin, I scattered some dirt and rubbed my hands clean and the congregation, such as it was, uttered the usual condolences and began to disperse, leaving me alone with Pip.

'How did Peg come to this?'

'She tried her best all her life, Jono. She just got worn out, that's all. She never gave up on life – life gave up on her. It just got too hard, even for Peg.'

'Where's Frankie?' I asked. 'Why isn't he here?'

'Don't know. He doesn't get in touch much these days.'

The rain was still coming down in sheets. Pip was drenched. I couldn't tell if it was the rain or if there were tears in his eyes. I pulled him towards me. As we hugged I could feel him shaking, sobbing.

'Can we go somewhere private, Jono? There are things I need to tell you.'

We left Spider to settle up with the priest and made for the theatre.

I led him to my dressing room and poured him a stiff drink. I sat at my dressing table, poured myself one and opened my make-up box.

'I have to get ready, Pip,' I said choosing an Egyptian tan pancake. I addressed his reflection in the mirror as I applied the make-up with a wet sponge. 'I want to know everything since you left, the full story; everything from this is my dog spot.'

I glanced back at his reflection. He looked furtive, ill at ease. He went to the window and looked out. He pulled a gun from his pocket.

'What the hell are you doing?' I said, spinning around to face him.

'There's a contract out on me, Jono.'

'Are you taking the piss?' Was this a fantasy? He always did have a vivid imagination.

'I'm in deep shit, was,' he said. 'I need somewhere to crash tonight. Will you help me?'

I studied his face. Something in his eyes told me he was in serious trouble. This was for real. I closed the blinds, locked my door and returned to my dressing table.

'I'm not doing anything illegal, Pip,' I said, picking up my eyeliner brush and continuing with my preparation. 'You got me into enough trouble when we were kids. I'm not falling for your shit this time.'

'You're the only one I can trust, Jono.'

'How do you know? I haven't seen you for fifteen years.'

'You never fucking clecked on me when we were kids, did you? Once a butty always a butty?' he said with a grin.

'Some fucking butty; you left without a word.'

The ancient tannoy crackled into life. '*This is your half hour call, ladies and gentlemen, your half hour call.*'

I rose from my seat, reached for my stage outfit and started to dress.

'We had to do a runner, Jono. Deakin was threatening Peg with eviction and worse. He wanted her to work off what she owed him at that shitty club of his and she knew what that meant.'

'Where did you go? You didn't even leave a note.'

He pondered, took a slug of his whisky and continued.

'I thought we were going back to Germany but Peg dumped us off at Benny's and pissed off. We were left standing on the doorstep like the fucking Bisto Kids.'

He paused. There were tears in his eyes.

'I felt lost like a bleedin' orphan,' he said continuing. 'Like being told my mother had died. She'd let me down. I hated her but loved her at the same time. She'd promised me we'd find my father. I knew he wasn't a prince for Christ sake, but was he even German?'

'Who knows? Knowing Peg, she could have pulled an aristocrat; she had all the airs and graces. How long did you stay with Benny?'

'Not long. It wasn't a barrel of laughs. Living with Peg wasn't great but at least she loved us. Benny's wife hated us.'

'She didn't mistreat you? Benny's wife, I mean?'

'No, but the screaming matches were bloody classic. "How can I be expected to bring up Peg's feral brood?" she would yell. I don't know whether it was guilt or duty but at least we were clothed, fed and educated. She sent me and Frankie to some poncy private school in Cardiff. It was a far cry from our school in Cwm Teg, I can tell you.'

He pulled out a cigarette and offered me one.

'No, thanks. I gave it up.'

'Since when?'

'Since Dyfrig nearly caught us wanking in the bus.'

Pip cracked up at the memory; it was the first time I'd seen him smile all day.

Another crackling interruption. *This is your fifteen-minute call, ladies and gentlemen, fifteen minutes.*

'How did you end up in London, Pip?'

He took a deep drag. 'The situation got worse; Stella gave Benny hell till he folded and sent us to his sister's in Hampstead. She was loaded, married a banker or something but she was as mean as hell. Okay, she sent us to a flash school but that was only for appearances. She loved all the bullshit, cap and gown and shit, but after the ceremony she told us we were on our own.'

'Bit harsh, wasn't it?'

'You could say that. Being a student with no bleeding readies was no fucking joke. I was skint. Frankie did okay though; he'd shacked up with his tutor. She was a lot older than him, obviously, but he'd sweet talked her and she'd put him through law school.'

'What about you?'

'I got a job as a night-watchman on the docks. It wasn't easy working nights and trying to study by day, as you can imagine. Then this guy called Ronnie turns up, says I could earn a few bob if I turn a blind eye to his comings and goings.'

I raised an eyebrow.

'Don't look at me like that, Jono… Living in London is hard. Money was short. The allowance from Benny didn't go very far. It's alright for you; you're a bleedin' la di da.'

It seemed he'd been fraternising with crooks for too long; he had their entire vernacular.

'What did you have to do for the extra Nelson's?' I said.

'What?'

'Nelson's… Nelson Eddy's… Readies? Don't you know anything?'

He smiled. 'Touché, Jono. Anyway, I did a bit of driving for some villains. When they found out I had a part-time job as a nightwatch-man on London docks, they bunged me a few quid to look the other way.'

'What the hell were you thinking?'

'I had to do something to keep body and soul together; I was bloody brassic.'

'You could've come to me.'

'I didn't know how to find you.'

'Don't give me that crap; my name is splashed all over the West End. It's even on the sides of buses for Christ sake.'

'It would have been no good looking for Jono Griffiths, now would it?' he said with a wry smile. I knew he was lying; he'd just been too proud to ask.

'Anyway, the bunch of readies Ronnie bunged me every week came in very handy. I didn't care what he got up to.'

'You were never averse to a little dodgy dealing, were you?' He hadn't changed; the old cliché was right – and *this* small wild cat had his original spots still firmly in place.

'Listen, if I'd known that I was about to be dragged into the biggest police corruption case in history, I never would have got involved with Ronnie and his cronies in the first place.'

'You could have bailed out.'

'You taking the piss?'

He drained his glass. 'Can I have another one of these?' I nodded towards the bottle. He poured another generous double and continued.

'Ronnie's a dangerous bastard; he's not someone you'd want to cross.'

He went to the window, looked through a chink in the blinds and nervously scanned the street below.

'I rang Frankie for advice, but he didn't want to know. Said in his position it didn't do to be associated with villains. Stuck-up toffee-nosed twat! He always was a wimp.'

'So, where does that leave you?'

'Don't know. The shit's hit the proverbial. The corruption goes all the way up to assistant commissioner. There's enough evidence to prosecute three assistant commissioners, nine chief detective inspectors and fourteen flaming constables. The word on the street is that a supergrass exposed the detectives at City of London Police, including members of the Sweeney.'

I shot him a quizzical look.

'The Flying Squad were all corrupt, all in the funny handshake brigade, looking out for each other, even the commissioner of police was involved.'

'How do you know all this, Pip? Are you winding me up?'

'Honest, Jono, you can check it out if you don't believe me; it was in all the papers. The Sweeney had been helping to arrange bank robberies for a percentage of the take and taking bungs from villains to lose evidence. These were the same bloody villains who were bunging me a bunch of white fivers every week to turn a blind eye while they nicked precious metal from the docks.'

'Fuck me, Pip, what have you got yourself into?'

'You don't know the half of it. One of Ronnie's boys got careless and got caught red-handed having it away with a stash of gold. I was hauled in and questioned for three days.'

'*This is your five-minute call, ladies and gents, five minutes please.*'

'I've got to go on in five, walk with me, Pip. You can watch from the wings if you like. So…what happened?'

'Fuck all. They couldn't pin anything on me. That's the good news.

The bad news is the bastards I'd been associated with swore blind I was the supergrass that grassed them up and they put a contract out on me.'

'Did you?'

'What?'

'Grass them up?'

'You must be fucking joking; I'm too fond of my legs; I like walking on them. So that's it, Jono, the whole story, spotty dog and all. I got to get out of town fast or it's my arse. Can you help me or not?'

I could see he was scared to death. I couldn't have *him* on my conscience as well.

'I only need to crash for one night, was. Somewhere they can't find me.'

'Okay, Pip, but just for tonight. It's not my house, you understand. I'm staying with a friend of mine. She's in the States at the moment but she's due back next week.'

'I promise, Jono. It'll only be for one night; I'm leaving for France first thing in the morning.'

'*Overture and beginners to the stage please. Overture and beginners.*'

The overture struck up.

'Stay here, Pip. Don't go anywhere till I come off.'

Chapter Thirty-Two

We caught the tube to Dolphin Square, picked up my car and made for Whitechapel.

'This is it. Stop here, Jono. Park it here.'

There were yellow lines everywhere. Pip pulled out a crumpled old parking ticket from his pocket and stuck it under my windscreen wiper.

'A little tip I picked up from the villains,' he said with a grin.

The old run-down building had been converted into flats and bedsits. We climbed the stairs to his third-floor apartment. I use the term loosely; the one-bedroom flat was a shit hole. Water ran down the stained walls, making puddles on the worn-out oilcloth that graced the floor, a dead mouse, which nobody had seen fit to remove, was curled up and decaying in the corner, and the whole place stank of damp and mould.

Pip grabbed what meagre possessions he had and took a last look around. We made for the car.

We drove in silence. I wanted to know more about him, Peg and Frankie but he wasn't in the mood to talk; he just sat there lost in his thoughts. I drove down the Old Kent Road and headed towards the A2. It was very late by now and there was virtually no traffic. I slowed as I approached some traffic lights at New Cross and happened to glance in my rear-view mirror. I noticed a BMW with its windows blacked out. It was a little too close for comfort for my liking. The lights changed and I accelerated away. The car followed, keeping its distance this time but matching my speed.

'I don't know why, Pip, but I'm sure there's a car following us.'

'Lose him, Jono.'

I slammed my foot down and jumped the next set of lights but the car was still on my tail. My heart was pumping like a jack hammer. I couldn't breathe. I could feel the sweat trickling down my neck. What the hell was I doing? What had he got me into? I raced down Shooter's Hill, ignored the lights at the Black Prince, raced through Bexley village and screeched into the circular drive of Salina's house. The pursuing car roared past. A couple of youths were hanging out of the window, giving us the finger, yelling abuse as they went. It had just been some kids playing dare but it had certainly put the wind up me. I reflected on how many times Pip had got me into trouble and I couldn't wait for the morning to see him leave for France.

Pip followed me into the palatial mansion. He'd been sharing with the cockroaches in a Rachman-esque flat with no hot water and rats for company. The contrast of this Victorian pile set in four acres with lawns sweeping down to the swimming pool and orchards beyond must have blown his mind. He stood gazing in awe at his surroundings.

'Is this your digs?' he said as he explored Salina's house with its *Gone with the Wind* staircase, nine bedrooms, oak-lined dining room, snooker room, library and bar as big as any pub. 'Who owns this place, Jono?'

'My friend, Salina... Salina Star. You might have heard of her.'

'Are you kidding? I've got some of her records. Are you and her...?'

'She's a friend, that's all.' I lied. It wasn't the first and it wouldn't be the last affair I'd have with an older woman. I showed Pip to one of the guest rooms but we were too wound up to sleep. We had a few drinks and sat shooting the breeze till the sun came up.

Salina's housekeeper made us breakfast in the morning and I drove Pip to Heathrow airport. As I watched him go towards passport control I had mixed feelings.

'See you, was,' he said, 'and...thanks.'

He looked furtively over his shoulder, shot me a roguish smile and turned away.

'See you, Pip,' I said almost under my breath. I watched until he was swallowed up by the surge of jostling passengers making for the departure lounge and, for the second time in my life, I wondered if I would ever see him again.

It was many years before I had anything more to do with Peg's boys, and thoughts of her and her boys had receded into the mists of my ever-diminishing memory. Then the phone rang. I ignored it. I was already late for my gig and I was hurriedly checking my props and putting my music in order as I did before every performance.

'Get that will you, Penny?'

'Get it yourself. It won't be for me.'

'I'm in the middle of sorting out my routine.'

'I don't know why you bother. You've been doing the same bloody act for eight years; you should know it by now.'

'I know you resent the fact I'm in this business,' I said, refusing to be drawn into yet another argument. 'But you knew what you were getting into when you married me.'

She shrugged, and reluctantly grabbed the phone.

Her manner was short, terse. 'Hello...yes... Who is it? Who?'

She turned to me and yelled, 'It's some guy...says he's looking for someone called Jono.'

She handed me the phone. I couldn't believe it. Nobody had called me Jono for years.

'Hello, Jono. Remember me?'

I hesitated, not knowing quite what to say. I hadn't heard from

Frankie since he'd left South Wales all those years ago. Why would he call me out of the blue like this? I was never his favourite.

'Jono? Are you there?'

'Frankie? Is that really you?'

'Yes, it's me. Can you meet me? It's important.'

I was intrigued; what could be so important after so many years?

Chapter Thirty-Three

Hanover Chambers

The suite of offices in Hanover Square was expensively furnished with soft leather chesterfields, polished mahogany side tables with Capo di Monte table lamps on them and deep pile carpets that you sank into when you walked. The neat receptionist said he was expecting me and buzzed me through.

He cut an affluent figure behind his huge mahogany desk. He was dressed in one of those well-cut pinstripe suits that all successful lawyers seemed to wear.

'It seems you've done well for yourself, Frankie.' He'd certainly come a long way from Cwm Teg.

'It's the wife's business,' he said dismissively. 'She inherited it from her father. When he died I took over.'

'Cigar?' he said, offering me a large Cuban.

This was a far cry from the skinny kid in patched pants I'd first met at Pip's birthday party puffing on a Woodbine and blowing smoke out of his navel.

'Don't smoke,' I said. 'Have to look after the voice, you know.'

'Ah yes, of course you're a famous performer now,' he said, a hint of sarcasm in his voice. It seemed his resentment of me hadn't faded with the years. I didn't rise to it.

'How did you find me?'

'Are you taking the piss? I'm a lawyer. I rang your agent, told him you'd come into an inheritance.'

'You said on the phone it was important. What's going on, Frankie?'

He hit the intercom. 'Emily, bring us some coffee, will you. Oh, and hold all my calls. I'm going to be some time.'

A blonde statuesque secretary in mini skirt and stilettos arrived bearing coffee and biscuits. She bent over and placed the tray on the desk, gave Frankie a seductive smile. His eyes followed her as she left, closing the door behind her.

'You needn't look like that,' he said, noticing my accusatory look. 'You're no bloody angel.'

'Is it serious?'

He lit up his Cuban, took a suck and slowly blew the smoke towards the ceiling. '*She* thinks it is. I can introduce you, if you like.'

'No, thanks. I'm in enough trouble with my wife already.'

'If *my* wife knew a thousandth of my misdemeanours it would be my arse, I can tell you.'

'Look, will you get to the point?'

'Okay, it's Pip. He's in trouble.'

'So, tell me something new.'

'This is serious, Jono. His wife phoned me. She's very worried about him. Ever since he retired he seems to have a death wish.'

'What do you mean?'

'He's not sleeping, he won't eat, and he's been hitting the booze like it's going out of style. He's been driving while he's pissed and been

190

banged up on drink-driving charges. He doesn't seem to care anymore. His wife's afraid his liver will pack up. I'm worried that unless we can do something he'll end up like Peg.'

'What can I do about it?'

'He might listen to you. He won't listen to me.'

'I don't know, Frankie. He'd never listen to me as a kid, just did what he liked.'

'Come on, Jono,' he cajoled. 'We'll only be gone for a few days. What do you say?'

'Where is he, anyway? I haven't heard a word from him since he did a runner twenty years ago.'

'He's got a dental practice in Paris.'

'How did he manage that? I didn't think he'd finished his time at Guy's.'

'It's a long story.'

'I'm listening.'

'More coffee?' he said, pouring himself another. I shook my head.

'He sneaked back into London via Jersey when he thought the heat was off and persuaded Guy's to accept him back. It turned out the gang were still looking for him. So he finished his course and went back to France 'tout de suite.' He got a job pushing stiffs about in a hospital until he'd learnt the language then set up a practice in Paris. That's when he met Janique.'

I shot him an inquisitive look. He put down his cigar and took a sip of his coffee.

'She was a nurse, older than him but very attractive. He fell for her big time. I think she reminded him of Peg.'

'Was she married?'

'Divorced. She'd been married twice before. She was a bit of a rebel by all accounts and Pip's unorthodox, if not bordering on criminal, ways seemed to appeal to her wild nature. He was involved in what he euphemistically described as his black operations.'

I raised an eyebrow.

'Basically, when gang members got shot he would patch them up.'

'He always was a mad bastard.'

'He loves the excitement and so, it seems, does Janique. He's famous, or should I say infamous, in criminal circles. He loves being seen in the best Paris restaurants fraternising with the Corsican Mafia. It's good for his twisted ego.'

'This is all very interesting, Frankie, but…'

He cut across me. 'I'm known as Francis now.'

'My, my, we have come up in the world.'

'It just sounds more kosher, that's all. Frankie sounds a bit…well, you know?'

'Yes… I know.' I wanted to ask him why he was ashamed of his background but I decided not to. I couldn't help but reflect on how different our paths had been and how diverse our lives had turned out, me as an actor, Frankie as an eminent lawyer and Pip, as Frankie had just revealed, was a dodgy dentist in Paris.

'Anyway, Frankie…' I was fucked if I was going to call him Francis. 'Why are you worried about Pip? What's he done?'

'It's not what he's done – it's what he's doing. He's down at his Pyrenean retreat drinking himself to death. It's in his genes, I suppose. He told me there's no hope; his liver's about to pack up. Okay, we weren't always the best of friends but I don't want him to end up like Peg. So…will you help me?'

'What makes you think he'll listen to me?'

'You two were close, perhaps even closer than he and I were.'

I didn't answer.

'Well…will you come?'

Visions of us as kids filled my head: Pip and his gambo, the tip, the Forge, Echo Valley Pond.

'Okay, for old times' sake,' I said. 'But I have to be back by next week. I've got a big show coming up. You've got to understand, Frankie, I've got commitments.' I was lying. Truth is I was between jobs. My last show in the West End had folded after some bad reviews.

Chapter Thirty-Four

Heathrow Airport

I boarded the plane with apprehension. I didn't know what to expect. Would I even recognise Pip after all this time? We landed in Barcelona late that afternoon with the intention of hiring a car and driving the hundred and sixty or so kilometres to Le Perthus.

Frankie called ahead. I was surprised to hear him speaking in fluent French. His expensive education in London had obviously paid off. He hadn't been much of a linguist at junior school; it was all he could do to get his tongue around Llangynwyd, and that was the next village. He put down the phone.

'I spoke with Janique. Pip's in bed. It seems he's just come out of jail.'

'What?'

'He was busted for drink-driving again. Janique said she'll tell him we're coming and he'll meet us in the village.'

We decided against taking the main road and drove along the Catalonian coast which ran all the way from Barcelona to the French border. The season hadn't started yet and the Costa Brava was unusually quiet. As we drove through the pretty coastal towns that fringed the Mediterranean it was easy to be lulled into a sense of being on holiday. We passed through the little resorts that had been popular in the sixties until we reached Girona. It was getting dark by now and it would have only taken us another hour to reach our destination but we decided to stay the night and leave first thing in the morning. We got up early, had a leisurely breakfast of croissants and delicious coffee – somehow coffee always tastes better in Spain and France; it must be something to do with the milk.

The road trip was the longest time I'd spent with Frankie since that unforgettable day when we'd walked to Cardiff. As we approached the Pyrenees, the mountains reminded us of that adventure and the memories of the little valley town came back to us clearly as if we'd only just left. We reminisced about the things we'd got up to and the characters of the town. We laughed as we remembered falling in Echo Valley Pond and smashing our socks against a rock to dry them, sliding down the mountain on tin trays, picking whinberries and eating them till our tongues turned purple, and running away from Dyfrig the nightwatchman. We were back there, ten years old again, like a couple of naughty kids.

'What happened to you, Frankie? After you left Cwm Teg, I mean.'

'How much do you know?'

'Not much. Pip told me you'd been dumped on Benny and he'd sent you to his sister. She put you in some poncy school or other, didn't she?'

'I didn't think so at the time but she did us a favour. I don't suppose I'd have ended up owning a law practice if I'd gone to Llwynderw Secondary Modern,' he said, shooting me a mischievous look.

'What about Pip?' I asked, ignoring his jibe.

'He hated it. Anything he could do to disrupt, he would. I think he was hoping to get expelled.'

'I can imagine.'

Frankie started to laugh. 'The little bastard let the white mice loose on open day. It was mayhem; the mice were running about the floor, teachers were trying to catch them and mothers were jumping on chairs like in some fucking *Tom and Jerry* cartoon. Pip was convulsing with laughter as usual and then Herr Schneider walked in.'

'Herr Schneider?'

'The science teacher, we called him the Führer behind his back; he was a bloody sadist. He'd taken an instant dislike to Pip, which probably had something to do with the fact that Pip had called him a fascist bastard. Schneider swished his cane and told him to bend over the desk. Pip wasn't having it. "You can't do this," he said. "It's illegal. I'm descended from German royalty." The whole class cracked up laughing. Schneider told us all to shut up and gave Pip six strokes of his cane anyway. He had to sit sideways at his desk for the rest of the day just to relieve the pain of his bruised and stinging arse. You'd have thought he would have learnt his lesson, wouldn't you? But no...'

'He was hardened to it, Frankie. He'd had plenty of practice. Peg's stick by the fireplace had seen plenty of use.'

'It was just as well, because he had another thrashing a few days later for impersonating the Führer.'

'Who? Schneider?'

'No, Hitler. When Schneider left the room, Pip stuck on a black moustache made of crape paper and was goose-stepping about the class room yelling "Heil Hitler" and giving Nazi salutes.'

'Do you fancy stopping, Frankie? There's a cafe up ahead. I need a piss.'

We pulled into the roadside cafe. It was all but empty save for a few truck drivers. The toilet was a hole in the floor and the whole place stunk of piss. I wondered what Penny would think of this primitive setup. I held my breath until I'd finished, gave myself a shake, then left, exhaling as I went. Frankie plonked a not-too-clean cup in front of me.

'I got you a café con leche, if that's okay?'

'Thanks, Frankie. Any more sugar?' I said, pouring the one packet into my cup.

'You can have mine,' he said, flicking me the large packet. 'I'm trying to keep my weight down.'

'There's one thing about Spain, they don't give you those piddling little packets of sugar like we get at home,' I said.

I poured the other packet in and watched it as it sank slowly through the thick foam.

'Do you remember doing this in Chico's Cafe?'

'Yes, they had some of those bottles with silver funnels on top that would pour a teaspoonful as you tipped it up.'

'They had brown sugar as well. I'd never seen brown sugar before; I thought someone had spilt their coffee in it. Happy days, Frankie... happy days.' I stirred the sugar in. 'Were you happy in London?'

He took a sip of his coffee and pondered.

'Yes, apart from Schneider I liked it. It was a bit of a culture shock though. For one thing it was a mixed school and sitting next to pretty, long-legged girls in short gym-slips as my hormones raged did little for my concentration. Pip had even less self-control than me; he was always staring out of the window watching the girls playing netball or in the cloak room chatting up some young nubile or other.'

'If he wasted his time, how the hell did he get to go to university?'

'He was bright. He could just do it. I had to slog my bollocks off to get my grades. Pip, on the other hand, just turned up on the day, winged it and the little sod passed them anyway. He was a natural.'

'Perhaps it was in his genes.'

'Who knows? The only one who knew who his dad really was was Peg and she wasn't telling.'

'Did she come and visit?'

'Who?'

'Peg.'

'No, she didn't know where we were; we were living with Benny's sister.'

'I don't suppose you wanted for anything, her being rich and all.'

'Hannah? She was tight as arseholes. She didn't even give us any pocket money. Pip accused her of having a financial philosophy inspired by the rectal constrictions of a duck. Ironic, isn't it? It was the expensive education she'd paid for that gave Pip a grasp of the English language that enabled him to insult her so eloquently.'

He took another swig of his coffee and continued.

'I was skint but Pip always seemed to be flush with cash. He had some scam going selling cigarettes to the other kids for double the price he paid for them on the black market. I'm sure if drugs had been about back then he would have been peddling those too.'

'And after you matriculated?'

'I went to the London School of Law. Pip went to Guy's. I didn't see much of him during the university years; I was too focused on making a life for myself.'

'Did you stay with Hannah?'

'No... I left before I graduated. But all I could find in my price range were seedy bedsits in the dodgy part of town. Pip hadn't fared any better; he was sharing with the cockroaches in a rat hole in Whitechapel. Living in squalor wasn't my idea of fun but I got lucky – my lecturer fancied me.'

'Pip told me. She was older than you, wasn't she?'

'Yes but very attractive. What was even more attractive, she owned a nice house in Hampstead. Her father was the senior partner in a high-flying law firm in the city. After my years at law school I joined the firm. But that's enough about me. What about you?'

'I went in a totally different direction from you and Pip. Well, I wasn't academic, was I.'

'So you followed your old man into show business. How is the old bugger?'

'We lost him a few years ago. I was doing a concert on the south coast – Dad was playing for me. I didn't know what was wrong with him at first. He just kept getting out of breath. I took him to the local hospital and they found this tumour in his pleural cavity and that was it. I still can't believe he's not here. He was always there, on stage, backing me whenever I needed him. I can still see him, immaculately dressed in his tuxedo, sitting at the piano behind me. You know, Frankie, I never failed an audition when he was in my corner; he taught me all I know. When he died I was devastated. I'm not a religious man – more of a daytime atheist, you might say – but when he died I went back to Cwm Teg, climbed Garn Wen and shouted to a higher being, "Why me, God, why me?"'

There was an awkward moment when neither of us spoke.

'I've often thought about you, Jono. I'd see your name from time to time in the press. You're doing okay, I guess?'

'Yeh, thanks to the old man. He always said, "I can open doors for you, Jono, but you've got to be ready. You got to get your gun loaded," he would say, "cos if you don't get your gun loaded you can't shoot those birdies."'

We sat in silence for a while, lost in our thoughts. Frankie lifted the coffee cup to his lips, drained the dregs then pushed the cup to one side.

'I'm sorry I haven't been in touch since we left,' he said. 'But I knew you were doing okay; I always knew you'd make it, was.'

Just for a moment I saw the old Frankie, the underdog following Pip's lead, not the high-flying lawyer in his pinstripe suit. I felt closer to him somehow. I grabbed the tab and paid the girl.

'Come on, Frankie. We'd better get going; there's a few miles to go yet.'

Chapter Thirty-Five

We arrived at Le Perthus late that afternoon. Being so near to the border, it was seething with tourists. The one main street was jam-packed with cars, bumper to bumper all looking for parking spots. We drove until we found a space in a narrow side street and wondered how we would find Pip amongst the throng of day-trippers. Then we saw him, staggering out of a nearby bar carrying a box full of wine.

The face was the same, save for a large Gallic moustache that he now sported, but he was twice the size. It seemed the years of overindulging in French cuisine and fine wines had really taken its toll.

'Jono? Is that you?' he yelled, his face lighting up. I couldn't believe it; he had a bloody French accent. He plonked the box of wine on a nearby tractor, crossed the road and hugged me till I thought my ribs would crack.

'I want you to hide this booze,' he said, grabbing the bottles and thrusting them into our hands. 'Frankie, put them in your car. If Janique sees them I'm fucked.'

'Where's *your* car, Pip?' I asked.

'The bastards have banned me again. I've still got an agricultural licence though,' he said with a wink and climbed aboard the tractor. 'Follow me,' he said, starting up his unusual ride. 'And watch how you go. It's pretty rough terrain.'

He wasn't kidding. After about a mile the road turned into no more than a rough track full of potholes; it was all I could do not to damage the car. After a while it was obvious that I could go no further so we abandoned the hire car, extricated the bottles of wine, and rode the rest of the bumpy way on his tractor.

'How much further is it, Pip?' I asked. 'My arse is killing me.'

'Just over the brow. Janique will be waiting for us so behave yourselves. She's not like us shit kickers. Her first husband was a minister in Georges Pompidou's government for Christ sake and her father was the Viceroy of Djibouti.'

'She's pretty rich, then?' I mused.

He shrugged. 'She inherited all this,' he said, indicating the land around us.

'Frankie told me you met in a hospital.'

'I was wheeling a patient on a trolley along a hospital corridor when I bumped into her, literally. "Bonjour," she said, "comment allez vous?" "Sorry," I said. "I don't speak French." "I'll teach you, if you like," she said. I knew she was flirting with me but what the hell. I needed to learn the language so I could open a practice here. She wasn't bad looking either which was a bonus. And that was it; the start of a beautiful friendship.'

The track came to an end at a five-bar gate that led to his estate – for that is what it was, an estate: two farm houses, a number of gîtes and the main house which was more like a baronial hall, befitting of the Viceroy of Africa.

'You'll be staying there,' he said, pointing to the main house in the distance. 'I'm still renovating the farm house. There's only room for Janique, my son and me but I'm sure you'll find Le Mas Reste comfortable.'

Pip's half-finished house was set amongst orchards and fields and surrounded by a rustic stone wall. Next to the house was a well-tended kitchen garden from where the aroma of aromatic herbs wafted on the air.

'I built this myself,' he said with pride, pointing to the rustic edifice. He dragged the case of wine from his tractor and proceeded to hide his bottles of contraband in various holes in the stone wall.

He yelled over. 'Janique… Janique…the boys have arrived. Janique is preparing a meal, wild boar. I shot it last week.'

Janique, a small, petite woman no bigger than a twelve-year-old child, greeted us like long-lost relatives with the French custom of kisses on both cheeks and one more for luck. The aroma of her Jean Patou perfume filled the air. The only jewellery she wore was an elegant string of pearls at her throat. The sliver strands running through her beautifully quaffed hair and the Chanel dress she was wearing seemed to radiate an elegance that all well-bred French women seem to have. She babbled on, not one word of which I understood. Frankie seemed to follow the conversation. I just nodded politely.

'She doesn't speak English, Jono. She understands a lot, though, so be careful what you say.'

I noticed a boy of about eighteen hovering nervously behind her. I shot Pip an enquiring glance.

'This is my son, Llŷr.'

I raised an eyebrow.

'I named him Llŷr, knowing full well that these arrogant French bastards would never get their Gallic tongues around the voiceless alveolar lateral fricative, even though the Zulus can do it.'

I looked at Frankie. What the hell was he talking about?

Llŷr was a dead spit of his farther when he was young: same height, same black hair, same hazel eyes; he even had the same lisp that Pip had worked so hard to eradicate.

Janique ushered us towards the orchard where a dining table had been prepared for lunch. My mouth watered at the sight of the wild boar, French bread, cheeses and carafes of fine wines. We'd had nothing since leaving Barcelona except for the coffee en route and I was starving.

It was hot for the time of year and the sun was already high in the early summer sky. The place was drowsy with the heady smell of fruit and herbs wafting from the kitchen garden and the boughs of the apple trees hung with their ripening globes in the sun.

We sat down in the shade of an ancient fig tree to the most sumptuous spread I'd seen outside a Michelin-starred restaurant. We ate with only the sound of birds and the drone of lazy bees collecting nectar from the garden breaking the otherwise tranquil silence. I noticed what looked like a cigarette burn on the polished surface of the table. Pip watched as I ran my finger over the mark.

'I remember exactly how this got there,' I said. 'This is…?'

A smile was playing about his lips. 'Yes, it's Peg's table. It's a long story, Jono. I'll tell you about it later. Let's eat first.'

Between mouthfuls of Janique's excellent wild boar stew he told me the story of the table.

'When Deakin died, Peg's old house went up for sale. I'd made a few quid,' he boasted, indicating the land around him. 'So, I bought it for Llŷr. I knew he wouldn't want it, the table I mean, so I had it shipped out for sentimental reasons. Remember, Jono, when we would hide under it when Peg was on the warpath or drunk or both? Or the parties she would throw for us. Do you remember? Knife, fork, spoon, cigarette and glass of wine?'

'It's all Peg's fault you ended up a lush, then!'

'No, Jono. It's in the genes, kid.'

I probed deeper. I was still in the dark about how Peg had ended up as she did. Pip tactfully changed the subject. If he knew, he wasn't telling. I think it must have been too painful for him. He loved her for all her faults. We all did.

'More wine?' he asked, filling my glass without waiting for a reply.

As we lingered over our long lazy lunch, sun on our backs, wine in hand, we were lulled into a state of nostalgia. My matrimonial misdemeanours, Pip's criminal past and alcohol addiction, and Frankie's humdrum life seemed to fade into insignificance as we remembered those long-lost heady days of our childhood. Pip lit up a gauloise and took a long satisfying drag and let the smoke escape through his teeth, slowly savouring the flavour. Pip had been hooked on nicotine ever since he'd been introduced to cigarettes by Peg. When he couldn't steal his daily fix from her handbag he would blag me into nicking some from my old man's pub.

'Do you remember when we nicked some fags from behind the bar and hid them under a loose floorboard, Jono?'

'I do, but when we went to get them some bloody mice had chomped their way through six packets of Player's Navy Cut.'

We laughed as we reminisced. Transported back to a time of hope, a time when all our dreams seemed possible. When the most heinous crime was nicking cigarettes from my father's pub and hiding them under a loose floorboard, or pinching apples from someone's tree, or stealing a kiss from an unsuspecting girl up the Forge. We recalled the times we'd sat on the stairs listening to the banter from the characters in the pub – Dan the Yank boasting about places he'd been to but never even seen and Jackie Manship thanking the men who had done a whip-round to pay his fine for swearing in the street. How times had changed. We remembered how we would tease Ben, the pot man who ran after us naughty kids for saying he stank a bit. We reflected with shame how we had been in part the cause of his demise. His one weeping socket, where his eye had been, let him down and he'd fallen down stairs while chasing us, and the plate in his head that he'd had since the war killed him. I can see his pathetic face as he sat waiting for the ambulance. I hope he doesn't die, I'd thought. We didn't mean him any harm.

The effect of a full belly, fine wine and the hot sun on our backs was starting to have a soporific effect on Frankie and me and we started to doze off. We were shaken out of our slumber by Pip; it seemed the excessive amount of red wine he'd swigged seemed to have had little or no effect on him whatsoever.

'Wake up, you bastards,' he said. 'I want to show you my second favourite place in the whole world.'

Rising, I thanked Janique for her hospitality. 'Merci, Janique, c'etait delicieux,' I said, dragging up the remnants of my schoolboy

French. Her face broke into a beautiful smile followed by a torrent of French and more kisses on both cheeks.

We followed Pip as he climbed over a barbed wire fence and scrambled down a steep grassy bank that led to a narrow stream. 'Come on, you sods,' he said. I marvelled at his surefootedness as he jumped from rock to slippery rock just as he'd done as a kid; even though he was three parts pissed and tipping fifteen stone, he could still do it. I remembered, as he jumped from stepping stone to stepping stone, the times we'd gone home from school the river way, and how I'd fallen in the water and dried my socks by slapping them on rocks.

We followed the stream until it emptied into a dark indigo pool. Shafts of sunlight shone through the canopy of trees overhead, making a dappled effect on the water. Over the pool, iridescent blue butterflies swarmed, a kingfisher dived for a minnow, frogs croaked, bees buzzed. I could see why he liked it so much; it must have reminded him of Echo Valley Pond and the colourful dragon flies that hovered over the water there. Although he'd embraced the French culture and spoke the language like a native, it seemed he still had nostalgia for the little valley town in Wales he'd left all those years ago.

'I come here when I'm pissed,' he said and pointed to a Welsh slate plaque next to the water. The inscription read, *In Memory of Peg, the best Mam in the world.*

The sun was going down by now and it was starting to get dark. As we clambered back over the barbed wire fence Frankie, never being the most athletic of us, caught his hand on the barbs and ripped it quite badly. It was bleeding profusely. Pip wrapped a not-too-clean handkerchief around it to stem the bleeding, swept the remains of our meal from the table and ordered Frankie to lie down.

'Stay put, Frankie. I'll go and get some equipment.'

I don't think I would have trusted him to operate on me knowing how scatterbrained he was as a kid. I watched in awe at the dexterity in which he cut and sewed the gaping wound, and this while he was still three parts pissed.

By the time we arrived back, Janique had brewed fresh coffee. I was lingering over my café au lait, musing as usual how coffee always tasted better in France and Spain, when Pip made an announcement.

'Come on, boys,' he said, downing his double espresso in one. 'Let's go to town. We'll take the four by four. Jono, you can drive.'

'Is Janique coming?' I asked.

'No, was. This is a boys' night out.'

I shot her a glance. Janique, seemingly quite used to his solitary sojourns, just smiled a resigned smile and shooed us out like the naughty boys we were.

Chapter Thirty-Six

The Bordello Debacle

Driving his antique station wagon was no picnic. Nothing seemed to work. The clutch was shot, the steering wheel had more play in it than the Wales rugby team and the brakes weren't too clever either. Negotiating the potholes on what loosely passed for a road was a nightmare.

'Where are we going, Pip?' I asked.

'We're going to the bordello on the border. I'll direct you.'

'I'm not going with any hookers,' I protested.

He indicated a nervous-looking Llŷr sat in the back seat. 'It's not for you. We got to make a man out of this one. Stop at this bar, Jono. He needs some Dutch courage. I don't know why they call it Dutch; what's so special about those fuckers!'

The bar was full of smoke and smelt of garlic, Gauloises, and dodgy drainage, which only helped to give the place its atmosphere. Gallic-looking guys, cigarettes dangling from their mouths, were playing bagatelle. A large television above the bar was showing a football match that no one seemed to be watching and some rowdy youths playing pool added to the jovial *joie de vivre* of the place.

The manager welcomed Pip like an old friend, kissed him on both cheeks then, turning to Frankie and me, repeated the process. Pip ordered two bottles of the house red, some strange-looking sausage, and garlic bread. He drew out his Breton fighting knife, the handle of which was disguised as the buckle of the special belt he wore around his waist. He started to dismember the sausage and pass it around.

'You always had a thing about knives and guns, didn't you, Pip?' I said accepting the morsel of sausage.

'Yeh, he broke into the hardware store back in Cwm Teg,' interjected Frankie. 'Nicked a bunch of air rifles then the little bastard asked me to fence them.'

'What's with the knife anyway?' I asked.

He grinned. 'I eat my food at some of the best restaurants in Paris with this,' he said, brandishing the wicked-looking utensil. 'I love to piss off the well-to-do clientele.'

He'd never admit it but it was an arrogance that he'd acquired to cover up what I suspected to be an inferiority complex.

Pip was holding court and being rather loud and obnoxious. He was reminiscing about the old days and laughing hysterically at one of his own jokes when a German announced, in a voice meant to be overheard, that 'Some people don't know how to behave.' Before I knew it Pip had him against the wall with the vicious-looking curved blade at his throat. The manager blew a whistle and jumped over the counter, yelling something in French. I didn't understand but he didn't sound happy. Frankie managed to pull Pip off the German and we beat a hasty retreat before the police turned up.

We made for the Spanish border, arriving at the bordello with Pip still fuming from his altercation with the German. Still pumped up, he turned his aggression towards the madam.

'I want the South American chica,' he yelled.

'Je suis desole, monsieur. She is with another client.'

'I don't give a fuck,' he screamed, his voice rising in anger. 'Where is she?'

He started bashing on doors and barging into the rooms. The said chica opened the door to reveal a large, hairy-arsed truck driver, wearing a dirty tee shirt, boots, and not much else. His member was raised up in anger.

'This gives a new meaning to the phrase "coitus interruptus",' Pip quipped. 'He's definitely had his coitus interrupted.'

The lorry driver made a grab for him. Pip pulled out his gun and waved it about in a threatening fashion. There was a struggle, the gun went off and everyone hit the deck. Frankie grabbed Llŷr and once again we headed for the car – this was becoming a bit of a pattern. The truck driver, fuming at having his night of passion cut short, gave chase. Pip took the wheel and we headed for the hills with the truck driver, his truck sans trailer, in hot pursuit. He was gaining on us. Pip went off-road but the truck kept on coming. I was amazed at Pip's driving skills; although he was drunk as a skunk he was driving like a rally driver. Pip knew the terrain like the back of his hand. He should – he owned half of it. He took the route least conducive for a ten-ton truck and the driver's wagon, not being built to go off-road, got stuck in a ditch. Pip, elated by his triumph, pulled out his gun and shot three rounds out of the window in defiance.

As we came over the brow of the hill the lights of Le Mas Reste were a welcome sight. The magnificent house overlooked a river that meandered through a wooded valley towards the coast.

'There it is, Jono,' he said, pointing towards the large house. 'You'll sleep well tonight.'

I doubted if I would sleep at all after that hair-raising ride. The last trip I'd done with Pip was bad enough but this had been ten times worse.

Chapter Thirty-Seven

Le Mas Reste

The ancient pile was a rectangular building with what looked at first glance like a flat roof with turrets all around it. It was surrounded by terraces and its fortified walls were three feet thick.

We entered through the kitchen. Inside was like going back in time. It still had the original flagstone floor, sinks hewn out of granite with a handle to pump the water from an artesian well, and an ancient cast iron range with a large copper hood standing in pride of place in the centre.

Pip led us through a maze of passageways lined with African spears and artefacts – booty from the Viceroy's exploits no doubt – until we reached a stone spiral stairway that led to the main part of the house. We passed the library. It was stacked, Pip informed us, from floor to ceiling with rare and first edition books that had belonged to his father-in-law, the late Viceroy. He pulled one of the books from the shelf, blew the dust off it and handed it to me. It was a collection of photos of artworks by Pablo Picasso.

'Look at the fly leaf, Jono,' he urged.

I turned to the page. There was an original pen and ink drawing by Picasso and an inscription which read 'To my dear friend from Pablo.'

'Is this real, Pip?' I asked in awe.

'Yes. Apparently Picasso was a great friend of the old boy. It's worth a bloody fortune. Can't sell it, though. It belongs to the family.'

The next room was every bit as awe-inspiring. The jungle room, as Pip called it, was stuffed full of priceless African art that had been plundered by the Imperial French forces: full-size elephant tusks mounted on plinths, a cache of gold trinkets and African death masks which, after all these years, still bore the traces of blood from the poor bastards who had been sacrificed by some long-forgotten witch doctor in some long-forgotten tribal ritual. Overlooking this treasure was the imposing life-size yellowing, dickey bird watching photo of the Viceroy himself being punted along a river on a barge by his natives. Jodhpured, gaitered, and wearing the customary pith helmet – it was as if he were still guarding his ill-gotten gains from the grave.

Pip showed us to our room.

'Sorry, boys, you'll have to share. The other rooms haven't been made up yet. I'll be in the next room if you need anything. I always keep one room as a crash pad so as not to disturb Janique after a boys' night out,' he said with a grin.

Our bedroom, furnished in French Empire style reminiscent of Napoleon's bed chamber, had a grandeur that I wasn't expecting. The boat beds of mahogany with their high headboards and footboards had a dignity consistent with Napoleonic majesty. They were decorated on one side with motifs and initials of the family inscribed within the family crest and figures of victory; palm branches, swans, lions, rose-wreaths and climbing grape vines. There was a simple, elegant writing desk under the wooden shuttered window and a marble-top wash stand, basin and jug. A free-standing psyche mirror added to the elegance of the room. The adjoining bathroom had a free-standing cast iron roll-top bath, WC and a bidet, all connected to an ancient plumbing system.

As we got undressed, Frankie mused that this was the first time we'd shared a room since those days back in Cwm Teg, when Peg would cram us all into bed with her and tell us stories of her showbiz exploits and all the famous people she knew. In retrospect, I'm sure she made half of it up but we hung in wonder on her every word. We reminisced late into the night – things we'd got up to as kids, the tricks we'd played, the girls we'd kissed – until, totally exhausted after our long day, we fell into a deep sleep.

At 3am the door burst open to reveal Pip, standing there, swaying from side to side dressed only in his boxer shorts. He was followed by an excited Beryl, the rough-haired dachshund, who leapt onto my bed, ran up my body until she reached my face and proceeded to lick me as if I were her dinner.

'Where's the booze?' he demanded, dragging Frankie's case from under the bed. Finding what he was looking for, he pulled out one of the secreted bottles of Beaujolais and swigged from the bottle as if his life depended on it.

'What the hell are you doing, Pip?' I protested, trying to extricate myself from the attention of the excitable Beryl, who was still trying to lick me into submission. 'Don't you know what time it is?!'

'Shut up, you. Go back to sleep – this is important. Frankie, wake up. How much is my house worth?'

'How the hell should I know, Pip? I'm not a bloody estate agent. Go back to bed.'

'You're a fucking lawyer, aren't you?' he yelled, anger rising in his voice. 'You should know.'

'Oh… I don't know…about two million?' Frankie said, trying to placate him.

'No, four,' he yelled.

I listened to Pip haranguing Frankie until the sun came up. 'What the hell are you doing, Pip?' I scolded. 'Look at the bloody state of you. Don't you care?'

'Fuck off, Jono; what the fuck do you know!'

'I know you're killing yourself. I've come all this way to try to help you but it's obvious to me you're beyond help. Trying to reason with you is like pulling teeth. If you don't care about yourself, think of Janique and Llŷr. Christ, Pip you've got it all: money, a beautiful place to live, a family that loves you. What the hell's wrong with you?'

'It's all bollocks, Jono. You always want what you don't have but when you get it it's fucking futile. It's just things.'

He was starting to get the shakes and it wasn't undulant fever either. He slumped onto the bed and took another swig from the bottle. He was calmer now, reflective, maudlin.

'You know when I was happiest, Jono? When I was back in Cwm Teg with you two little sods. Life was simpler then. This,' he said, indicating his surroundings. 'It's all shit.'

'You can't go back, Pip.'

'I know, was, I know.'

I looked at him hunched over, head in his hands; he was a sad case. He had everything to live for and he was throwing it all away.

'Come on, butty, time you were in bed.'

Frankie and I eventually manhandled him back to his room. Complaining that he wanted another drink, he slumped awkwardly onto the bed and his wedding tackle flopped out from under the leg of his boxers. Frankie yelled, 'I've just seen your privates.' Frankie and I burst into hysterical laughter. Pip, seeing the funny side of the situation, started to laugh too, then fell back onto the bed and descended into a deep coma.

We were woken up by Janique's sister, struggling with a tray loaded with an assortment of delicious-looking croissants and steaming coffee. She was even smaller than Janique; at a guess I'd say she was no more than four foot six. Pip, she informed us, had left some time ago. After the much welcome breakfast we attended to our morning ablutions, as best we could, in the antiquated bathroom and then made our way up to the farm house. There was no sign of Pip. Janique told us that he'd gone to town on his tractor for provisions and she didn't expect him back until the afternoon, if then.

'You know what he's like,' she said with a sigh.

'Sorry we couldn't have been more help, Janique,' I said. 'We'll come over again if you need us but we have to leave for Barcelona. The flight home is this afternoon so there's no way we can wait for Pip to return.'

Chapter Thirty-Eight

We arrived back in London that afternoon and resumed our respective lives. Frankie made for his office, his boring life and even more boring wife. I caught the six o'clock train from Heathrow to the West End and went to my agent's office in Dolphin Square.

Like a lot of men of breeding, Bunny didn't care what he looked like. He was sitting behind his leather-topped desk, his ill-fitting toupee slightly askew. He was puffing profusely on his cigarette. He always did this when he had some good news to impart. The ash had fallen from his Balkan Sobranie, decorating the front of his jacket that sported frayed cuffs and leather patched elbows. In sharp contrast to his dishevelled appearance were his expensive handmade shoes from Jermyn Street.

'I've fixed you a pantomime in Cardiff,' he excitedly announced.

'I know Penny will be pleased.' Bunny was more of a family friend than a business associate and he knew that me being in London and the family being in Cardiff was putting a strain on my already rocky marriage. He paused, stubbed out his colourful cigarette and immediately lit up another before dropping the bombshell. 'I've also fixed you an Australian tour.'

I didn't answer. He looked at me expectantly, waiting for my reaction. I knew I had to take it. Work in Britain was drying up. There was a sad decline in the club scene. The Government had brought in a law banning gambling in places of entertainment, which put musicians, croupiers and the likes of me out of work. What was I to do? I had to look further afield. Penny was going to go ballistic.

'It's extremely lucrative,' he enthused, sensing my apprehension.

'The Cardiff pantomime would be great, Bunny, but I don't know about Australia.'

In retrospect I should never have got married. I had my old man's genes after all. It was doomed from the start. I'd been going out with Penny forever. It had become a habit; I'd just gone along with it to keep her and her family happy. She wasn't in show business. She said she understood but she never got used to the fact that I was surrounded by the temptation of good-looking long-legged showgirls. When I'd gone to Monte Carlo with four beautiful dancers, I was given an ultimatum for the second time; this time it was either showbiz or her.

'What kind of life is this?' she'd yelled. 'You're never here. You rush in, dump your washing, pack a bag and you're off again. If you go again, don't expect to find me here when you come back.'

I remember my old man having to make the very same decision and returning to Wales. Don't get me wrong, I love Wales. No... I'll rephrase that, I'm in love with Wales, and the contract to do pantomime in Cardiff seemed like the answer to all my problems. I decided to grab the lifeline and return to my roots. This way was a compromise but at least I could stay in the business and be home every night, for a while anyway. Australia? Well. I'd cross that bridge when I came to it. What I didn't foresee was that playing Dick Whittington would change my life forever.

The voice came from the darkness of the wings.

'You don't remember me do you, Jono?'

I turned. The woman with long black hair and deep violet eyes smiled. I'd never forgotten those eyes. My stomach flipped. Was it really her?

My cue came and I made my entrance. My head was all over the place. I glanced back into the wings; she was still there, giving instructions on the talkback system. The tabs flew in at the end of the first act and I went looking for her. She was nowhere to be seen. I grabbed a passing stage hand.

'Where did she go?'

'Who?'

'Jennifer Jones?'

'No Jennifer Jones here, mate.'

'The girl who was in the corner?'

'Oh, Jennifer Campanini, you mean? She's gone to the green room.'

She had her back to me, making coffee when I entered. She turned on hearing me. My stomach flipped. She was as beautiful as I remembered. I just stood there, not knowing quite what to say.

'Hello, Jono,' she said.

'Is it really you, Jennifer?'

'Have I changed that much?' she said, offering her hand.

I noticed the wedding ring. 'Who's the lucky guy?'

'Chico Campanini; do you remember him from school?'

'Chico? Vaguely.'

I remembered him alright. I was hit by a pang of jealously at the mention of his name. With his slip-on shoes and Tony Curtis haircut, he thought he was bloody chocolate. All the boys wanted to be him and all the girls fancied him and he knew it. The last time I'd seen him was outside his mother's cafe with Jennifer all those years ago.

'How is he?' I asked not too convincingly.

'Same as ever, still thinks he's God's gift. To tell you the truth, Jono, he's a bloody philanderer.'

'Why do you stick with him, then?'

219

'I never had a reason to leave.' She paused then shot me that same shy smile.

I couldn't take my eyes off her – love at first sight it wasn't. I'd loved her when we were kids and from the way I was feeling now I still did. A voice told me to forget it, she was married and so was I, but I couldn't get her out of my head. I was hooked.

Last-night parties are melancholy occasions. A theatre family that's been together for months go their separate ways. We were dancing to Stevie Wonder when I kissed her. She didn't resist. I asked her if she would like to see the phosphorous, not one of my best lines but the only one I could think of at the time. We drove to a deserted beach, and made love as the luminous plankton sparkled on the crashing waves.

'Not bad for a first time,' she said.

I started to laugh uncontrollably. I can't explain why. I was as high as a kite, not from drugs but from the euphoric feeling of making love to the girl I'd thought of every day since that first kiss.

I was driving home with my arm around her when a police car flagged me down. The cop got out, did his John Wayne walk back towards my car and tapped on the window.

'You the driver of this vehicle?'

'Well, it's automatic,' I said. 'But I've got to go with it wherever it goes.'

'Comedian are you, sir? Do you mind stepping out of the car?'

I did as he asked and blew into his bag. It was negative.

'Don't see many of those on a Saturday night,' he said, looking a little peeved at not getting his Saturday-night quota. He shot a glance at Jennifer, looked me up and down then handed me a ticket. 'Present yourself at the nearest police station in the morning. And I suggest you drive more carefully in the future, sir; the last time I looked, driving one-handed wasn't in the *Highway Code*.'

I dropped Jennifer off at the end of her road and drove home. I crept in unnoticed and crashed on the couch. I came round with Penny standing over me. She had a cup of tea in her hand.

'What time did you get in last night?' she asked accusingly.

'Oh…er…not sure. About one…one thirty.'

'You lying bastard,' she screamed, brandishing the police ticket. 'I found this in your pocket. It says you were stopped by the police at 3.30am. You're in love with her, aren't you?'

'Who?'

'You know very well who, the love of your bloody life,' she screamed. 'I've seen how you look at her.'

I tried a look of contrition but I was failing miserably. I couldn't deny it. I didn't *want* to deny it. She flung the tea at me and stormed out.

The next day the shit hit the fan. The bush telegraph got back to Jennifer's husband and all hell broke loose. He threatened to kill me and himself, in that order. I was due to leave for Australia the next week. I'd signed the contract but I was loath to go. Leaving Jennifer to face the music alone was a bad idea; I knew Chico would be putting the pressure on her to go back and there wouldn't be a thing I could do about it.

'Don't worry, Jono. I'll be fine,' she said. 'You can't break your contract. It will damage your career.'

This was a far cry from the attitude of my wife who would have gladly seen my career crash and burn.

'But how will you cope while I'm gone?' I said.

'It's only for twelve weeks. I'll cope. I'll move out. I'll go to my mother's.'

Chapter Thirty-Nine

At eight o'clock on a cold February morning Pan American Flipper Flight One lifted off from Heathrow. My head was spinning; my heart was thumping. I was on the verge of a nervous breakdown. I went to the toilet and locked myself in. I stood motionless, looking at my reflection in the mirror. I started to chastise myself. What have you done? You've left your wife and two little children for a juvenile infatuation. It was no good. I couldn't see reason. I was incapable of rational thinking. I was infatuated.

They say that love is madness and I have never been so close to going mad as on that twenty-four-hour flight to Sydney. I returned to my seat and sat staring at the cumulus clouds below. I could see the faces of my children in those changing forms of floating cotton. I was about to face the loneliest journey of my life.

'Are you okay?' he asked.

I turned. It was a man of about my age. His hair was long and matted, Rastafarian style.

'Are you okay?' he repeated. 'I noticed you looking down at the clouds. Are you into clouds too?'

With the relief of having someone to talk to, my tale of woe spewed out of my mouth like a torrent. He nodded knowingly.

'My wife's just left me,' he confided. 'Taken the baby back to Canada. Have you got anywhere to stay in Sydney?'

'My agent will have booked a hotel, I expect.'

'I don't think you need to be alone tonight,' he said, looking at me with concern. 'Come and stay with me.'

It never ceases to amaze me how kind most people are. This was a total stranger taking me into his home without a second thought. Under normal circumstances I would have been suspicious of his motives and declined his offer but this wasn't a normal circumstance.

Bob, that was his name, lived in a conventional house in a tree-lined suburban Sydney Street. But there was nothing conventional about Bob. It looked as if he were living in the middle of the bush. The adjacent houses all had manicured lawns and pretty flowering borders but Bob's garden had all the original eucalyptus trees and scrub. There was a hammock strung between two of the trees.

'I'll sleep in that,' he said, pointing towards the hammock. 'You can sleep in the spare room.'

He rolled a thin joint, lit it, took a lungful then offered it to me.

'Want a drag?'

'No, thanks,' I said.

'Go on. It's good stuff – I grow it myself.'

'I don't even smoke tobacco. Do you mind if I crash?'

'Sure, no problem. Sorry I haven't had time to change the sheets.'

He wasn't kidding; they looked like the world and his wife had slept in them but I was past caring. I awoke to the smell of brewing coffee; it seemed Bob was an early riser.

'Can I use your phone, Bob? I need to call a cab.'

'Take my car. I don't need it today. The keys are in it.'

This was either the most trusting person I'd ever met or he had no value for possessions. I drove his ancient Volkswagen to the agent's office. I was greeted by a not-too-happy secretary.

'Where have you been? We sent someone to meet you at the airport. We thought you'd missed the plane.'

'I'm sorry,' I said. 'I should have called.'

'You're on at the South Sydney Juniors' Club tonight,' she said without waiting for an explanation and handed me my date sheet for the week.

'You're booked in at the Chevron Hilton in Charing Cross. Go back to the hotel. The driver will pick you up at seven.'

I drove back to Bob's house, thanked him for his kindness and left.

'I'll come to see the show tonight,' he yelled after the departing taxi.

The shiny new Chevron Hilton at Kings Cross looked totally out of place surrounded by bars, restaurants, nightclubs, brothels, strip clubs and massage parlours. The Cross, as it was known, was Sydney's red light district. Flashing neon signs invited you to enter venues offering adult entertainment. Touts standing in doorways of sleazy clubs were advertising their wares; 'Come inside – they are naked and they move,' they were bawling to anyone within earshot. The area looked decidedly more interesting than the hotel I was about to enter.

I hate hotels. I'd spent half my life in them. Once inside, they were all the same; you couldn't know where you were in the world until you opened the curtains. The ubiquitous wall-mounted television, the packets of tea, coffee and biscuits, the band of paper around the toilet seat, proving it had been cleaned, and the chocolates on the pillow – chocolate on the pillow? What the fuck was that all about? I sat flicking through the channels, looking for something vaguely interesting to watch. It was the usual dross: game shows, talk shows and local news. I eventually found a channel showing back-to-back episodes of *The Flintstones* and settled for that.

Kanga, my driver, a grizzly-looking guy in a shell suit, sporting a three-day stubble, arrived about six thirty.

'You ready, mate?'

'As I'll ever be.' I sighed.

As he drove he filled me in on the details. 'The band call is at seven thirty. You'll be on about ten.' He pulled out a packet of Winfield's and offered me one. I shook my head. 'What's the matter? Not good enough for you?'

'Don't smoke. Bad for my health.'

'Tell that to Paul Hogan… I hope you'll be better than the pop group we had last night,' he said, taking a drag of his Winfield. 'They were real fuckin' shithouse. So it's down to you, mate; if you don't do any good tonight we'll lose the fuckin' club.'

My stomach churned as I entered the South Sydney Juniors'; the thought of facing a hostile audience didn't do much for my already battered confidence.

The club was an eye-opener. I was amazed at the size and opulence of the place. It wasn't like any rugby club I'd ever been in. Its cabaret room held about five hundred people. There was a ballroom, restaurant, indoor swimming pool and a gambling casino. Pictures of the host of international stars that had appeared there hung on the walls. Normally I would have been buzzing about working this great club. But as I walked through the casino, with the sound of the rows of one-armed bandits, or 'Pokie' machines as the Ozzies called them, ringing in my ears, I wished I were somewhere else.

I was doing the band call when Bob turned up. He'd made the effort. He'd put on what passed for his best suit but his hair was still like an explosion in a mattress factory.

'Where've you been?' I asked.

'Up a fuckin' tree by the looks of him,' quipped Kanga, with his usual Ozzie humour.

The compère started to introduce the next act and I started to get the shakes.

'Get me a double vodka will you, Kanga? And put some orange juice in it.'

'Why didn't you just ask for a bloody screwdriver?'

'Is that what they call it?'

Kanga came back with my drink. I pulled out a Valium from

my pocket and downed it with the screwdriver. I'd never needed any stimulant to get me on stage before, adrenaline was enough for me, but this was different. I did my performance on autopilot. According to Kanga I had a great reception but I was unaware of it. It was as if I were in a trance. I stuffed another Valium in my mouth, said goodbye to Bob, and Kanga drove me back to my hotel in the Cross.

I ordered a steak sandwich from room service and sat flicking through the TV channels. Tears were involuntarily streaming down my face. I'd never felt so alone in my life. I missed my kids; I missed Jennifer. I was consumed with guilt and self-pity. I'd faced the rat race, the back-stabbing, played all the shit holes. I'd worked my guts out and hit the big time but it all seemed to mean nothing now. This was a new low for me; as the song goes, 'Is That All There Is?'

I stared at the phone, willing it to ring. I had to speak to Jennifer. I grabbed it and dialled her number. No reply. A letter arrived the next day. It started with 'Whatever happens I'll always love you' – a Dear John letter if ever I'd heard one. I knew what was coming. The text had overtures of sadness. I was sure she was going to go back to Chico.

I paced around the room like someone demented. How could she do this to me after all I'd sacrificed? I saw the photo I kept of her on the table; I grabbed it and ripped it into pieces and threw it on the floor. My heart was breaking. I sat looking at the Sydney Harbour Bridge through my window. The beautiful vista meant nothing to me. All I could think of was how could I get home to sort things out. I picked up the torn pieces and was trying to stick them back together like some mad jigsaw when the phone rang. I grabbed it hoping it was her.

'Jono…? It's me…Frankie.'

'How did you know where I was staying?'

'I rang Penny. She told me to ring your agent and slammed the phone down on me. What the hell's wrong with her?'

'Don't ask.'

'I've just heard from Pip. He wants to invite us to Llŷr's wedding.'

'Who?'

'Llŷr. You remember Llŷr, don't you…? Pip's son?'

Of course I did but I wasn't thinking straight; my head was all over the place.

'Are you still there?'

'Yes…yes, I'm here.'

'Well…what do you think? We can take the wives, make a trip of it.'

'Things are a bit difficult at the moment. I'll let you know,' I said without much conviction.

'Okay, but let me know soon, okay? We need to arrange tickets and stuff.'

I told him I would and ended the call. Frankie didn't know it but it had been my darkest hour. I hoped I would never reach that level of despair again. I thank him to this day for his timely intervention, however unintentional.

The next six weeks were a blur; I was just going through the motions. Every day I'd wake up, and for a brief moment I felt normal then reality would kick in and the familiar knot in my stomach would be back. Every day I'd go to the same steak house for lunch and order the same steak served by the same waitress.

'Nice accent,' she would say. 'Where you from?' She wanted me and another time I would have taken her up on it but not today. I didn't even have the heart to flirt. I'd lost my entire spirit.

I'd been on the road with Kanga for weeks and I was at breaking point. On the long journeys I bent his ear about my troubles. He was sympathetic but in the long run he still worked for the agent and his main priority was to get me to the club.

We arrived at Wagga Wagga – a name I thought he'd made up – and entered the Return Service League Club. A pop group, famous in the sixties, was on stage churning out all their past hits to a not-too-interested audience. Then it was my turn. I knocked back the now customary screwdriver and went in search of the band. It consisted of a drunken pianist and a Maori band banging on hollow logs. How I got through the act was a mystery. I did the best I could and walked off the stage to sparse applause.

I went back to my dressing room, grabbed a bottle of vodka and poured a stiff one. I sunk it in one. I was pouring another when Kanga snatched it from me and handed me a glass of water.

'Don't you think you should take it easy, mate?'

I nodded towards the stage. 'I need the shots just to get up there. I'm not performing, Kanga. I'm just going through the motions.'

'Listen, mate, you can't go on like this.'

'I'll be okay,' I insisted.

'Don't come the bloody raw prawn with me, mate; you're having a nervous fuckin' break down.'

His words hit the spot. Tears welled up in my eyes and started to stream down my face. 'What's happening to me, Kanga?'

'Look, mate, this can't go on; you're gonna have to sell your trousers and get on that big bird home.'

'How can I? My contract runs for another six weeks. I've never broken a contract in my life.'

'Listen…leave the agent to me. I'll just tell him you've made a blue with the wife and you got to go home. I'll sort it out.'

I sat in silence as we drove back to Sydney. It was a dark night; the road through the bush had no street lights. Kanga was concentrating hard not to run into any stray kangaroos. I was being lulled into a state of sleep when he jammed on the brakes.

I jolted awake. 'What's up, Kanga?'

'My bloody lights have gone out.'

He got out of the car to investigate and stood in front of his SUV, hands on hips. He shook his head.

'You wouldn't fuckin' read about it, would ya; both my bloody headlights have been smashed by flying stones. I won't be able to see a thing.'

'What now?'

'We're gonna have to stay put till the sun comes up.'

When we arrived back in Sydney it was the morning rush hour. Shops and offices were opening up. I looked at the people going about their daily lives, doing normal things, and wondered if my life would ever be normal again. Kanga was right; I had to get home to sort things out.

'Drop me off at the office, Kanga. I have to explain the situation to the agent. I can't let you do my dirty work.'

Chapter Forty

The next available flight to London was via Los Angeles, stopping at Auckland and Hawaii. It was a long way around but I had to get home. I paid with my credit card, grabbed my ticket and went towards departures. I walked through the shopping precinct that all airports have before you can reach passport control – I'm sure they do this so you'll buy some of the crap they are peddling. I bought some perfume for Jennifer and some toys for the kids, went through passport control, and boarded the plane.

'What time will it be when we land in London?' I asked.

The pretty flight attendant on Pan Am Flipper One looked at her double-faced wristwatch.

'Let me see...we land in LA in an hour... You know there's a seven-hour lay-over, don't you?' she said.

'Yeh, I know.'

'Where you staying?'

'Holiday Inn.'

'So am I. What we gonna do for seven hours?' She left the words hanging in the air. I knew where this was going.

'So…what time do we land in London?' I said, reminding her of my question.

'Yeh… Sorry. It will be 06.20 in LA and 09.20 in New York. New York is six hours different so it will be 14.21 in London.'

'Ain't ya glad you asked,' quipped a passing camp steward.

I landed in Heathrow feeling and looking like shit. I waited impatiently, listening to the thumping of bags as they were thrown onto the conveyer belt, and watched them as they spewed out of the opening onto the carousel. How long was it going to take? One by one the passengers jostled for position, grabbing for their bags as if their lives depended on it. Where the fuck was mine? When it came the locks had been damaged and some of my stuff was hanging out. Could anything else go wrong with my life?

The arrivals hall was rammed, I scanned the crowd. The usual suspects were there: men in chauffeurs' hats, girls from travel agents holding placards with names scrawled on them, anxious-looking women waiting for their other halves, and girls rushing to meet and kiss their boyfriends. I searched the melee for any sign of Jennifer. Perhaps she hadn't come. Then I saw her. Her hair was tied up in a scarf, she was wearing no make-up and her eyes were all puffed up like she'd been crying. She pushed herself through the crowd and ran to me. I pulled her towards me; tears were coursing down her face.

'I had to go back to him,' she sobbed. 'He was threatening to kill himself. I couldn't have it on my conscience, Jono.'

'He won't do it,' I reasoned. 'The ones that say they will never do.'

She didn't answer. There was a pause.

'Where does he think you are now?'

'He doesn't know. I just said I was going out to post a letter.'

We booked into an airport motel. It was the worst time of my life. After three days of crying and cajoling I was exhausted. I couldn't convince her to leave him; I didn't want to convince her; she had to want to. I asked her to take me home. I needed to see the kids.

I arrived at my house to be welcomed by a sour-faced mother-in-law nursing my two-year-old daughter.

'What do you want?' she spat. 'Don't you think you've done enough?'

She put the little girl down. She ran to me arms outstretched and clung to me like a limpet. I looked at Penny. She was crying. What had I done? It broke my heart but what could I do? I didn't love her anymore. I packed a case and made for the door.

'Daddy!' I turned. It was my little boy behind me. He was holding a small suitcase.

'Where are you going?' I asked.

'With you, Daddy,' he said. I could feel the tears prickling behind my eyes. I picked him up and kissed him.

'Sorry, son,' I said. 'I've got to go now but I'll come to see you whenever I can.' I put him down gently and ran to my car.

I was driving in a trance, going nowhere. I'd been on the road for about an hour when I realised I was back in the little valley town that had been my home all those years ago. I drove until I reached the bottom of Garn Wen Mountain. I left the car and walked the overgrown path to the top. I gazed at the familiar vista. Nothing had changed. The air was still, not a sound, just as I remembered it. A crow's raucous call broke the silence. I sat amongst the couch grass and whinberry bushes and reflected on my fucked-up life.

From the top of the hill I could see Peg's house. Memories of Frankie, Pip and me were whirling around my head; just three scruffy kids sliding down grassy slopes on pieces of cardboard, climbing cliffs, falling down trees and swimming in Echo Valley Pond, the Dormobile, Bates' Field, Dan the Yank, and Jennifer Jones – the lovely Jennifer Jones who'd gone back to Chico. My heart was breaking.

I don't know how long I sat there. Time didn't seem to matter. Nothing seemed to matter. The sun was setting and there was a damp chill creeping into the early evening air. The smell of the couch grass and the resinous smell of the pine trees, damp from the forming dew, evoked long-lost memories of my childhood. Where better to end it all than here, I thought. This is where I'd been happiest. I unscrewed a bottle of painkillers and poured the contents into the palm of my hand. This was the only way out, the only way to stop this constant gnawing pain in my stomach.

'You okay, *was*?'

There was that word again. I turned. A man about my age, holding a couple of dead rabbits on a piece of string and a shot gun cracked over his arm, was looking at me. There was a look of concern on his face. His whippet leaned into me as if he knew me. I could feel the warmth radiating from his smooth, fine skin as he pressed against my leg. I shot the man an enquiring look.

'He likes to feel your warmth,' the man explained. 'Milgis have got thin skin, see. Hey...don't I know you? It's...Jono isn't it...Jono Griffiths? Don't you remember me? Islwyn? You sat next to me in school.'

I remembered his smelly daps more than him but I didn't let on.

'You okay?' he probed.

I was far from okay. Little did he know it but his interruption had probably saved my life.

'Yes...yes, I'm fine,' I lied. 'Just had to see the old place again and completely forgot the time.' We shot the breeze for a while, talked about old Lefty, the headmaster, and Viper, our form master, and I promised to meet him later for a drink if I had time.

'See you in the Collier's Arms later, then,' he said. 'You won't recognise the old place now. It's a bloody Wetherspoons.' He set off down the hill, his faithful milgi trotting obediently by his side.

I sat for a while longer watching Islwyn's diminishing figure as he descended towards the town. The sun was getting low in the sky now, sending fingers of shadows up the slope to meet me. It was getting cold. I started to shiver, not from the cold but from realising how near I'd been to ending it all. I climbed further up the hill to a quarry just below the summit.

Our cave, as we called it, although it was no more than an overhanging rock that we'd built a dry-stone wall around, was still there. Some of the wall had fallen into disrepair and, judging by the droppings littering the floor, its last occupants had been of the woolly kind. I gazed up at the overhanging rock. The names we'd scratched into it all those years ago were still there: Pip, Frankie and me. I reached up to touch them; how simple things were then. I looked down on the town. It was getting late; the lights were coming on one by one; it was time to walk the trail back to my car.

I wasn't sure what to do or where to go. I needed space to think. I didn't want to go to my mother – she would only smother me – and I couldn't go back to my wife. I moved in with Robin, an actor friend. He was in London most of the time so I had the place to myself. Jennifer would visit but the few snatched clandestine meetings we had at the flat only seemed to make things worse. When she left to go home to Chico I felt like shit.

It was becoming harder and harder to meet. Chico wouldn't let her out of his sight. Since the affair had become public he followed her everywhere, scuppering any chance I had of seeing her. It was destroying me. I was going through hell. Jennifer was unhappy too; she was just going through the motions of being the dutiful wife.

Breaking in to the BBC wasn't the best idea I'd ever had but desperate times need desperate measures and I was desperate. Jennifer was working on a production and I saw a window of opportunity.

'How did you get past security?' she said.

'I borrowed Robin's car, put a wig on, parked my car across from the park, climbed over the perimeter fence, went through the scene dock and here I am.'

'And all because the lady loves Milk Tray,' she quipped with a smile. She was making light of the situation but she knew things couldn't go on as they were.

During the following year, apart from the odd meet at Robin's flat or clandestine meeting at some out of the way pub, we didn't see much of each other. She kept promising that we would be together in the end but as the weeks turned into months I was losing hope that it would ever materialise. I didn't want to give her an ultimatum. It had to be her choice: stay or leave. How could I be responsible for breaking up her marriage? Breaking my own was bad enough. But I couldn't live like this anymore; I wasn't in control of my life. Drastic measures were needed. I picked up the phone and dialled her number.

'Jennifer? Ble mae e?' I spoke in Welsh for fear he was listening.

'He's in the garden but he'll be back any minute.'

'I'll make it quick, then. I'm going to France to see my friend Pip. I've been invited to his son's wedding. I'll probably stay, try to make a new life for myself. I understand you can't leave Chico but I can't live like this either. I have to get my life together. Will you tell Robin I've left the key to his flat with a neighbour?'

She didn't answer. Then, after a long pause, 'I'll always love you,' she whispered. 'Always have, always will.'

I could hear her crying. I replaced the receiver and dialled Frankie's number. I didn't have much to pack; I'd left home with the clothes I stood up in and a few changes of underwear. I stuffed them into a holdall and took a last look around the flat. I was about to leave when the doorbell rang. It was Jennifer.

'I'm coming with you,' she said.

We clung to each other, tears cascading down our cheeks.

'What about Chico?'

'He's thrown me out. I didn't have the guts to leave, so I told him I was in love with you in the hope that he would.'

The next day I called Pip. He sounded pretty drunk.

'Jono, I want you to get me a new passport and driving licence. Mine have been taken off me again.'

'What the hell!'

'I'm out on bail. I was driving pissed drunk while disqualified and smashed into a shop window. The bastards have taken my French passport to stop me skipping the country. I got to get out of here, Jono. I'm going down this time as sure as hell. I can't go back inside, Jono. I'll fucking die. Being in a cell with villains, sharing one spoon to eat with, is not all it's cracked up to be. Will you help me? I'll send you my birth certificate.'

'I'll try, but wouldn't Frankie be the best bet? He's the bloody lawyer.'

'Frankie's up his own arse,' he scoffed. 'Won't do anything dodgy
– says it's his fucking reputation.'

He ranted on for another fifteen minutes about the bastards who'd
banged him up. He was slurring badly by now. I heard him taking
another swig.

'My liver is failing, Jono; I'm very ill.'

'Surely there's something they can do? You've got connections.
What about a transplant?'

'It's too late, was. There's no getting out of this one. It's too late,
mate…too fucking late.' There was a long pause; I thought he'd gone.
Then…

'I must see you guys before…' Another pause, then he started to
ramble on again. 'I'll go to Roscoff and pay someone to sail me to Jersey.
I can get into the country from there without a passport. I've got money
in a bank there and in Argentina. Speak soon.' The line went dead.

Chapter Forty-One

We met with Frankie and his long-suffering wife, Connie, at the airport.

'You remember Jennifer, don't you, Frankie?'

'How could I forget?' he said, eying her up. 'Everyone in school fancied *you*.'

Connie shot Frankie a look that could kill. She didn't look at me. I think she tarred me with the same brush as the philandering Frankie.

Connie was a lovely girl if a little taciturn; it was easier to get a conversation out of a tailor's dummy than get a conversation out of her. Apart from her looks I couldn't see what she and Frankie had in common. She had a resigned look about her. I'm sure she knew of Frankie's dalliances but for the sake of the family she never let her dignity slip.

We arrived in Barcelona with a day to spare, so we decided to make the most of the wonderful city. While I waited for the bags to be unloaded Frankie went to hire the car. I'd booked us into the Hilton Hotel before leaving. Frankie wasn't happy about it. He said it was too expensive. When we came down in the morning Frankie informed us that he was going to eat at a small cafe on the corner. No wonder he was rich – he was too bloody mean to spend anything, except on his fancy women.

Jennifer was unusually quiet at breakfast. We'd made love that morning but she seemed distant as if her heart hadn't been in it.

'Is something wrong?' I probed.

'No, I'm just tired, that's all.'

I didn't believe her. She'd become more and more withdrawn as the weeks had gone by and her mood swings were affecting me. I loved her but I was starting to realise that apart from an adolescent infatuation and an affair that had only been a few months long, I didn't really know her. Had I done the right thing? Or to be more specific, had she made the right decision?

We caught the metro to the centre of the city. The carriage was full to bursting; people were jammed together like kippers in a box. A woman, who looked like a Romanian gypsy, was a little too close for comfort. She was looking at Jennifer, face to face. Jennifer opened her bag to check what stop we needed, pulled out her wallet, checked the details and then put the wallet back in her bag. At the next stop, the Romanian woman got off and a band of buskers got on.

I'd seen buskers in the London Underground but this was the first time I'd seen them busk on a train. They were a happy bunch: two guitarists, a drummer with a snare drum, and a girl singer. They launched into their set. The music had the infectious percussive beat that all Spanish music has and I started involuntarily to tap my foot. The girl beckoned me to join them and I launched into a full-on tap routine much to the amazement of the crowd and embarrassment of Frankie. The place erupted and they started to toss money into the hat that had been put on the floor. Before we arrived at our stop the hat was overflowing. The band thanked me. We got off the train on a high, and made for the Las Ramblas.

The Ramblas was alive, a vibrant place. Throngs of tourists were vying with locals, hustling to find a vacant table at one of the street cafes. We found a table outside the colourful Gaudi Hotel, its curly turrets and colourful facade reminiscent of a child's sandcastle. We ordered tapas and a jug of sangria and watched fascinated as the human statues in their exotic costumes and make-up went through their well-practised routines. Excited children dropped coins into their hats then squealed in delight when the statues moved to pick them up. We could have stayed there all day watching this pantomime but it was getting late. We had to get an early night. We had a long drive the next day.

The waiter dropped the bill on the table and Jennifer picked it up. 'I'll get this,' she said and opened her bag to pay. Her passport was still there but the cash had gone.

'Oh no! It must have been the woman on the train,' she said. 'I should have noticed the signs. Why would she leave the passport? It doesn't make sense.'

'They only want cash,' said Frankie. 'No way of tracing them. Anyway, it's only money. They're dying in Africa,' was Frankie's flippant remark. I gave him a sour look and paid the bill with my credit card.

The next morning we picked up the hire car and drove to the French Catalan border. We booked into a hotel in Figueres, found our rooms, unpacked and showered, then went to the bar. Frankie went to call Pip to let him know where we were and Jennifer, Connie and I ordered a well-earned gin and tonic. Frankie finished his phone call and joined us.

'What you having, Frankie?'

'A large glass of red for me. I've spoken with Pip, told him we'll be up in the morning but he said he'd pick us up in his Hummer, whatever the hell that is.'

'I thought he'd lost his licence?'

'Well you know Pip… Anyway, let's relax for now. It's been a long day.'

We waited until gone noon the next day but there was no sign of Pip. Frankie was getting impatient and decided to call again. A torrent of French followed, none of which I understood, then, in English:

'What do you mean he's in jail again?' There was another stream of French, culminating in Frankie slamming the phone down.

I shot him a 'what-the-fuck's-going-on' look.

'The stupid bastard has got himself banged up again. Apparently he went out pissed and turned his car over. If that wasn't bad enough he was already banned from driving from a previous offence. Janique is afraid he'll miss the bloody wedding.'

'He'll never change,' I said. 'He's still a delinquent, just not so juvenile anymore.'

Chapter Forty-Two

It was late August. France had suffered an unusually hot summer and it hadn't been kind. The landscape had been charred from forest fires that had raged for weeks, made worse by 'the mistral' fanning the flames. We'd decided to avoid the busy motorway and took the much quieter country roads. It was a sorry sight. On both sides of the road, blackened skeletal shapes of trees stood smouldering like burnt matchsticks and acrid smoke still hung in the air. The ecological massacre had laid waste to houses, crops and orchards alike. I couldn't help feeling for the people who'd lost homes and in some instances family members and hoped that the devastation hadn't reached Pip's estate.

As we followed the signs for the Pyrenees, my fears were allayed; the countryside became greener. Glad to be leaving the scorched landscape behind us, we drove the last few miles of winding road in a brighter mood. We reached the little town and took the narrow track that Frankie and I had driven previously with Pip. If anything the track was even more perilous than I remembered.

We arrived at the gate leading to the big house; it was locked. There was a handwritten note on the gate telling us to come to the farm house. We drove the rough track once more, dodging the potholes for fear of damaging the hire car. We arrived at the farm. There were no cars in the drive. It was very quiet; the place looked deserted. There was a cow bell hanging adjacent to the front door, masquerading as a door bell. Frankie pulled on it. A dog barked somewhere in the house but no one seemed to be responding. We were about to leave when the door creaked open. Beryl the dog bounded out, greeting us like long-lost friends, followed closely behind by a very small woman, no more than four feet six tall. Another sister, I thought. Were all Janique's family members this small?

She shooed Beryl back in and looked up at Frankie.

'Bonjour, tu es Frankie?' she asked with a smile.

'Oui.'

'Janique est dans le village La-bas,' she said, pointing us towards a small hamlet in the distance. Some more rapid French followed. Frankie, noticing the blank look on my face, explained.

'Janique is performing in a play in the next village; some summer festival or other if I understood her fully.'

We thanked the woman for her help and made our way back up to what euphemistically passed for a road, and drove the rest of the potholed track until we eventually arrived at the small hamlet.

It was a hive of activity. Cars were parked nose to tail in a field high above the village but we managed to squeeze into one of the last remaining spots. We took the steep winding steps down to the square below where the small civic hall in the corner of the square had been adorned with flowers ready for the impending wedding ceremony. The far end of the square had been set up for the al fresco performance.

A makeshift stage had been dressed with a set and some old furniture. Plastic chairs in rows had been set out for the expectant audience and trestle tables laden with delicious-looking food had been laid out for the after-performance refreshments. The play was a French farce with Janique taking the lead role. I couldn't understand the French script but from the roars of laughter from the local audience it was obviously a big hit.

The show over, we made our way back to the farm house. The next day's preparations for Llŷr's pending wedding were well under way. There was still no sign of Pip who, I assumed, was still banged up in Perpignan jail.

Janique was nowhere to be seen the next day. She'd left early in the morning to oversee the final arrangements at Le Mas Reste. Frankie, I and our two spouses were left to our own devices. We ate a leisurely breakfast prepared for us by Janique's sister, got dressed for the wedding and drove the same death-defying route as the day before.

We arrived at the small village where the wedding was to be held and joined the villagers as they crammed into the small hall. Janique, being the Maire de la Commune, or mayor of the small hamlet, was to officiate at the ceremony. I remember thinking how nice it must be to have your mother carry out the official duties at your wedding.

Where the play had been performed the night before, trestle tables had been laid out with canapés and champagne. Wedding guests were being served by men wearing tall chef hats and long white aprons. In my ignorance I thought this was the wedding reception. I couldn't have been more wrong. This cold collation had been laid on as a gesture for the villagers who hadn't been invited to the main reception.

Feeling full, we drove back to the farm and changed for the next soirée. We arrived at the big house. It was a grand affair. Even more champagne and canapés were served to the accompaniment of a string quartet. If I thought this was to be the end of the celebrations I was in for a rude awakening; in the court yard a huge marquee had been set up for what can only be described as a banquet. More chefs with tall hats and long white aprons had flown in especially from Perpignan to serve us the five-course meal: foie gras, salmon, poussin, wild boar, etcetera, all washed down with a selection of grand cru wines from the local vineyards.

Everyone had been allocated different tables. Frankie and Jennifer were on a table with members of the French Government and relations of Janique. Connie and I were sitting with the vineyard owner, his Mexican wife and local dignitaries. No one at my table spoke a word of English. Connie, being rather a tacit person at the best of times, sat looking into space and I spent the whole evening speaking my fractured Spanish to the Mexican wife of the vineyard owner, who translated into French for the rest of the table.

I avoided explaining to the rather bemused company why the groom's father wasn't present by pretending I didn't understand. Llŷr had told me that Pip was being released that day and with the wind in his favour, he would at least make the reception.

Frankie and Jennifer, who were also being quizzed as to Pip's whereabouts, were sliding under the table, metaphorically speaking, trying to stifle laughs. Someone had noticed the bride's mother hadn't shown up either, to which Frankie had quipped that perhaps she'd been banged up with Pip in Perpignan jail. Jennifer had stuffed a napkin into her mouth in an effort to smother her guffaws and Frankie was almost choking on his foie gras.

The speeches were next, not a word of which I understood. Wedding speeches always go on too long and this time was no exception. Llŷr was last to speak. Thankfully, he kept it short, switching seamlessly from French to English. He apologised for his father's absence and hoped he could join us soon. I hoped so, too, but in my heart I knew it was a slim chance. Turning to me he announced that his friend from Wales would sing a folk song from his home village. Press-ganged into singing for my supper, I took the microphone.

'Pip loves this song,' I explained. 'It's only a shame he's not here to hear it. Llŷr will translate for me as I explain the story. It's not really the right sentiment for a wedding but it's Pip's favourite so here goes.

'It tells the true story of Will, a poor thatcher who won the heart of Ann, an heiress. Their relationship was forbidden and Ann was confined to her room. She wrote to Will on a sycamore leaf, with a pin dipped in her own blood, and trusted the precious love-token to the mercy of the wind. Will, believing he'd been rejected, left, only to return years later to find Ann dying. She died in his arms and his heartbreak is expressed in this haunting love song.' Llŷr translated and I started to sing.

Mi sydd fachgen ieuanc ffôl
Yn byw yn ôl fy ffansi,
Myfi'n bugeilio'r gwenith gwyn,
Ac arall yn ei fedi.

The first I knew that something was wrong was seeing blue flashing lights bleeding through the canvas of the marquee. From my vantage point on the stage I could see two gendarmes at the entrance. There was a buzz around the audience by now but I kept on singing.

Pam na ddeu i ar fy ôl,
Ryw ddydd ar ôl ei gilydd?
Gwaith 'rwy'n dy weld, y feinir fach,
Yn lanach, lanach beunydd.

Someone pointed in the direction of Janique's table and she was called over. Llŷr came towards me. I could see by the look on his face something was terribly wrong. He mounted the stage and whispered in my ear. His hand shook as he took the microphone from me.

Chapter Forty-Three

I couldn't make Pip's funeral. Six months later Frankie, Connie and I caught the plane to Perpignan. Jennifer wasn't with me; we'd broken up just after Llýr's wedding. Jennifer's mood swings had deepened. Chico had been calling her, begging her to go back, putting pressure on our already fragile relationship. She was consumed by her Catholic guilt about leaving Chico. I knew what that was like. My mother was a Catholic, albeit a lapsed one, but she still cooked fish every Friday and genuflected whenever she saw a funeral cortège pass by. Jennifer insisted that whatever happened she would always love me but had to do, in her mind, what was the right thing. I loved her too but the writing was on the wall. I had to own up. It's true what they say – you can never go back. I was foolish to think I could. I was in love with the past, that first kiss, the link to my first sexual awakenings, Cwm Teg and Pip.

Frankie booked us into a hotel, hired a car and I drove the forty-six kilometres to Le Perthus. We travelled in silence.

Connie was her usual taciturn self. Frankie was just staring out of the window, lost in his reflections. I broke the silence.

'Killed by a drunk driver… The bloody irony of it!'

'He was on borrowed time, Jono. His liver was about to pack up. At least this way it was quick.'

My mind was full of thoughts, thoughts of what might have been, what had passed and why Pip had ended up like Peg. Frankie had been Pip's brother after all and I, well, I might as well have been. I would never have friends later in life like when I was eight and Pip and Frankie were the best friends I'd ever had.

I'd been driving on autopilot for about an hour. Before I knew it we were in Le Perthus. I turned right onto the now familiar track that led to Pip's farm house, trying to dodge the same potholes that hadn't been fixed since the last time. On arriving we were welcomed by an excited Beryl who, tail wagging, ran back and forth excitedly from her compound, proudly trying to introduce us to her newborn litter of pups. There was a note on the door from Janique.

'Gone to the village Hall, Go to Big house. Llŷr will meet you there.'

We were met by a sombre Llŷr. A girl I didn't recognise was hovering behind him. There was an awkward silence, the last time I'd seen Llŷr he was getting married, to a different woman.

'This is Michelle.' he said, sensing our discomfort.

She wasn't pretty in a traditional sense. She was what my grandfather would have described as a handsome woman, which was in sharp contrast to Llŷr's wife who was pretty in a mouse-like way but devoid of any personality. Michelle, on the other hand, was full of it. She took my hand with a firm grip and flashed a warm smile.

'Come and join the barbecue,' she said. 'You must be hungry after your journey.'

I didn't much feel like socialising; it had been a very long day. All I wanted was a shower and my bed but it would have been churlish not to accept. She led us to where members of Janique's family, who'd flown up from Paris for the memorial, were sitting around a long trestle table with friends. The atmosphere was jovial, which seemed strange to me. I had been brought up in a Welsh family where memorials were usually quite sombre occasions. Copious amounts of half-empty wine bottles and remnants of what had been nothing short of a banquet littered the table. Someone proposed a toast to their recently departed friend. Bottles were glugged, glasses were clinked and food was chomped, followed by cries of 'Bravo, Philippe. Á vous, nous buvons á votre mémoire.' It seemed the wake had already begun.

It was late afternoon and the heat of the day had abated somewhat but there was a feeling of an impending storm in the air. The sun was going down in a bank of angry purple, and a large drop of rain splattered across my plate – a harbinger of what was to come. Fork lightning strafed the sky, tearing the dark heavily laden clouds apart, then, without warning, the rain came down in torrents. Abandoning the barbecue, we all made a dash for the house.

Apart from Llŷr and Michelle, only Pip's brother-in-law had any command of English. Frankie made small talk; I nodded and tried to look intelligent. Llŷr went to telephone Janique to see what was keeping her and I hijacked Michelle; at least she was someone I could converse with. Her English was impeccable but there was a trace of an accent I couldn't quite place.

'You have very good English,' I said.

'My mother's from Cornwall,' she explained. 'I suppose that must be the attraction, Llŷr and I both being Celts.'

After the usual niceties, I neatly steered her towards the subject of Llŷr's marriage; where was his wife? I was curious to know what had happened.

'He'd been going out with Françoise since they were teenagers,' she said. 'I think it just became a habit. She came from a privileged background as did Llŷr and it was expected by both families that they would eventually marry.'

'But if he didn't love her…?' I left the question hanging.

'Llŷr just went along with it to keep the peace.'

I nodded. Hadn't I done the same thing?

'Most men are weak,' she continued, 'and Llŷr is no exception.' She gave me a knowing smile. What did this charming girl know? Had someone told her of my chequered love life?

'When Llŷr and I met it was instant,' she said. 'Love has toppled kings from thrones, Jono,' she said, flashing me another of her engaging smiles. I could tell what Llŷr saw in her.

It was getting late and there was still no sign of Janique, so we decided to have an early night. Michelle showed us to our rooms. I had the same room I'd shared with Frankie, and Frankie and Connie had Pip's old crash pad up the hallway.

The storm was really setting in by now but I was so tired I fell into a deep sleep. I was awoken by the wooden shutters banging, wind howling and the rain coming in through an open window. I looked at my watch; it was six thirty. I must have dozed off and was woken up again by sounds coming from the kitchen and the smell of percolating coffee. No point in going back to sleep, I thought, so I followed the aroma of the coffee to find Frankie and Connie, sat at a kitchen table, mugs of steaming coffee in hand.

Frankie, who was always thinking of his stomach, suggested we go for breakfast to Pip's favourite restaurant, which was high up on a mountain overlooking his estate. Rain was still coming down in sheets as we negotiated the narrow winding road. The higher we went the worse the visibility got. As we neared the summit, the apparition of what looked like a Swiss chalet, clinging to the side of the mountain, swam into view through the swirling mist.

With its trestle tables and wooden benches, it was more of a bar than a restaurant. As we entered, the aroma of coffee and Gauloises assailed my nostrils, stirring my taste buds. Frankie took charge as usual and ordered the full monty. A girl, struggling with an obscene amount of cold cuts and cheeses, croissants and coffee, plonked them on the table in front of us. Connie chose a croissant and Frankie attacked the spread like he hadn't seen food for a week. I didn't know where to start.

'Go on, Jono. Get stuck in,' he urged, sensing my apprehension.

I didn't feel like food; my heart wasn't in it. I could feel Pip's presence, visualise him surveying his land below, croissant in one hand, glass of wine in the other. I strained my eyes to see the family mausoleum through the swirling mist. The thought of the forthcoming interment of his ashes brought tears to my eyes; I couldn't believe I would never see Pip again. I sat there lost in nostalgia for the old days – to be as we were, Peg's boys. I could hear his voice.

'Give us a go on your bike, was. Go on, Jono – take a drag.'

I thought of that little kid sitting on his gambo with his elbows poking out of his jumper and what he'd become, what he'd achieved. I wondered what he might have done had he had a conventional upbringing. Living with the eccentric Peg wasn't easy. He had to fend for himself most of the time but perhaps it made him stronger, who knows. He'd succeeded against the odds. He had it all: family, money, kudos. But it seemed this wasn't enough; he was programmed to self-destruct. Was it in his DNA? I don't know and I don't suppose I ever will. All I know is that I will miss him.

Breakfast over, we wended our way towards the family's vault where it had been the tradition for Janique's family to be interred for over a hundred years. When we arrived the family were already there. There was a short service conducted by the local priest followed by eulogies from Janique and Pip's brother-in-law. This was all done in French as one would expect. Llŷr was the last to speak; he did this bilingually for our benefit then asked if I would sing a Welsh song.

'Pip was proud of his Welsh heritage,' he said. 'His favourite saying was, "*There's only one thing better than a Welshman and that's another Welshman.*"'

As Pip's ashes were interred in the mausoleum, the sound of my acapella rendition of 'Lisa Lan' broke the respectful silence. It didn't matter that no one understood the Celtic lyrics; the poignant sound of the folk song, rising like a lark in the tranquillity of the cold morning air, brought them to tears. Turning to Frankie, I sang the last verse in English.

Will you come to bid goodbye,
When in the earth my form must lie?
I hope you too will there be found,
When men shall lay me in the ground.

When I finished they all stood in silence, consumed by their thoughts. It was Llýr who broke the impasse.

'Philippe wouldn't have wanted us to be sad. Let us remember him as he was – a wild spirit.'

We made our way back to the farm house where Janique had prepared yet another banquet in Pip's honour. The huge refectory dining table was groaning with the weight of food: deep tureens filled with wild boar stew and vegetables, just as Pip would have liked it, freshly baked bread, copious amounts of wines and spirits, and every cheese you could imagine. There was even a plate of stew for Beryl the dog and smoked salmon for the cat. As we ate the mood lifted and Janique, in her broken English, proposed a toast.

'This is the wine Pip kept for de special occasion,' she said, filling her glass.

'To Pip, my husband and the best lover I ever had.'

We rose as one. 'To Pip,' we chorused in unison.

Chapter Forty-Four

I met Llŷr off the Paris flight and made for Hanover Chambers. We were shown into Frankie's office by his PA. He rose from behind his large desk to greet us. Hugs were exchanged and he waved us towards the leather chesterfield. We took a seat.

'Tea, boys? Coffee?'

'Coffee will be fine,' I said.

He buzzed through to his secretary.

'Some coffee, please, Emily, and hold any calls. I'll be in a meeting for a while.'

He went to his safe, hesitated for a moment then punched in the combination. He came back with a large envelope and some keys. He gave the keys to Llŷr.

'For the house,' he said, then offered me the envelope. It was addressed to Pip and Frankie. I recognised the handwriting; it was Peg's. I shot him a quizzical look. Why was he giving it to me? He avoided my eyes. I took the envelope and held it for a moment.

He cleared his throat. 'Before you open it,' he began, 'I've got a confession to make.'

He sat down behind his desk. I could see his right leg involuntarily bouncing up and down like a jackhammer; he was obviously stressed about something. He pulled out a Cuban from a box on his desk, lit it and took a drag. He let the cloud of blue smoke slowly escape from his lips. I looked at him, waiting for this grand revelation. He took the cigar from his mouth; his jowls were pulsating as he clenched and unclenched his jaw. He took another slow drag.

'I've had this letter since before Peg died,' he said at last. 'Not even Pip knew of its contents.'

He gestured for me to open it and took another drag of his cigar. I ripped open the envelope and emptied the contents onto the table. A book, a letter and a gold chain with a Welsh love spoon attached to it fell out. I opened the letter and read it aloud.

> *Hello, my lovely boys. If you are reading this letter then you know I've kicked the bleedin' bucket. The book belonged to Bert, Jono's dad; he leant it to me when we were young and I've had it ever since. Reading it again and again just brought back memories of the old bugger; and somehow it kept me close to him.*

I opened the book and read the fly leaf. It read, 'To Peg from Bert with all my love. Xmas 1951.' I shot a look at Frankie. He avoided my eyes. I paused then continued reading.

> *You will also find a gold Welsh love spoon pendant with an inscription on the back; you'll see it says from Bert to Peg with all my love – It's not what it seems boys. It wasn't just an affair; we were very much in love and you, Pip, were the result.*

I stopped reading and looked at Frankie again. He gestured for me to carry on. I continued to read.

You were always close to Pip, weren't you, Jono? But you were much closer than you knew – you are brothers. Bert passed away without knowing he had another son. I always meant to tell him but he'd made it plain that his future was with you, Jono, and your mother, and I didn't want to fuck up your lives; mine was bad enough. So, my dear boys, don't hate me for not always being there for you. Look out for each other. Think of me from time to time.

Your loving, if not always considerate, mother, Peg xxx

P.S. Sorry you're not a prince, Pip. Although I did shag a prince once, at least that's what he told me.

I was gobsmacked. I glared at Frankie. I didn't know whether to be angry or cry.

'Why did you keep it secret all these years, Frankie? Didn't you think we had a right to know?'

He gazed down into his lap then looked up at me; he was struggling to find an appropriate response.

'I'm sorry, Jono… I meant to tell you but I suppose I was jealous of your closeness to Pip. As time went on it became harder to own up to the truth.'

He took another suck at his cigar and slowly shook his head.

'My biggest regret is that I never told Pip before he died. I meant to but it never seemed like the right time. The last time he contacted me he was drunk as usual. He told me he was having legal problems and he wanted me to help him out. I'm a respectable lawyer, on paper at least, and there was no way I could get involved with any of his dodgy dealings. I'd taken the rap for his petty crimes too many times when we were kids and I couldn't be seen as anything but squeaky clean. Especially then – I had a case pending against me.'

'What case?' I asked.

'My partner, unbeknown to me, had embezzled money to the tune of two hundred thousand pounds by ripping the top off the wills that came through the office. If I couldn't pay it all back we were both facing jail. I was at my wits end; how could I find that kind of money? Apart from the fact it was a fortune, I was living a double life and keeping two women in a manner to which they very quickly became accustomed. But enough of my problems.'

Frankie shot Llŷr a sheepish look. 'This may come as a shock to you, Llŷr, but he wanted to disinherit you. He said you'd fallen out big time. He didn't say what had gone on between you two but he was as mad as hell.'

'It was something and nothing, Frankie. He was pissed drunk at the time and banging on about how much the grand wedding was going to cost him. When he'd sobered up he forgot all about it. He was always threatening to cut me off. He didn't like the way I always told him what he didn't want to hear. I told him booze would be the end of him. The irony is, the one time he was sober he was killed by a drunken driver.'

'I told him he couldn't, Llŷr – cut you off, I mean. It was complicated. It wasn't my field of expertise but as far as I knew he couldn't disinherit you. Under French law a certain amount of the estate is reserved for the children and half goes to the first child. And as you are his only child... well, it speaks for itself.'

'Did you explain that to him, Frankie?'

'Of course I did, Jono, but he kept going on about being a British citizen. I tried to reason that he was resident in France and Llŷr was born there. If he'd been a non-resident perhaps I could have opted for the law in this country rather than French law, but it was a bloody long shot.'

'So, what did you do about it?'

'He had money stashed in Jersey, Panama and God knows where else.' He turned to face Llŷr. He looked uneasy. 'I'm not proud of it, kid, but the thought crossed my mind that if he transferred his money to me it could be the answer to all my problems. He'd confided in me that he was dying and he didn't want you to get it, so I thought what the hell?'

There was an awkward silence. How were we supposed to react to a revelation like that? Frankie reached into his pocket and handed Llŷr a cheque.

'I'm sure he would have wanted you to have it, Llŷr. It's all there, every penny.'

I looked at Llŷr. Tears were welling up in his eyes. I grabbed him and held him close.

Chapter Forty-Five

The following day, Llŷr and I caught the train from Paddington to Cardiff then changed onto the valley line. As we walked up the main street of Cwm Teg my heart sank; evidence of the government's austerity was everywhere. Where once there had been full employment there were now men sleeping rough. Hypodermics, fast-food cartons and sleeping bags littered the doorways. The last time the valley had seen such deprivation was during the miner's strike back in the eighties.

The strike had lasted a year. Men, having to feed their families, had continued to work and were branded scabs. There were violent confrontations pitting friend against friend, brother against brother, and neighbour against neighbour. It was the most bitter industrial dispute in British history and the crackdown on the proud miners and the closure of all three of the pits in the valley had taken its toll on the community.

The present government's policy was having the same effect. Where there had been shops and businesses in a bustling community, charity shops and fast-food joints now pervaded the high street. Mrs Tucker's bakery, which sold the best iced buns I'd ever tasted, was now a charity shop, and the local book shop, where I'd bought my Enid Blyton books and Superman comics was a Chinese take-away. The Bracchi's Cafe where we'd drunk our frothy coffee was still there but under new management. The Italian name had been painted over and replaced with a new sign proudly announcing the Twenty One Cafe. We stopped for a coffee.

'How many sugars, love?' the waitress asked, while operating the same hissing Gaggia machine.

'Two, please,' I said.

'I thought you looked a bit cheeky,' she quipped with a toss of her head.

We walked towards Peg's old house, passing the market place on the way. It had once rung with the sound of barrow boys balling out their wares, but it was all but silent now. Phyllis the Fish's shop was now peddling pakoras and poppadoms, and the Collier's Arms, where my old man could sell at least two barrels of beer on a Monday morning to the thirsty miners dodging a shift, had been taken over by one of the poncy pub chains and turned into a gin palace.

A block of soulless flats had replaced the old dressed stone building that had been my school; the school where, as I was riveted to my ancient oak desk, Viper's dramatic description of the Roman invasion of his Celtic land had fired my fertile imagination. I remember to this day his stories of how the Silures stood rattling their swords and shields in defiance as the Roman centurions marauded uphill towards their circular Silurian defences. He spoke with passion of how the Silures, brandishing their swords and spears, threatened to kill every Roman insurgent who dared to invade their homeland. 'With their fierce woad-painted faces,' he would say, 'they looked like they could do it too.'

Llŷr wasn't saying very much, just gazing at the down-at-heel town. The stories Pip had told him of the valley and the adventures we'd had as kids must have seemed like a fantasy to him now – just some of Pip's drunken melancholic ramblings seen through nostalgic eyes.

In one of his more sober moments, Pip had made me promise to make sure that Llŷr knew of his heritage. What would he make of it, I wondered, and the house that held so many memories for me?

'Penny for your thoughts?' I asked.

'What do you mean, Uncle Jono?'

'This is a far cry from your life in Paris, isn't it?'

'Pip wanted me to know where I came from.'

From the outside the house looked much the same as I remembered it but it had been neglected. The garden where the Dormobile had lain was even more overgrown than before. I noticed something sticking out from the long grass. I grasped it and it came away in my hand. On further inspection I realised it was a piece of Dan the Yank's old wheelbarrow. Llŷr put the key in the door. It worked but the door was swollen with damp, jammed tight. He put his shoulder to it and gave it a shove. It creaked open, pushing the pile of old junk mail and flyers into a heap. As we stepped over them into the hallway, I half expected to see Peg in one of her flamboyant outfits, sparkle in her hair, her Celtic eyes shining. In my head I could hear the kids' voices, see the table laid out with knife, fork, spoon and glass of wine, and hear Peg's throaty laugh as she plonked her eggs Benedict in front of us. But the place was empty. It smelt musty, damp; it looked like it had been empty for years. I walked through to the kitchen; there were still remnants of Peg's art work littering the floor.

'Did Pip ever come back here, Llŷr?' I asked.

'No. He just got Frankie to buy the house for him and have what furniture he wanted shipped out to France.'

I looked through the grimy windows to where Garn Wen loomed in the distance; at least that hadn't changed. It was timeless. I was lost in my thoughts when Llŷr spoke.

'Is that the mountain Pip always talked about?'

'Yes, that's the one... Come on, Llŷr. Let me show you.'

We climbed steadily towards the summit, passing the crater where Echo Valley Pond had been. My heart sank; it was full of choking water weeds and a barbed wire fence had been erected around it. I reflected that the sign shouting 'Danger Keep Out' wouldn't have deterred the intrepid Pip.

We reached the overhanging rock we'd called our den and I pointed out our childish signatures scratched into the rock. From where we were we could see Peg's house in the distance. We didn't speak; we just listened. Not even a skylark broke the silence this time. I looked at Llŷr. He was the image of his father, and I was back there again, an innocent age when everything was an adventure. Our childhood was a time of hope; a time when all our dreams seemed possible. Maybe we expected too much, but if Peg taught us anything it was that through all the shattered dreams and broken promises, you've got to carry on. Llŷr opened his holdall that he'd been clutching all day and pulled out a small urn.

'What's that, Llŷr?' I asked.

'It's some of Pip's ashes,' he said. 'They weren't all interred in France. Before he died he made me promise I would bring him home.'

I watched as Llŷr scattered the ashes to the four winds. There were tears in my eyes. I couldn't speak. Llŷr placed a sympathetic hand on my shoulder.

'Well, Uncle Jono,' he said. 'Where do we go from here?'

I looked at my new-found nephew, the dead spit of his father, and thought of my own kids who are now grown up, and my one regret is that they never had the chance, as we did, to slide down this mountain on a tin tray.

Epilogue

Present Day

It's late June, whinberry-picking time in Cwm Teg. It's been years since I was there with Llŷr and I'm ready for my nostalgic fix. As the train clanks its way towards the old parish I'm transported back to those first days when, with my mother, I had taken the same journey. Things have changed somewhat. The once black tips that had scarred the landscape have been reclaimed and grassed over, erasing all memory of the coal mines that had fuelled the economy for so many years. I wonder if the people, who now have green hills to look upon and clean air to breathe, yearn for the old days and the coal that had given them their livelihoods, even though it had polluted their valley.

The train jolts and shudders to a stop, breaking my daydream. The station seems smaller than I remembered it, as does the town. I walk towards the Forge. The crumbling old stack is still there. In pride of place, above the many fly posters, is a plaque with an EU flag, stating that the Cwm Teg Iron Works Furnace No. 4 was built in 1850.

Standing incongruously next to this reminder of a time long past is a twenty-four-hour supermarket. I stand motionless, staring at the ruins at what had been the foundry wall. My stomach flips; the butterflies of love I thought were long since gone are still there. I tell myself that it's stupid. How could an inanimate object like this old brick wall emote such strong feelings? It's been sixty years since that first kiss against that wall, but still the emotions stir. I don't know how long I've been standing here; time doesn't seem to matter. An elderly woman outside the supermarket is sitting with her dog. She's looking at me. There's concern in her eyes.

'Lost are you, love?'

'No, not lost,' I say. 'Just lost in a memory, that's all. I used to live here once. I just thought I'd like to see the old place one more time.'

I walk back towards the town. The tip where I'd first met Pip has been pulled down and replaced with a car park. I pass Mrs Flannigan's shop; it's a hair salon now. 'Walk in appointments available all day', it announces. On further inspection I see that it's closed. There's a bill stuck on the wall outside announcing the arrival of an American Circus. I wonder if the travellers still use Bates' Field.

I walk towards the once coal-dust-polluted river that now runs clean and clear, past where the blacksmith who made us hook and wheels to play with used to be. Opposite is a tanning studio. A young girl sitting outside in the sun playing on her phone acknowledges me.

'Nice day,' she says, flicking her long black hair from her eyes.

I take the river path for old times' sake. It's now a paved walkway with park benches punctuating the route. I pass the cricket ground and swimming baths. The once open-air pool where I'd met Jennifer and spent so many happy hours has been covered over like so many faceless sports centres.

'Hello, butty,' says a man passing on his bike. Everyone talks to you in the valleys. I'd forgotten how friendly they were – the salt of the earth, valley people. I scan their faces to see if I recognise anyone. Do

I know them? Then I realise I'm looking at the wrong demographic; everyone I knew back then would be as old as me – white haired and wrinkled.

I walk past Jennifer's old house, knowing she doesn't live there anymore but I just can't help myself. I pass a kid playing with his toy sword. Two other kids have dumped their bikes and are throwing stones in the river as Pip and I once did. The familiar miners' cottages that back onto the river still stand, whitewashed and pristine, their gardens still opening up on to the same river bank. I stop at a general shop to buy a plastic carton then walk the familiar trail to the top of Garn Wen Mountain. I find the spot where as a kid I'd collected whinberries amongst the couch grass. A skylark calls from somewhere above; does he remember me? I sit and pick and think.

Old visions spin in my head: I remember my first cigarette, my first kiss and the lovely Jennifer – I wonder where she is now – the mad journey to Cardiff with Pip and Frankie and breaking into Lefty's office. I remember Patch the gypsy horse I'd ridden and making log cabins out of pit props to be just like Dan the Yank. I reflect on those formative years, the things I'd got up to, the adventures I had with Peg's boys and most of all, the vision of Peg, glitter in her hair, plonking eggs Benedict in front of us. That vision of her is still as clear in my memory as the day she left.

But that was a long time ago now and I've seen and done things since then that most ordinary people can only dream of. I've performed to millionaires on their yachts, gambled in Monte Carlo and San Remo, played the major concert halls and theatres of the world, had record contracts and West End triumphs. I've been admired by my peers, loved by my fans and rubbed shoulders with the great and the good. But of all the memories there is one that's as vivid and poignant today as it was back then – the sight of Peg in that bus stop.

The town hall clock strikes twelve, dragging me back to reality. I realise my carton is full of the purple fruit. It's time to catch the train back to my life which, for all the fame and fortune I've achieved, is all just a bunch of memories now.

'Don't believe your own publicity, Jono,' my old man used to say.

'Show business isn't real.' I should have listened; he was right. It wasn't real. Now that I'm nearing that final curtain I realise that my life has been far richer for that fateful meeting with Pip, Peg and Frankie and being brought up in this valley.

I'm sure there's a time in everyone's life that's unforgettable and that summer, the summer I spent with Peg and her boys, that was my time. But things are different now; everything has changed, attitudes have changed, the only thing that has never changed is the mountain, which is still as I remember it.

Lightning Source UK Ltd.
Milton Keynes UK
UKHW011946211220
375642UK00002B/112